CORPORATE
Affair

Linda Cunningham

OMNIFIC PUBLISHING
DALLAS

Omnific Publishing
10000 North Central Expressway, Dallas, TX 75231
www.omnificpublishing.com

First Omnific eBook edition, March 2013
First Omnific trade paperback edition, March 2013

The characters and events in this book are fictitious.
Any similarity to real persons, living or dead,
is coincidental and not intended by the author.

Library of Congress Cataloguing-in-Publication Data

Cunningham, Linda.
    Corporate Affair / Linda Cunningham – 1st ed.
    ISBN: 978-1-623420-16-1
    1. Contemporary Romance — Fiction. 2. Vermont — Romance.
    3. Office Romance — Fiction. 4. Small Town — Romance. I. Title

10 9 8 7 6 5 4 3 2 1

Cover Design by Micha Stone and Amy Brokaw
Interior Book Design by Coreen Montagna

Printed in the United States of America

This book is dedicated to my mother, Betty Waidlich,
because she was the first one to read it
and she really liked the story

Chapter One

Aiden Stewart stood with his head bent, letting the pulsating hot water of the shower beat down on the back of his neck. He remained there, motionless, for a minute or two before he reluctantly turned the water off and stepped out onto the soft, white bath mat. He grabbed one of the fluffy towels and began to dry himself.

Aiden was just vain enough to pause as he caught his image in the large, gold-framed mirror opposite the shower. He took pride in the tall, lean body he saw reflected there. His muscles were not bulky like those of a man who spent too much time trying to outdo his last bench press. Instead, they were the long, supple muscles of a true athlete, the muscles of a healthy, thirty-two-year-old man who was comfortable in his own skin, who was used to doing anything physical with ease and grace. He towel-dried his dark brown hair and glanced into the mirror again. It fell attractively around his face, framing his black-lashed, clear brown eyes. He smiled at what he saw, fondly recalling some of the compliments women had offered concerning those eyes, as well as the way his long nose and high cheekbones were softened by the curve of his full lips.

Aiden was just vain enough to take pleasure in his own physical attributes and, whenever he had the opportunity, use them to get what he wanted. Especially from women. He reflected on this as he picked up his toothbrush. He sighed, feeling the game was getting a little out of control. He was juggling four women in four locations at the moment, and that was a little much, even for him.

A bold knock on the bedroom door jolted him out of his self-serving reverie.

"Yes?" Aiden called out, wrapping the towel around his waist and going to the door.

"You in there, son?" his father asked. Aiden loved visiting his parents' gracious home outside of Portland, Maine. The house was welcoming, soothing, and beautiful, much like his mother herself. A visit always made Aiden feel secure and comforted, just as he had felt growing up there.

"I'm here."

"Well, open the door and let me in!"

A visit with his mother, however, also meant a visit with his father. The cantankerous old Yankee had built his life from the ground up and was careful not to let anybody forget it. Aiden sighed, and opened the door.

"You're not dressed yet!"

"It'll take me two seconds," said Aiden calmly as he began to pull on his clothes. "What's the big hurry?"

"Are you prepared for this meeting?"

"Ah, yes, I guess so."

"Now, Aiden, you've got to be prepared. I need to acquire this company to keep us on top. Trade Winds is still the biggest communications company in northern New England, and I want to keep it that way! Acquiring ChatDotCom will give us a greater range and a jump on where the growth will take place over the next twenty years. Gene Palmer is a savvy businessman. I've known him for years. He took off to Vermont where he could be a big fish in a little pond, and he's done real well for himself. Created and sold two businesses before Chat, but now he's old and it's no secret he's sick. He wants to retire. Palmer will cave. And we have to be there when he does."

"Dad, I know all this. We talked about it last night."

"You've got a three-hour drive ahead of you. Why did you stay out so late last night? Was it that Webb girl?"

"I was out with Jennifer Webb, yes."

"Well, you stayed out too late."

"Dad, I'm thirty-two."

"Is it serious between you? You've been seeing her off and on since high school."

"That's just it, Dad, off and on."

"Well, I'm not that impressed with her. Never was. She thinks she's entitled, like so many kids your age. She thinks because her father is head of the finance committee at the hospital and she went to Harvard she's better than everybody. I'm not that impressed with her father, either, if you ask me."

"I didn't ask, Dad," Aiden muttered as he threaded his belt through the loops of his gray slacks. He picked up a blue and yellow striped tie and turned toward the mirror over the dresser.

"When are you going to find yourself a real woman and grow up?"

"Dad—"

But his father was not listening. The older man sputtered as he changed the subject back to business. "The only thing we have to be careful of is this guy Christopher Fenton. He's—"

"I know, Dad. He's president of Fenton Industries."

"He's more than that! He's the power behind Fenton Industries! He's ruthless. A corporate raider. Frankly, I don't think he's mentally sound, but he's smart—and not in a good way. As soon as he finds out that Palmer's ready to retire, he's going to make his move and try to snatch up ChatDotCom. He knows we don't have a lot of cash right now and we're expanding. It's my opinion he has the wherewithal to outbid us."

"Now, Dad, you don't know that."

"Trust me, I know. Fenton is smooth and cagey. Just a little older than you. Clawed his way up. And he's not a spoiled rich kid, either, like you. That makes a difference. Aiden, you're a grown man now. It's your job to make sure Trade Winds acquires Chat before Fenton gets wind of it. If he found out we were going after it, he'd try to steamroll us right under. And believe me, that guy will stop at nothing! We want Chat for what it is: communications. That's what we do. Fenton is just a jackal. Feeds on dead things. He'll just buy it up and chop it up and sell off the pieces. That's how he makes his money."

Aiden glanced at his father as he straightened the knot of his tie.

The old man's eyes bored into his. "Trust me," he repeated, "I know the type."

Aiden sighed. It was pointless to argue with his father. It was like trying to drown a fish. Instead, he slipped on his sport coat—a dark blue linen and silk blend appropriate for the warm spring day. "Hey, Dad, what do you know about this Fitzgerald guy? Is it mandatory that he come with the company? What if we don't want him?"

Aiden's father shook his head vigorously. "I don't know anything about him," he said, "except that Gene Palmer won't consider a sale from anybody unless Fitzgerald goes with it, in full capacity as CEO and for five years. I got that much from talking to one of their board members on the golf course yesterday."

"So that means he's in control of ChatDotCom for the next five years, even as part of Trade Winds?"

"Yes, unless we find a loophole. Now, if the guy's doing his job, then we leave him right where he is. It's your job to find out what's going on. And don't forget, before you start worrying about this Fitzgerald guy, we've got to acquire the company first."

A female voice called up the winding staircase. "Gordon, are you up there bothering your son?"

Immediately, Aiden saw the old man soften.

His father called back down. "We'll be right down, Nellie." He leveled his eyes at his son again. "Hurry up, Aiden, your mother's waiting breakfast for us."

Aiden followed his father down the stairs and into the large kitchen at the back of the house. They sat down at the big antique farm table in front of steaming mugs of coffee, and Nell Stewart set their breakfasts of sausage, scrambled eggs, and English muffins in front of them as she had been doing since Aiden could remember. Then she took her own seat opposite her son.

Nell Stewart was seventy-six years old, still lithe and active. Her few gray hairs softened the color of her thick wavy hair from its original dark brown to a lighter, tan color. She wore it caught in an elastic, low on the back of her neck. Her face bore the wrinkles of her age, but it was easy to see the beauty she had been. Gordon Stewart reached over and squeezed his wife's hand. It was a gesture of affection familiar to Aiden. He watched them in silence for a minute as they all started to eat, and his mind wandered.

Aiden was the youngest child. His two older sisters were nearly grown when he was born. They had been raised during the lean times.

He had heard the stories of how his father's business dealings had nearly failed several times, threatening the family with bankruptcy. His sisters had told him how they'd had to move into this now beautiful, gracious home when it had been an old, decrepit, and neglected house with a leaky roof and no insulation against the Maine winters. It sat on a spit of cliff so close to the Atlantic's waters that the salt spray coated the windows during the autumn storms. The family had lived downstairs in the house for the first ten years, heating it with wood stoves, but both Gordon and Nell knew the value of ocean view land and the potential of the house itself. They just had to stay afloat till the potential became a reality.

Aiden's sisters had lived through the hard times, but Aiden was the child of his parents' success. Born right after his father's first real profitable business coup, Aiden had been raised in the lap of luxury. He had foggy memories of the house being renovated and his mother's careful planning and execution of those renovations. He also remembered his father asking her repeatedly if she didn't want to move and build a new house. Aiden was glad his mother had wanted to stay where they were. It always impressed people, especially the women he brought home, to see the place with its magnificent views of Casco Bay. Aiden liked to bring them down the steep wooden stairs, gray with age, that ran across the face of the cliff to the small private, pristine beach. He enjoyed watching how obviously impressed they were when he opened the boathouse door and revealed the sleek and shining *Nellie Bly*, his father's prized wooden sailing yacht.

"What are you thinking about, Aiden?" asked his mother. "You're staring off into space."

"Oh, uh, I was just looking out the window. It looks like spring is finally here. The lilacs are blooming. They weren't even budded the last time I was here."

"Yes! And about time. It's been a long winter. I'll open the windows today and let the smell of lilacs fill the house. Are you coming back here to your condo, Aiden, or are you staying in Vermont?"

"I think I'll just wrap it up and come back to the condo. I have a date."

Gordon snorted. "You had a date last night."

Aiden laughed "Well, I have another date tonight."

"You should date less and tend to business more."

Aiden cut the conversation short. "I better get going," he said, rising from his chair. His parents stood, and hand in hand, followed him to the door. Aiden bent down and kissed his mother on the cheek. "Love you, Mom," he said.

Gordon caught him in a great bear hug. "Do your best, Aiden! Get this thing in the bag!"

An hour later, Aiden was driving through New Hampshire on the old Route 4, headed for central Vermont. His thoughts drifted. He thought about his date the previous night with Jennifer Webb. They had gone to Hugo's, one of Portland's finest restaurants in a city of fine restaurants. He didn't know why he couldn't work up any enthusiasm for Jennifer. He genuinely liked her. They had known each other a long time and had dated sporadically — sometimes seriously, sometimes not — since high school. Jennifer was a tall, attractive girl, Harvard educated in economics, a broker for the upper echelon clientele at Greater Bank of Maine in Portland. Her family, although not close friends with his, was a familiar entity. She had an abundance of energy and they shared similar interests in sailing, skiing, and hiking, but the relationship would not progress beyond a certain point. Last night they had had sex, which Aiden could only describe as rather clinical, on the sofa of her house on Cape Elizabeth. She had not invited him to stay the night, and he had been relieved because he hadn't wanted to.

Then there was Alexis, the cool blonde he would sleep with tonight. She lived in Boston, and he had met her at a business seminar there. She had driven up the night before and had spent the day with her college friend. He'd had only been on two dates with her, but Aiden knew she was ready. She had a body most men would salivate over, and he knew was in for a night of physical pleasure. He had even called his cleaning lady to ask her to put flowers on the dining room table and in the bedroom and to have the bed freshly made. He was that sure of himself.

Aiden's thoughts moved on to his parents. Perhaps they were part of the reason he went from woman to woman, or juggled two or three at once. Where, he thought somewhat sardonically, would he ever find a woman who made him feel the way his mother obviously made his father feel? Where could he possibly find a woman who loved him as completely as his mother loved his father? It was hard, especially these days, to live up to such an example. Every time Aiden thought of marriage, he thought of his parents. That was what marriage was. It was love, respect, sticking together through all the ups and downs of everyday life. It was someone who squeezed your hand at breakfast. It was being kissed on the top of your head as you sat brooding over your books.

Aiden stared at the ribbon of road stretching out ahead of him. He heaved a deep sigh and dismissed his idea of marriage, one like that shared by his parents, as unattainable.

Chapter Two

Aiden pulled into Clark's Corner, Vermont, exactly three and half hours after leaving Portland. The BMW's GPS instructed him to turn left and follow the road along the river for two-point-four miles. He slowed to the posted speed limit of forty miles per hour.

"Destination on right in point-one miles," said the metallic voice of the GPS.

Aiden saw the sign on the front of an old brick factory building that followed the edge of a canal that came off the river. CHAT.COM *Communications For Today and Tomorrow.* He turned as instructed and crossed a narrow bridge to a newly paved parking lot, pulled into a spot marked for visitors, and shut the engine off. He opened the door, stepped out into the sunny spring day, and stretched. It was ten thirty in the morning.

Aiden looked up at the building. It had obviously been an old paper mill or perhaps a tool company, built along the rushing river during the heyday of the New England industrial boom. The building had been skillfully renovated, and the artistic details imparted by bricklayers of long ago were again visible. It was quite a grand structure, curving gracefully along the lip of the canal. Whoever had overseen the renovations had done so with an eye to not spoiling its original character, and the many windows winked once again in the morning sun. Aiden could almost see the droves of immigrant Irish, Poles, Italians, and Scots who came to this country early in the twentieth century for jobs in factories like these and the new lives such jobs would provide. He had always liked history, and he felt oddly comfortable as he walked through the door into the spacious lobby.

The floors were the original hemlock wood of the factory. In those days the floors were oiled and swept daily until they weathered to a dark mahogany-colored finish. Today it was easy to see that they had been meticulously redone, shining brightly with the original dark-blond color of the natural wood. In the middle of the lobby was a circular, marble-topped desk, behind which sat a pretty young receptionist.

"May I help you?" she asked politely. Her hair was long, unmoving, and unnaturally jet black. Her eyes were rimmed in smoky shadow, and the mascara had not been spared.

"I'm Aiden Stewart. I'm here for a meeting with M. Jordan Fitzgerald."

"Oh. Oh my," said the receptionist, warming ever so slightly, "you're from Trade Winds. The company that wants to buy us. I'm sorry I didn't recognize you, Mr. Stewart. I'll announce you right away. Just wait here. Can I get you coffee or anything?"

The girl's agitated manner amused him. *My reputation must have preceded me*, he thought.

"It's okay," he said. "Take your time. I'll wait. And I prefer to call it a merger, rather than 'buy.'"

The girl hurried away through two big glass doors behind her desk, muttering, "Merger, yes, merger. That's the word."

Aiden put his hands in his pockets and looked around. He wondered if CEO M. Jordan Fitzgerald was as excitable as his receptionist. He gazed at the reproductions of historic photographs that hung on the walls. Some were pictures of rows of men in front of the behemoth machines that once filled the building with their clanking metal voices. Others showed teams of horses bringing in wagons filled with hay, while still more were of the river, jammed with logs upon which balanced wool-clad men wielding their cant-hooks. How odd it was that one of the most successful small Internet providers should be cloistered away in the backwoods of Vermont. *Well, the Internet could flourish anywhere*, he thought, *and that's why we want to own these companies. We have to own them.* As much as he tried to dismiss his father's irritating lecture before he left Portland this morning, Aiden couldn't. He knew in his heart that even at his advanced age, his father was still a consummate businessman. Aiden squared his shoulders as the receptionist came back through the big glass doors.

"Follow me," she said.

Aiden walked after her around the reception desk and down a short, wide hallway. On either side of him were glass walls through which he could see people working in their cubicles or gathered together around conference tables. At the end of the hallway was a solid wooden door with M. JORDAN FITZGERALD printed on it in gold letters. The receptionist opened the door, slipped through, and shut it again, leaving Aiden standing, and rather surprised, in the hall. Soon she reappeared, slipping back through in the same manner and closing the door behind her again.

"You may go in now," she said formally, stepping aside to allow him access to the door. "You are actually early. Your appointment is for eleven o'clock."

Aiden found her comment strange as he reached for the handle of the door, making him wonder what Fitzgerald would be like. "Thank you," he said pleasantly to the receptionist as he gripped the handle.

He pushed down, opened the door, and stepped into the room.

Aiden felt the shock hit him between wind and tide. A young woman who appeared to be not yet thirty stood behind a large desk. Her dress might have been too casual for office wear, except for the blue linen blazer she wore over it.

"He" was a "she." Fitzgerald was a woman. Aiden grappled visibly with his surprise, having assumed something entirely different.

"Welcome, Mr. Stewart," she said, extending her hand over the desk. She didn't smile, but her expression was not unfriendly.

Aiden blinked and closed the door behind him. He crossed the room, offering his hand in reciprocation. She took it in a firm grasp. He noticed she wore no rings. She gestured with an open palm to a seating area at the end of the long room. On an oriental rug, two wing chairs faced floor-to-ceiling windows that proffered a beautiful view of the river as it flowed between the old factory and the wooded bank on the opposite side. A bottle of Pellegrino, an ice bucket, and two crystal glasses sat on a low table between the chairs.

"Let's have a seat over here. It's so pleasant to look out on the river," she said and then she smiled warmly. "It helps the powers of concentration."

Aiden was having problems with his powers of concentration at that moment. As she came around from behind her desk, he tried to remain professional and not stare at her long, shapely legs complemented by high heeled pumps. He tried to keep his eyes fixed on her face, but there was little relief there for a man trying to keep his mind on business.

He hadn't imagined it. She was beautiful. Her eyes were bright blue, like the sky, and her deep auburn hair, worn pulled back in a conservative twist, was so thick that her head seemed to tilt backward ever so slightly with the weight of it. Her skin was fair without being pale, yet it seemed to glow with an inner blush. Her mouth was soft with inviting full lips.

"Why are you staring at me?"

Her remark jolted him, and he felt the heat of embarrassment creeping up his neck. He quickly recovered his composure. "I'm sorry," he said smoothly, "I wasn't staring. I was only — "

"Surprised I was female?" Jordan Fitzgerald gave a hint of a smile. She had been here before.

Aiden chuckled self-deprecatingly and looked down at the floor. "Well, to be honest, yes. I had you pegged as a cranky old man on the verge of retirement."

This time her smile was spontaneous. "I can assure you I am not on the verge of retirement."

"And you're obviously not a cranky old man. Jordan is an unusual name," said Aiden as he followed her across the room to sit down in one of the wing chairs. "What does the M. stand for?"

Jordan continued to smile sweetly as she answered him. "That's really not what we're here to talk about, is it?"

"Ah," Aiden countered as he took his seat in one of the chairs. "Put in my place. Fair enough. Let's get down to business, then. I'm here representing Trade Winds, the communications company. We've admired ChatDotCom for a long time now. Its successful growth over the past five years is a testament to a solid foundation and talented management."

Jordan sat gracefully in the other chair and smoothed her dress over her lap. She leaned forward to open the Pellegrino, and Aiden caught a brief glimpse of ample cleavage sheathed in black lace. It was the black lace that would keep him awake later that night.

Jordan smiled a little as she plunked a few ice cubes into a glass and poured the sparkling water. Aiden took it from her. "Go on," she urged, pouring the second glass for herself.

Aiden swallowed a sip of water. "As I was saying, your company's success is exceptional, and we at Trade Winds would welcome the opportunity to work with ChatDotCom in this rather mercurial business."

Jordan gave a little half-laugh, half-snort. "Mr. Stewart, you needn't waste your time buttering me up. I know what ChatDotCom is, where it's been, and where it's going. You don't want the opportunity to work with us. You want to acquire us. Isn't that right?" She stared at him with those clear blue eyes, and now she wasn't smiling.

Aiden glanced down into his glass, then looked up and met her gaze. He was silent for a moment, trying to pigeonhole her, trying to gauge the best way to continue the conversation. He set his glass down, sighed deeply, and ran his hand through his hair. The best way, he decided, was to meet her head-on. "Yes, you're right, of course. Trade Winds is prepared to offer a sizable amount of cash in order to merge with ChatDotCom. We feel your company is the perfect vehicle for our own expansion. The merger would be beneficial to both parties."

"That's rather presumptuous of you," said Jordan, a noticeable edge to her voice.

And now, Aiden's temper flared a little. Her beauty had taken him off guard, and he had been acting foolishly. It was time to get tough. "Look," he said, trying to keep his voice low and calm, "just hear me out. Everybody in the industry is looking at Chat right now. It's strategically located. Its track record with its clientele is extraordinary, as are its profits. And—" Aiden paused to give his words emphasis before he delivered the punch. "And," he repeated slowly, "everyone knows Gene Palmer is fighting cancer and wants to retire."

There was a flicker in her eyes, a nanosecond as a shadow crossed her face. He was not mistaken. She recovered almost immediately, however. Folding her hands demurely in her lap, she met his gaze fearlessly.

"Mr. Palmer has never tried to keep his condition a secret," she said quietly, steadily. "Everybody in the industry in this part of the country knows about it. Isn't it strange how people like to spread bad news? Or take advantage of someone else's misfortune?"

Aiden's teeth clenched instinctively. What was it about this woman that she could cut him down to size so effectively and with so little effort?

Aiden collected his thoughts. "I assure you, Trade Winds is not out to take advantage of anyone's misfortune. I'm sure we would have approached ChatDotCom in any case. The truth of the matter is, we're expanding. We started in Portland. Our headquarters are there. We want to expand into northern New England, and we see your company as the perfect partner in such an expansion. Now, would you like to hear our proposal?"

Jordan seemed to relax. "I would be very interested to hear your proposal, your offer, and to pass it on to Mr. Palmer. As you know, ChatDotCom is a privately held company. Mr. Palmer owns the company flat out. In his absence, he's appointed me to handle all the details of these offers as they come in. He knew as soon as word got out he was sick that this would happen, but I can tell you I think he's rather looking forward to retirement. His illness seems to be under control at the moment, and his outlook on life is a little different now. He has a close family—wife, children, grandchildren. He'd like to spend more time having fun with them. I don't mind saying that I think very highly of Mr. Palmer. He has been more than generous to me, and I'm honored to have the opportunity to oversee ChatDotCom. We—we work closely together. I know him quite well, and therefore I'll ask my questions and make my decisions based on my perception of what his actions would be. I must tell you, though, there's another offer on the table as we speak, and I will be presenting that to Mr. Palmer as well."

Her last statement took Aiden by surprise. He was sure Trade Winds would be the first to step up. He smiled a little. "May I ask who beat us to the punch?"

"I see no reason why you shouldn't know that Fenton Industries emailed us a proposal late last week. I have a meeting with Christopher Fenton later today."

Aiden was once again reminded that his father was almost never wrong about a business scenario. "I believe you received *our* proposal late last week," he said, taking another drink of his water.

Jordan laughed. "It was really quite funny," she said lightly. "They came within an hour of each other, but Fenton's came first."

Hilarious, thought Aiden sarcastically. "Well, then you know that our offer is ten million cash up front, followed by five installments over the next four years of four million each. That's a total of thirty million. That's a lot of money for a small company in a backwater town."

"I'll just ignore that last remark, Mr. Stewart," Jordan replied. "I will tell you, however, that Fenton Industries has offered fifteen million up front, followed by two installments of ten million each over the next three years. I think you'll agree that's a significantly more attractive bid. I guess our backwater location wasn't as much of a concern to Christopher Fenton. Do you have any more questions, or are you prepared to raise your bid?"

Aiden had lots of questions. He wanted to ask her how old she was. He wanted to ask her how she had happened to be hired by Gene Palmer. He wanted to ask her where she came from, where she went to school, how it was she was so self-possessed and cool in the face of brokering multimillion-dollar deals. And he wanted to know why she had to be so maddeningly beautiful. Instead, he consciously thought of his father and said, "Very interesting, Ms. Fitzgerald. Your company seems pretty high on everyone's popularity meter, and it's nice to be wanted. I see we're outbid at the moment, but I'd like the chance to get back to my father and our board. We want the affiliation with ChatDotCom. I'd like to discuss the situation with them and have the opportunity to talk this over with you again. You see, my father and Gene Palmer were cut from the same cloth. Trade Winds is a privately owned company too. There may be points to Fenton's deal that we could trump, and I'm not saying we couldn't raise our offer." *Anything to keep Fenton out of our territory,* he thought to himself.

"Competition is a healthy thing, Mr. Stewart," Jordan said, and she laughed again. "I certainly would talk over the matter with you again. The only thing I must encourage is speed, however. Mr. Palmer did say to me that any offers were to be weighed, analyzed, and decided upon within the month. His mind is made up, Mr. Stewart, and when that happens, he moves ahead. He's not one to drag his heels."

"That presents no problem to me," answered Aiden. "I'll talk with my company this afternoon. I can meet with you later today."

"I'm afraid the rest of the day is booked for me, as well as the evening. I could meet tomorrow sometime. I'd have to ask Ashley. She's the receptionist you met on the way in. She keeps me organized."

"Is there a place to stay here in town? I can reschedule my day tomorrow. I'll meet you at your convenience."

"The Inn On The Green in the center of town should have a room. It's a good choice because they have a dining room and a bar. There's also a bar across the green if you feel like stepping out. If the Inn doesn't have a room, there are a couple of bed and breakfasts where you could stay."

"Thanks," Aiden said. "I'll drive into town and look around." He put his glass down on the table, sensing their meeting was over—for now.

He was right. Jordan Fitzgerald rose from her chair. "And I should tell you," she said as he stood also, "the Inn is almost two hundred years old. It's a nice old place, clean, good food, but it's probably not what you're used to. It's kind of, well, in your own words, small town."

There was a playful twinkle in her eyes that Aiden couldn't miss. He hung his head for a second in mock self-reproach. Then he looked up and smiled back at her. "I wasn't being derogatory," he said. "Your town is beautiful. I grew up in Portland. That's not a big city, even today. I just meant—"

She laughed her musical little laugh as she met his eyes. "I know exactly what you meant, Mr. Stewart. No offense taken. Have a good rest of the day. I'll see you at some point tomorrow. Ashley will call you with a time. Oh, and call Ashley if you can't find a room. We'll arrange something."

"Thanks," said Aiden, holding out his hand. "I'm sure I'll be fine. I know we can work this out to our respective advantages, Jordan." Her first name just slipped out. He cringed inwardly, waiting for some kind of repercussion but she let it slide.

"It was nice meeting you, Mr. Stewart," she said quietly as she took his hand, all the while maintaining her formal demeanor. He felt it light and cool within his own, and he held on a little longer than was professionally necessary. She didn't pull away.

"Nice meeting you, too," he replied. "I look forward to seeing you tomorrow." He relinquished his grip on her hand and left the room, closing the door behind him.

Jordan stood still, watching Aiden Stewart leave the room. A minute later, Ashley opened the door again and stuck her head in a little way. "He's gone, Jordan."

"Thanks, Ashley. Crap! These meetings are hard. I'm so tired. And it's only noon. Did you call my mother and tell her I'll be home for lunch?"

"Yes, I did. Don't worry, Jordan. You look fantastic today. I know you just bowled him over. You gave him something to think about, I'm sure. He was really cute, though, wasn't he?"

Jordan laughed. "Yes," she said, shaking her head and returning to her desk, "he was very good looking. It just makes things harder, though."

"Jordan, you're lonely. You've got to have some fun. You need a guy."

"Ha! Not now! Not with what I have on my plate. No way! It's not the time."

"Maybe a significant other would make things easier. It does for me."

"Well, that doesn't seem to be the way it's worked out for me." Jordan sighed. "Besides, I do have what you could consider a significant other."

Ashley smiled. "Yes, I suppose you do."

"Okay," said Jordan, grabbing her purse, "I'm going to take a quick lunch at home. I'll be back in about an hour. If Christopher Fenton calls, tell him to call me back at two."

"I will."

The warm sunshine of the spring day bathed Jordan's face when she opened the big front doors. The scent of lilacs was in the air. As she walked to the parking lot, her mind whirled. This Aiden Stewart had really gotten to her. True, he seemed a bit arrogant, but he certainly was handsome. Maybe Ashley had been right. Maybe she was finally caving in to loneliness. Most days, she didn't feel she even missed having a boyfriend. Her life was so busy, so full of things to do for the business and her personal commitments, sometimes it seemed she barely had time to brush her teeth, let alone take on the responsibility of a relationship. If it wasn't for her mother and father holding the fort and helping her at home, she would be adrift. And if it hadn't been for Gene Palmer's faith in her head for business, she would be in the poorhouse, too. As it was, she wasn't doing too badly. She made good money running the business alongside Mr. Palmer.

She was able to contribute to the financial commitments of herself and her family, and she was currently in charge of putting together a multimillion-dollar merger which would benefit so many people.

Still, Jordan thought, sighing again as she got into her car, *a dinner date with a handsome man who picked up the tab would be nice once in a while. Every girl likes to be taken care of sometimes.* She smiled ruefully to herself and drove out of the parking lot.

She turned left, crossed the river over the little cement bridge, and took the next right. The pavement ended, and the road turned to dirt. A quarter of a mile more and Jordan slowed and swung the car into the driveway of the modest, ranch-style house where she had grown up. The house sat back against the rise of a small hill. It was painted brown, the windows adorned with red shutters. A wooden deck stretched out from the back door, and a stone walk led across the neatly kept lawn to the front door. Jordan brought the car to a stop in front of the attached garage. She stepped out and walked up the side path into the breezeway. Just as she was reaching for the interior door that led to the kitchen, it opened. Jordan saw her mother standing there, smiling broadly.

"We have such a surprise for you!" she said.

Jordan smiled back quizzically. "What is it?" she asked.

Her mother stepped back. Jordan peered past her into the kitchen. Her father was standing across the room, holding a plump little girl with a riot of curly red hair. "Watch this," he said as he set the barefoot child down.

The little girl teetered momentarily as Jordan's father let go of her hands, smiling as she caught sight of Jordan. Slowly she took a step, then another and another.

"She's walking!" exclaimed Jordan, kneeling down and holding out her arms to the child. "Grace, you're walking!" Jordan encouraged the little girl.

The child held out dimpled hands. "Mama," she cooed as she stumped on her fat little feet all the way to Jordan's outstretched arms, "Mama!"

Jordan hugged her baby close. This was why she got up every morning. This was what motivated her each day of her life. And for the next hour at least, she would not give business or handsome strangers another thought.

Chapter Three

Aiden drove into the center of town and parked in front of the long rambling building that was the Inn On The Green. A broad porch ran the length of its white, clapboarded front. Aiden went up the steps and through the big oaken door. The registration desk was to his right, nestled in an old-fashioned alcove off the lobby. An old touch bell sat on the counter. Aiden *dinged* it rather loudly. A small, thin, dark haired man appeared from an open doorway in the back of the alcove. He peered sternly at Aiden over half-glasses balanced on the end of his beaky nose.

"Can I help you?" he asked.

"I don't have a reservation," said Aiden in explanation, "but it turns out I'll have to stay the night here in town. Do you have a room?"

"A double?"

"No, there's only me."

"Just a minute." The nervous little man disappeared back into the recesses of the alcove. Aiden could hear voices and the shuffling of papers. About two minutes later, a smiling woman came out. In her hand she carried a key, which she handed to Aiden.

"I'm Susan Noyes. I own the Inn with my husband, Bill," she said as she cocked a thumb toward the back room. "I think you'll like room twenty-one. It has a queen-sized bed. Just go to the top of the stairs, turn right, and it's two doors down. Lovely view out the window out toward the hills. We start serving breakfast at six, and breakfast is included with the room."

"Thank you," said Aiden gratefully as he took the key.

"Now if you can fill out this registration form while I take an imprint of your credit card." Susan smiled pleasantly as Aiden reached for his wallet and handed the credit card to her.

She peered over the edge of the desk. "Bags?"

"In the car," answered Aiden. "I'll go get it while you finish up with the registration." He took his card back and went outside to get his overnight bag that he had packed for just this particular scenario. The afternoon was warming up considerably. He would be glad to change into jeans and a T-shirt, explore the town, and stretch his legs a little. He had been sitting most of the day—it was not his natural tendency.

Susan spoke as he re-entered the Inn. "If you need anything further, either Bill or I will be down here. We close the desk at ten p.m. The bar opens at four, and we start serving dinner at five. If I must say so, we serve good food."

Aiden smiled and nodded. "Thanks," he said. "Actually, I'm feeling a little hungry now. Is there a place to eat here in town that I could walk to? I need to stretch my legs."

"Sure. MacTavish's Pub is diagonally across the green. They make a great hamburger and have some really good microbrews on tap, too. If you just want to pick up a sandwich, you can walk about a mile out over this street here. There's Chandler's Grocery. They have a pretty good deli, and it's a pleasant walk."

"Hm. A microbrew sounds good to me. Thanks a lot."

Susan nodded politely, and Aiden continued up to his room. He turned right down the narrow hall, and there it was, a big oak door with gold letters screwed on: Room 21. He held up the old-fashioned key and smiled. Aiden reckoned it just might be the original key to the two-hundred-year-old door. He turned it in the lock, opened the door, and stepped into the room. Two lace-curtained windows faced west, and the afternoon sun had just begun to filter in under the half-lowered blinds. Aiden set his bag down and crossed the room. He pulled up the blinds and looked out over the little town. The room was on the back side of the Inn. A wide lawn, sprinkled here and there with groupings of white Adirondack chairs with small tables for drinks, spread gracefully out from the old building. It wasn't a large area, but it was tastefully maintained with small perennial beds and bird baths. Two old maples kept it comfortably shaded. The perimeters of the yard were defined by a thick lilac hedge punctuated by two white picket gates on opposite sides. From his view on the second floor, Aiden could see the quiet little tree-lined streets that stretched beyond the Inn's garden. Neatly kept houses with ample back yards nestled between the tall trees. It was an older neighborhood. Aiden guessed most of the houses were probably built between 1920 and 1930.

Aiden opened one of the windows. A whisper of lilac-scented breeze drifted into the room. Unbidden, Aiden thought of his mother's house in Maine. It was the same scent, heady and comforting. Now he turned and looked around the room. The focal point was the big brass bed. It was highly polished and featured a gracefully curved headboard and footboard set off by cannonball spheres on each corner. A puffy, blue and white quilt and shams made up the bed, and there was an extra down comforter folded on the small chest at the foot of the bed. A narrow door led to a tiny bathroom on the left. Aiden thought it had probably once been a closet or a stairwell. All in all, it was a simple room, but it was clean and pleasant with a bureau, nightstands, faux-Tiffany lamps, and some turn-of-the-century prints on the walls. One of the prints was of a four-in-hand stage coach pulled up to an inn. The other was of a young couple in nineteenth-century dress, holding hands in an apple orchard in full bloom. It was entitled "Banns."

Aiden stood quietly for a moment, pondering the picture. It was the portrayal of a marriage proposal. People married young back then, before they hardly had a chance to know one another. He was glad that these days you could sleep with a girl and make up your mind later. Still, the sweetness of the picture had strangely touched him. He shrugged and crossed the room, throwing his bag on the bed.

Aiden changed into his jeans and T-shirt. He would go out to MacTavish's Pub and on the way make a phone call to his father. Strategies had to be worked out—and fast.

"Hello?" Gordon Stewart barked into the phone.

"Dad, it's Aiden."

"How did the meeting go?"

"It appears that you were right. Fenton's on top of it. He's already put in an offer."

"Of course I'm right! I'm always right about these things! I said he was a sneaky bastard. Has Chat accepted the offer?"

"Not according to Jordan Fitzgerald. She did say the offer was better than ours, though."

"She?"

"Ha! Yes. Jordan Fitzgerald is a woman. A young woman. She's sharp, Dad. I got the feeling she's at the helm and Palmer's pretty much out of it."

"You can bet Palmer's not out of it, Aiden. Maybe he's not there physically, but he'll hang on till his dying breath to get what he wants. She must be sharp for Palmer to trust her with this."

Aiden sighed. "What do we do now?"

Instantly, the old man exploded. "Damn, Aiden! Pay attention! You've got to play this. We need this! Offer another approach. Offer more money if you have to. We'll work it out as you go. Just keep reporting to me. And keep in mind that Fenton is pond scum. He'll stab anybody and everybody and climb up the bodies to get to the next level. Fenton Enterprises will eat that company alive. He could be putting together a package to resell for all we know. That's been his history. He'll buy up these small places and turn around and foist 'em off on AT&T or Verizon for millions in profit. He's smooth, though, and he's got assets to use. Are you on your way home? Because if you are, turn around and get back there! Stay until you get this deal!"

Sometimes, Aiden's irritation at his father seemed to collect at his temples. A slight throbbing told him he'd better take a deep breath or a full-blown headache would ensue. "Dad," said Aiden, forcing patience, "I'm still here. I got a room at an inn, and I'm meeting with Jordan Fitzgerald tomorrow." *Thank goodness for microbrews*, he thought. MacTavish's was only a few steps away. He walked faster, letting his father rage on.

"And don't forget that! Aiden, are you listening to me?"

"Yes, Dad," Aiden replied steadily. "I'll call you tomorrow after the meeting or maybe tonight to go over some things. I'll map out another offer and let you know. Bye, Dad."

"One more thing," the old man barked over the phone again.

"What's that?"

"Is she pretty?"

The question took Aiden by surprise. He was revisited by his stunned feeling earlier when the door had opened and revealed the opposite of the image he'd held in his mind's eye. "What?" he responded a little weakly.

"You heard me. She's pretty, isn't she?"

Exasperated, Aiden snapped, "Dad, what's that got to do with it?"

"My point exactly," said Gordon. "Call me tonight." Then he was gone. Aiden shook his head slowly as though to clear it, shoved the phone back into his jeans pocket, and looked up as he approached his destination.

MacTavish's Pub was in one of the old Victorian houses that lined the main street. It was a fanciful building, adorned with a wide, wrap-around porch and decorated with gingerbread molding. Aiden pulled the heavy door open and walked inside. He felt better instantly. The pub took up one side of the house. A small, neatly lettered sign on the stairway opposite the front door that said "Private Stair" indicated the proprietor probably lived above the pub. Aiden walked down the short hall and into the public room.

It was pleasantly cool and was paneled in the original dark chestnut of the time period. The turret room, that essential fixture of the well-appointed Victorian, bowed out from the main room and overlooked the green. Small tables were scattered comfortably about the room. Against the far wall was the bar, made of cherry and polished to an almost reflective finish. A shiny brass fender ran the whole length of it on the bartender's side. Behind the bar on the wall was a huge mirror in a magnificent gold frame, and on either side sat colorful liquor bottles on glass shelves. At the end of the bar were the beer taps. There were six stools at the bar; two were occupied by men dressed in jeans, dusty work boots, and sweatshirts. It was almost three o'clock; these guys were probably building contractors who were either finishing a late lunch or had decided to stop for a beer on the way home. Aiden walked in and straddled one of the stools.

A stocky young woman suddenly appeared from behind the row of beer taps. She held frosty mugs in each hand and set them down in front of the two men. Then she wiped her hands on the white apron she wore, picked up a small pad and pencil, and took two steps to stand in front of Aiden.

"What can I getcha?" she asked without smiling.

"What do you have on tap for local brews?" he asked.

"We got Long Trail, Magic Hat, and Otter Creek today," she answered, pencil poised over the pad.

Might as well go for the familiar, thought Aiden. "I'll have a Long Trail."

The girl nodded, went to the taps, and expertly pulled a frothing glass mug. She returned, set it in front of Aiden, and gave the barest hint of a smile.

Aiden smiled back. "Thanks," he said.

"You're welcome," she answered and exited through a door in the back to what Aiden assumed was the kitchen.

The man sitting nearest to him at the bar leaned over and spoke softly. "You gotta get used to Vanessa. She's just shy."

His buddy laughed out loud, raised his glass to Aiden, and said, "Shy my ass! She's mean as a snake!"

Aiden laughed along with them, then picked up a bar menu. He scanned it, but decided not to eat. He would have dinner a little later on. Right now his mind was spinning about how to handle the situation that loomed over him. By tomorrow afternoon he would have to have an offer on the table that would convince Jordan Fitzgerald of the wisdom of merging with Trade Winds. She seemed so serious for such a young woman. There was nothing of the ingénue in her, or so it seemed. Something about her told Aiden his offer would have to include perks for her employees, guaranteed growth at her location, and most assuredly more money. He would start by matching Fenton's offer and sweeten the deal with more cash up front. The rest he would have to work out tonight, in the hotel.

The big door creaked behind him. Instinctively, Aiden glanced over his shoulder, as did his two compatriots at the end of the bar. Two men dressed in business suits walked into the room. Clearly they were not local, and they stood awkwardly, hands in pockets, until Vanessa came crashing through the kitchen door. She grabbed up two menus from the end of the bar, saying to the men, "Where do you want to sit?"

"Any place is okay," answered one of them. "Are you still serving lunch?"

"We serve anything all day long," she responded tersely. "Follow me." She led the two men to a small table just at the bend of the bow window. "Drinks?"

"I'll have iced tea, no sugar," Aiden heard one say.

"Heineken for me," said the other.

Aiden heard the chairs scrape the floor and the rise and fall of their voices, but he was too engrossed in his own thoughts to pay any more attention. As he drank his beer, Aiden built up and knocked down scenario after scenario in his mind. He was putting together the third "contract" when the words "Chat dot com" caught his ear. He didn't move a muscle, but he was instantly alert and listening.

He had overheard a bit of the conversation between the two men who sat at the table by the bow window. What could they have to do with Chat?

"I don't think we'll have a problem with her," Aiden heard one man say. He wished he could turn around unobtrusively to see which one was speaking, but the room wasn't large enough and there were too few people for him to make a move and not be noticed.

"She's pretty quick, Chris," said the other man. "She'll scrutinize every word of any document before she signs it or even before she takes it to Palmer. I wish we could just deal with Palmer."

Chris! Christopher Fenton! Aiden's pulse kicked up a notch. He strained his ears, not wanting to miss a word. "Ha! That's all you know!" Aiden heard Chris Fenton laugh through his nose. "You were there this morning. She's wet behind the ears. She may be bright, but she's a neophyte. I Googled her. She doesn't even come up, except under the personnel column of the ChatDotCom website. And at that only as 'assistant to Eugene Palmer.' I think Palmer's made a mistake. He's sick and he's tired or he wouldn't have left such an inexperienced girl at the helm."

"We can't underestimate Palmer. She'll do whatever he wants her to do. The reason he put her in charge is just for that reason. She's self-less. Probably has a massive hero-worship crush going on with him."

Aiden heard Christopher Fenton snort again. "He's probably banging her. I know I wouldn't let something like that get by me, no matter what kind of salary I had to pay her. She could call herself whatever she wanted! Sick or not sick, Palmer's a fortunate bastard if he got to screw that before he's dead."

Aiden surprised himself with his sudden flush of anger. He took a large swallow of the beer and drained the glass. The conversation was offensive to him. Christopher Fenton was offensive, but then, his father had warned him. He looked up from the bottom of his mug. Vanessa had materialized in front of him. She held the two drinks for the table in her right hand. "Another?" she asked.

"Please," said Aiden. He wanted to leave, to get away from these men, but he felt he had to stay just to see if they gave up any pertinent information he could use when formulating his offer.

"Be right back," Vanessa said.

Aiden strained his ears to hear more.

"What can I getcha?" Vanessa addressed the men.

"I'll have the burger, medium, with a salad instead of fries."

"House, ranch, French, blue cheese, pepper Parmesan?"

"Ranch."

"And you?"

"Fish and chips."

Before she disappeared into the kitchen, Vanessa set her pad and pencil down on the bar and pulled Aiden another beer. Aiden lifted the frosty mug to his lips and continued his eavesdropping.

Christopher Fenton, whom Aiden still had not positively identified, said, "This is a valuable little niche up here in New England. Right in the middle of ski country."

"It's an escape area for the cities, that's for sure," said his companion.

"It's more than that. This is the new expansion territory. This part of the East is going to grow and be prosperous. The wealth will flow north into these areas. I have to get my hands on this company. It'll be worth five times what I pay for it today. Just give it five years. That's my prediction."

"Think she'll go for the proposal?"

The kitchen door crashed against the wall again as Vanessa bulled her way through, both hands held high with dishes of food. Aiden turned then and watched as she set the food down. The hamburger went in front of a large blond man, tall, with broad shoulders. He looked to be in his late thirties, and he wore rimless glasses. His hair was cut short and slightly spiked, and his neck was thick, as if he weight trained frequently. So this was Christopher Fenton. He turned back to the bar.

"She'll go for it. I've got my ways. There's never been a deal I couldn't close."

There's always a first time, thought Aiden.

Fenton continued, "I don't think she's as smart as she seems. I think she does exactly what Palmer tells her to. I say she's in it for the money. All I've got to do is up the ante, and I'll be the one putting it to her!"

"What about that clause about keeping her five years?"

"It'll make checking on business up here in the sticks all the more pleasant. And five years is just about the timeline I'm counting on."

"What makes you so sure she won't choose Trade Winds? She said their proposal was more of a merger than a real take-over."

"Ha! Trade Winds! Nothing to worry about. Old Stewart is just like Palmer. Stewart owns Trade Winds outright. Although it appears to be one of the biggest communications companies in New England, it just doesn't have the capital to work with that we do. In the end, I can just flat out offer more cash. Money talks. It's about the only thing that does. Besides, I plan to maneuver Miss Fitzgerald into a position of, how shall I say, *submission.*"

Aiden was lifting his glass to his lips and stopped. This was very nearly a threat. It sounded sinister. Was his imagination running away with him?

"And how do you propose to accomplish that?"

Aiden heard Christopher Fenton give a nasty little laugh. "That is something that's just going to have to remain a corporate secret. Suffice it to say, I've used it before to fire people, to get information, to turn the situation for the benefit of Fenton Industries. Works every time."

Aiden was boiling over with impotent rage. He had to finish his beer and get out of there. What was that his mother had said? *Eavesdroppers always hear unpleasant things.* Well, he had heard some unpleasant things. He took another gulp of the beer just as one of the men at the end of the bar motioned for Vanessa, who was writing up Aiden's tab, to come close.

"What'd you want now, Larry?"

The man leaned in over the bar and spoke in a low voice. "Hey, are those guys here to talk to Jordan about Palmer and Chat?"

Aiden watched as Vanessa looked over to the two men. "Don't know," she said. "I never saw them before. Could be."

"Sounds like they are. Hey, you call your cousin Ashley and tell her to tell Jordan to watch her step. Don't trust these guys. They ain't good people."

"Huh," said Vanessa. "You been eavesdropping?"

Now the other man spoke up, leaning close over the bar like his friend. "Not intentional," he said, "but it seems these guys are too stupid to keep their voices down. They been running their mouths, and we don't like what we hear. Just tell her don't trust 'em."

"I'll do that," said Vanessa, sliding Aiden's check along the bar. He picked it up and reached into his back pocket for his wallet. So this was a small town in action. Palmer must be a big fish in a little pond, like his father had said. Everybody seemed to know his business. And perhaps that wasn't such a bad thing. It could work in Aiden's favor. He left cash on the bar and included a healthy tip for Vanessa.

"Thanks," he said.

"Any time," acknowledged Vanessa.

Aiden walked out into the late afternoon. The sun was in the sky a little later these days. It would be flooding his hotel room with light as it set over the hills to the west. He walked slowly back to the Inn, hardly seeing as he walked.

Aiden's emotions were never a very active part of his life by day—or by night for that matter. Now they were in total chaos. He was struggling with something, some feeling he couldn't quite identify, yet it was familiar at the same time. Jordan Fitzgerald had confused him somehow, and he caught himself thinking about her constantly. Was it pity? Was it sympathy? Was it just animal attraction? His natural reaction to a pretty girl? He thought about his meeting with Jordan Fitzgerald, his surprise to find she was female. But had he been surprised that she was female or surprised at her beauty and youth? He had thought that despite her self-control and professionalism, her obvious competence and intelligence, she had looked almost fragile in the huge office. Those big blue eyes—there was something behind them, something guarded, something vulnerable.

Aiden shook his head and ran his fingers through his hair. He climbed the front steps to the Inn, nodded to Bill Noyes, who stood behind the desk, and went up to his room. He kicked off his sneakers and sat cross-legged on the bed, like he used to do when he was a student, his laptop balanced on his knees. He typed furiously for a while, making lists, highlighting, crossing things out, adding a balance sheet. Finally he looked up and out the window.

The last of the evening sun was indeed pouring into the room, washing the floor in gold and making the brass bed gleam. It was a warm room. In spite of the reason for his finding himself in the little town, Aiden felt content and at home. His phone rang, snapping him out of his daydream.

"Aiden!"

Aiden's stomach sank. He had totally forgotten. "Alexis," he said dully.

"Where are you? You were supposed to pick me up early so we could miss the traffic out to Cape Elizabeth. We'll be late, Aiden!"

Aiden listened to the edgy voice, tinged just a bit with hysteria and anger. Better get this over with fast, just like ripping off a Band-Aid. "I-I've had to stay in Vermont. I've got continuing business here, and it can't wait."

There was silence. Then, the woman's voice again, "Are you telling me you're not picking me up? Are you telling me we're going to miss the party? The party on the yacht? Where the other guests include the governor of Maine and a United States senator? Aiden? Aiden, are you there?"

"You can still get there. I'm just not able to go."

Now her voice became deadly quiet. "Aiden," she finally continued, "I'm disappointed. I'm angry. I drove up here from Boston for this. This is absurd, and I'm not going to waste my time a second longer. Don't ever call me again. Good-bye, Aiden!" She clicked off. Aiden sighed, looked at the blank screen of his phone, and ran his fingers through his hair. Oddly enough, he felt relieved. Alexis was just another diversion. He didn't realize until now that he hadn't actually cared that much for her personality anyway. All he had thought about was climbing into bed with her and having some fun sex. Suddenly he reflected. Fun sex. Then he thought about that, realizing it had been a while since he'd had any real fun. At any rate, the deed was done. He would not see her again. There were other fish in the sea, not that that seemed to matter at the moment. Aiden was once again aware that his emotions were in tumult. He was getting very involved in this merger deal. It seemed to mean more to him than his work usually did. Maybe he was getting like his father. He bent his head to the computer and began pounding the keyboard once again.

Chapter Four

Struggling with conflicting feelings, Jordan drove back to work that afternoon. She was elated that her daughter was walking, yet it had been Jordan's mother and father who had seen those first steps, not her, Grace's own mother, and certainly not Grace's father. Jordan fought the burn of tears at the back of her eyes.

Jordan gripped the steering wheel and clenched her teeth. *Focus on what you do have instead of what you don't*, she told herself. Consciously, she willed herself to think positively. Certainly, she was lucky to have her parents. Grace was lucky to be cared for in a real home by her grandparents. And it wasn't as though Jordan wasn't doing her part. Her job at Chat was everything to the family now that Jordan's father had been laid off from his construction job. Not only was she paying the mortgage, but she was contributing to her brother's university tuition as well. Her father and mother chipped in with savings and unemployment checks, but Jordan was shouldering the bulk of the family's expenses. She was glad she could do it. It made her happy to help her family, to be the one upon whom the rest could rely. That was what family was all about. Whoever was in the strongest position at the moment helped the rest weather the storm until they were back on their feet. If missing her daughter's actual first steps was the price she had to pay, then she would pay it.

She wheeled into the parking lot at ChatDotCom, pulled into her parking place, and hurried into her office through the private back door. She wanted to go through both the proposals from Trade Winds and Fenton Industries once again before she met Christopher Fenton this evening for dinner. Ashley could help her. Together they could compare the offers and make a list of non-negotiable issues in selling Chat so as to reap the greatest benefits for the employees of the company and for the Palmer family.

Jordan threw her blazer and bag into the chair at her desk and crossed the room to call Ashley in from her desk, but the door opened before she could reach it. The two women nearly collided.

"Oh, Ashley," she said, somewhat startled. "I was just coming out to get you. Will you help me go over these proposals? I've got to know the ins and outs of each one, especially the Fenton one because I'm meeting him for dinner at the Inn tonight. I want to get finished in time to get home so I can shower and change."

"Of course I'll help," said Ashley. "Actually, I was coming in to talk to you about Fenton."

Jordan blinked to cover her surprise. "Well, come sit down." She gestured to the wing chairs and turned to take two portfolios off her desk. As they sat down, Jordan said, "So, you have some ideas about the Fenton proposal?"

Ashley and Jordan had gone to high school together. They had not been close friends, but they had always been friendly. Ashley had worked at Chat for a year before Jordan started, and they had developed a professional friendship that soon grew into a personal one. Ashley was a tiny girl, almost a head shorter than Jordan. She was slim, quick, and efficient. She seemed to have an uncanny knack for anticipating things before Jordan asked for them. Ashley's appearance seemed to be of great concern to her. She was always dressed as well as her income level would permit. Her long, color-enhanced black hair was always done in a smooth, low pony tail, or draped artfully over her forehead and down her back. And, Jordan noticed jealously, it stayed draped all day, with never a single hair out of place. Jordan was bound to reflect on the fact that if she ever tried to wear her own hair like that, her curls would burst forth of their own accord, giving her the look of a crazy person. Ashley wore way too much makeup for Jordan's taste, almost as though she was performing on stage. Her blue-gray eyes were heavily lined in black. Her lashes were coated with black mascara, and the three shades of artfully blended eye shadow made her eyes seem abnormally large. It was obvious she frequented tanning salons, but her gentle nature was her own, and little by little, it was this that Jordan came to see.

Jordan had initially remarked to Gene Palmer that Ashley seemed nervous, almost on edge, but Mr. Palmer had only laughed and called her "watchful" instead. And, as Jordan got to know her better, she found herself relying more and more on Ashley to keep the everyday details of the business in order. She found her quite up to the task. "Watchful" had been a good word. Nothing seemed to escape Ashley Hart. However, it was very unlike her to read through a proposal without express permission or a request to do so from Jordan or Mr. Palmer.

Jordan settled herself back into the comfortable wing chair, the proposals on her lap. She looked up at Ashley.

"So you've read the Fenton proposal. Tell me, then, what did you think?"

Ashley's large eyes grew larger. "Jordan! Of course I didn't read the proposal. You know me better than that!"

"I thought you said you had something to say about the Fenton proposal?"

"I said I wanted to tell you something about Fenton. Christopher Fenton."

Jordan was brought up short. "Oh, sorry. I didn't understand."

"Vanessa called me this afternoon," Ashley continued. "Just before you got back."

"So? What does that have to do with Chris Fenton?"

"Well, it seems he came into the pub this afternoon for something to eat. Larry Sample was at the bar with somebody else. Vanessa didn't say who. Anyway, Larry told Vanessa to call me and have me tell you not to trust him. He said Fenton was saying things he didn't like."

Jordan's brow furrowed ever so slightly. "Hm," she said. "What did Fenton say?"

"Larry didn't specify. Just don't trust him."

"Well, I wouldn't, anyway. Both these companies only want what they can get out of Chat, which is territory. It's my job to see that a deal gets closed that's beneficial to us, not them. Because no matter what they say, no matter what they sign, eventually they'll do whatever they want. I do wonder what Larry Sample heard, though."

"Do you want me to call him?"

Jordan laughed sardonically as she leafed through the proposal. "Oh, no. Don't bother. You know Larry. He's always digging up dirt somewhere."

They worked over the proposals for a full two hours. Finally, Jordan looked at the clock. "It's getting late," she said. "I need to get ready. Can you get these properly printed and bound? I want to have it as ammunition. I know what I'm talking about, but with these guys you have to have everything on paper and you have to back up all your convictions with hard arguments. Also, I want to leave in time to stop in and see Mr. Palmer."

"How's he doing?"

"He just finished up another round of chemotherapy. He's got a break now for a while, but he wants to get this wrapped up soon." Jordan sighed. "He's only seventy-four. That's not that old."

Ashley shook her head slowly. "My grandfather died when he was eighty-six, and we thought he was too young to die. Eighty-six is ten years past the average. It's just that we didn't want to let him go."

"I suppose so," said Jordan as Ashley shut her laptop and stood up.

"I'll be right back," she said to Jordan and left the room.

Jordan watched her. Sometimes she envied Ashley. She was so steady, so kind. She saw the truth in everything—she and her husband, Kyle, had been together since eighth grade. They had both attended The Community College of Vermont, and when they graduated, they got married. For three years they had lived in a tiny, three-room apartment up over MacTavish's Pub. Ashley worked as a waitress; Kyle held the job he'd had all the way through high school as a mechanic at Rick's Garage. When Ashley finally secured her position at ChatDotCom, they bought a small Cape-style house from Kyle's cousin on a pretty side street in town. Everything seemed to fall into place for Ashley. Jordan was sure there would be children, probably two. Probably a boy and a girl, two years apart.

Jordan truly didn't begrudge Ashley a thing. That was just the way things worked out for some people. She sighed again. Other people were destined to travel a more circuitous route. She slipped into her jacket and picked up her bag.

Ashley returned with the document. "Here's the portfolio," she said, handing the bound paper to Jordan. "I made extra copies. They're in my desk if you need them, but I think you should only need the one for tonight. Good luck, Jordan!"

"Thanks," said Jordan, smiling. "I'm kind of weak in the knees. Maybe I'll feel better after I talk to Mr. Palmer."

"You'll do just fine. You always do. Tell Mr. Palmer I'm thinking of him."

"I will. Good night, Ashley."

Jordan walked out the front door to her car. Going to see Mr. Palmer was always a bittersweet experience. She missed him, gone from the office for six months now. On a daily basis, she missed his guidance, his friendship, his mentoring. She tried to see him every chance she got. They had a regular meeting every Monday afternoon and Thursday morning, but she tried to squeeze in extra visits too. She knew he was always glad to see her.

On the other hand, it pained her immensely to see the once large, boisterous dynamo of a man compromised by disease. He had lost almost fifty pounds. His hair was thin and his skin gray. His face bore the pinched look of a man struggling with serious illness and pain and the rigors of the treatment protocol. When Jordan had accepted the position as his personal assistant two years ago, right after her internship, he had been one of the strongest, surest people she had ever known. He taught her to trust herself, in spite of her circumstances. And in spite of her circumstances, she had rallied, found her niche, and come to know and trust her own judgment. Her confidence had grown until she knew she could depend upon herself. She could do it, whatever needed to be done. And she owed that confidence, that self-awareness, to Gene Palmer.

When Grace came along, Jordan was cognizant of the gossip that swirled around her, but she steeled herself and gave it no credence. She showed up to work every day and did her job with skill and finesse, just as she always did. She made it a rule to discuss her private life with no one. Mr. Palmer knew the truth, and Ashley and her family knew the truth. They were the only people who mattered to her. Everybody else could think what they wanted.

She turned off the main street and drove slowly up the long, curved drive. At the top of the hill sat the Palmer house. Built at the turn of the century by a wealthy factory owner, it was a large, imposing, two-story brick square. A white portico softened the front, and a meticulously pruned juniper hedge bordered the lawn. A garage had been added much later, and a greenhouse-style solarium connected it to the house. Jordan parked in front of the garage and entered through the solarium door. Gene Palmer's wife of fifty-one years looked up from where she sat at the small table in the garden-like room. The late afternoon sun warmed the space. Jordan closed the door on the encroaching chill of the spring evening.

"Hi, Mrs. Palmer," said Jordan softly. "How is he today? Is he up for a quick meeting? I'm having a business dinner with Christopher Fenton this evening. I just wanted to speak to him for a minute."

Marie Palmer, dark circles under her eyes, gave a tired smile and stood up, smoothing the front of her skirt. "Hello, Jordan. Actually, he's doing pretty well today. He sat out here with me for lunch. He asked for grilled cheese sandwiches and some soup. I gave it to him, and he kept it down. Then he went in for a nap—"

"And here I am!" Gene Palmer called out as he walked into the room. In spite of his compromised physical state, Jordan was still aware of the old man's dignity, sharp intelligence, and curiosity. He moved slowly but steadily toward Jordan and gave her a quick hug. "Have a seat, Jordan. We'll sit out here. The sun feels good." Gene sat down heavily on the cushioned wicker sofa with a groan. "There," he said with a little gasp as he settled himself. Jordan flashed him a warm smile to cover her own sadness and sat down in a wicker chair opposite him.

"Shall I leave you two alone?" Marie asked. "Would you like something to drink?"

Her husband scoffed. "You sit right beside me, Marie." He patted the cushion on his right and then said, "I would like some ice water, though, please, dear."

"I'll get it right away." Marie left the room.

Gene leaned in toward Jordan and winked at her in mock conspiracy. "I like to keep her as close to me as possible these days," he said with a grin. "Don't want her running off with the gardener!"

"Oh, Mr. Palmer!" laughed Jordan.

"Well, things like this change the way a man thinks about things. Marie and I spent too much time apart when I was building the business. She had her hands full working and raising the kids. It wasn't much help, my being absent. No more. Better late than never."

"Here you are, dear." Marie returned with a tall glass of ice water and set it on the low table in front of the sofa. She sat down beside her husband.

"So what's happening with this sale, Jordan?" asked Mr. Palmer.

Jordan laid the proposal down in front of him. He picked it up and scanned through it while she talked. "This morning I met with Aiden Stewart from Trade Winds. This evening I'm having a dinner meeting with Christopher Fenton from Fenton Industries. I have a feeling that Trade Winds just doesn't have the cash to throw around that Fenton does, but Fenton seems to have too many fingers in too many pies. At least Trade Winds is focused. It's the only thing they do. I have a feeling that Fenton Industries goes around buying up companies and then sells them off in pieces to the highest bidder."

"Hm," said Gene, not looking up from the proposal. "What makes you say that?"

"Christopher Fenton is flashing around a lot of money. The offer I received from him was heavy on the cash. It made me think he wasn't that interested in ChatDotCom itself, just the territory it's in. I didn't get the impression he was concerned with the same things we are."

"And what are we concerned with, Jordan?" He glanced up from the portfolio and looked at her sharply.

Jordan was past being afraid of Gene. It was just his way to react like this. He wanted to hear her say exactly what she thought. He always made her follow her plans through mentally before trying to carry them out. It was an exercise they went through together whenever a decision had to be reached.

"Well, ChatDotCom is one of the largest employers in this area. We employee over four hundred people, and that represents a lot of the area's economy. There's the college, there's the two hospitals, and there's Chat. Together we employ most of the population. For any of those institutions to close would devastate the work force. And that's not good. I know."

"Your father isn't working yet?" Gene asked suddenly.

Jordan shook her head. "No, but there are a couple of jobs, finish carpentry things, that he's interviewing for next week. He's really hoping."

"Nothing for him at Chat?"

Jordan smiled and shook her head slowly. "No, really, there isn't. Thanks, anyway, Mr. Palmer. We're doing all right."

"Well, your parents are fine people, and you're lucky to have them helping with the baby," Marie added. "How is Grace?"

Jordan smiled broadly. "Oh, Mrs. Palmer! She took her first steps today!"

Marie clasped her hands. "Wonderful! Such a magical time!"

"Hey, we're getting off topic, here." Gene let out a short huff. "What is it about women and babies?"

Marie looked at him fondly. "Go sharpen your pencil, dear."

"Ouch!" he exclaimed. "I've just been told to shut the hell up!"

Jordan laughed and said, "Anyway, back to business. I know we need to get the best price for Chat, but we also need to have a deal that will secure everyone's jobs. We need to know that Chat will continue. And it's important to get this deal done before something—" Jordan broke off, and her face blanched. *Before something happens to you,* she thought.

Gene Palmer waved his hand in the air. "You're right, Jordan. I don't know how long I'll live. Hopefully, I'll keep going for a while, but you're right. It would be nice to know that the business will continue to support the segment of the population that it's supporting now. And grow. That's why I put that caveat in there protecting your job. You're the one to carry this into the future. Still, cash is king, and the more money we get up front, the cleaner things will be."

Jordan nodded, fighting back tears. He always did look at things head on. And he forced her to do the same. She cleared her throat and continued. "I just think, and keep in mind this is only a hunch, an instinct, but I just think that Trade Winds is more sincere in its claim to merge with us and bring the communications industry farther into the north country. I kind of liked Aiden Stewart."

Gene was visibly tiring. "Hm. Is that the kid? I've never met him. I know the old man. Hard-bitten Yankee, but a good businessman."

"Like somebody else I know," said his wife.

"What's the kid like? Does he have a head on his shoulders, or is he just his father's puppet?"

Jordan looked perplexed as she remembered the clear eyes, the wavy hair, the athletic body that even the business clothes couldn't hide. "Well, I," she stammered, "I got the impression he was a pretty smart guy, um, man."

Gene Palmer's eyes narrowed as he looked at her, but he only said, "You go to your meeting. You've got a good understanding of what's important and what we need. You'll have to find the balance. You let me know how it turns out. I'll be here."

Marie stood as Jordan got up from her chair, but Gene remained sitting. His breathing was a little heavier now. Jordan hugged Marie and bent down to give Gene a quick embrace. "I'll call first thing in the morning," she said. "See you later."

At seven thirty that evening, in room twenty-one in The Inn On The Green, Aiden sat on the bed, propped up on pillows piled against the headboard, with his computer balanced on his lap. He was staring at the opposite wall, looking at nothing. Aiden felt uneasy. Suddenly, overnight, things didn't seem so simple. Aiden struggled to understand just what had happened. He had only been in this little town less than twenty-four hours, but he was involved somehow. He had gone on similar missions for the company, but they hadn't affected him so personally. The other times, he met with the usual suspects, they banged out an agreement, and Aiden was in his car or on a plane, on his way to bed some current girlfriend. Easy.

Not this time. This time there was competition. Competition from an undesirable source. The conversation he'd overheard at the pub resonated with him—and not in a good way. It was unsettling. Christopher Fenton gave every indication of being ruthless and dishonest, even dangerous. Aiden wondered what drove the man. Why would he care about a small communications company enough to scheme to get it? If scheming was what he was doing. Maybe it really was a gold mine in the resale business. Aiden couldn't be sure. He just knew he hadn't liked either the look of Fenton and his cohort or the way they had been discussing Chat.

And then there was M. Jordan Fitzgerald. Not the usual suspect. Not a suit. Not even close. In fact, she was the antithesis of any of the other business types, male or female, that Aiden had ever encountered. She wasn't the sterile accountant type who went from business to business, playing with numbers. She wasn't a hard-boiled survivor like his father or Gene Palmer who had fought for their niche and pulled themselves up by their bootstraps within it. No, she was something else. Aiden unconsciously twisted his mouth, trying to pigeonhole her, to label her. She was obviously smart. She was surprisingly young. And, she was so arrestingly pretty in such a unique way. Jordan was an enigma. She seemed friendly enough, but there was an unmistakable guard around her, a parameter past which, it seemed to Aiden, she let no one enter.

Aiden rubbed his tired eyes, and as he did so, his stomach growled. He set the computer aside and stood up, stretching. He was hungry. He glanced at his watch and suddenly felt as though he was starving. He crossed the room to the mirror and ran his fingers through his hair. Grabbing his white shirt from where he had draped it over the foot of the bed, he put it on and tucked it into his jeans. He threw on his sport coat, made sure his wallet was safely in his back pocket, and slipped his cell phone into his coat pocket. Then he headed out in search of something to eat.

The hall was empty, and as Aiden walked toward the stairwell, the hundred-year-old floorboards under his feet creaked. It was an old Yankee establishment, Aiden thought with a smile. There were no carpets wasted on the hallways. As he approached the stairs, Aiden could hear the clinking of silverware on dinner plates and the *ting* of glassware coming from the dining room. He had been planning to go back to MacTavish's Pub, but as he descended the stairs he thought he might as well try out the Inn.

Aiden strode across the lobby and waited at the door of the large dining room. A high schoolmaster's desk held menus, but there was no sign of a hostess or maître d'. He stood patiently until he saw Susan Noyes, dressed in a white tuxedo shirt and black slacks, walking through the dining room toward him.

She smiled cordially and said, "Mr. Stewart, can I get you a table?"

"Yes, thank you," answered Aiden, his eyes wandering around the huge room. "Looks like you're busy tonight."

"Thankfully, we are. It's usually quiet here most of the month of May. The summer people get here in June, but hey, I'm not complaining." She picked up a menu. "Anybody joining you?"

"No, just me tonight."

"Well, follow me. We've got a nice small table over here by the fireplace." As she turned to lead him to his table, she looked back over his shoulder. "Oh, dear, and here comes another couple."

Aiden smiled and turned to follow her gaze. "Well, busy is good," he started to say, and then he saw the couple.

It was Jordan Fitzgerald, and she was in the company of the man he had overheard at MacTavish's Pub that afternoon. Christopher Fenton. Aiden's heart gave a little leap. Jordan's thick auburn hair cascaded over her shoulders and down her back. She wore a dark green slightly shimmery dress that dipped low over her chest, exposing the plump tops of her ample breasts. The dress was shirred on one side and hugged her body, accentuating all her curves and stopping mid-thigh. Her black stilettos made her legs go on forever.

Aiden's head began to swim with a thousand thoughts at once. *She's beautiful. That hair, those exquisite legs! What's she doing here with Fenton? Had she closed the deal?* He felt his right hand raise slightly in an unconscious motion as he instinctively thought about how it would be to stroke those thighs. Quickly he recovered, spun on his heel, and followed Susan to his table, hoping she hadn't seen him.

"Here you go," the innkeeper said, handing him a menu. "I'll send your server out right away."

"Thank you," said Aiden, and he sat down heavily.

"May I have her bring you a drink?"

Aiden had planned on a red wine, but things had suddenly changed on so many levels. "I'll have a Scotch, a double with a splash," he said. "Talisker's, if you have it."

"We do," said Susan. "Enjoy your dinner."

Aiden was relieved the table was in a good location. Nestled next to the wall, it was close enough to the fireplace to feel the comforting heat, but inconspicuous at the same time. He opened the menu and peered over the top, watching Susan Noyes lead Jordan and Fenton across the room. Fenton's eyes darted all over, but Jordan centered her gaze politely on the back of Susan's head and walked gracefully to the table.

Aiden felt the rush of adrenaline as they came closer. He didn't want Jordan to see him. Fenton didn't know who he was, but Aiden had no desire to meet him under these circumstances. Susan sat them at a table diagonally across from Aiden's. Fortunately for him, Jordan chose the seat facing into the room and her back was to him. Aiden watched them carefully as they sat. He heard Susan ask for their drink orders. Fenton ordered a Dewar's on the rocks, but Jordan simply asked for a ginger ale.

"You don't drink?" asked Fenton.

"Well, not tonight," Jordan answered. "Guess I just don't feel like it."

Aiden's server, a plump high school girl, broke the bubble of his concentration. "Are you ready to order, sir?"

"Ah, yes." He spoke quietly, lest Jordan hear him and recognize his voice. "I'll have the prime rib, rare."

"A starter?"

"Just the salad will be fine. With blue cheese dressing."

"Baked, mashed, or French fries?"

"Baked, please, with sour cream."

"Thank you. I'll bring your salad right out." She turned and left him. Aiden brought his drink up to his lips and sipped the smoky Scotch. The peat flavor of the imported liquor stayed in his mouth, imparting a comforting burn that lingered. The server returned with his tossed salad and set it down in front of him. He ate it, and the garlic roll that came with it, all while trying to eavesdrop on Jordan and Fenton.

When his prime rib came, it was perfectly done. Ordinarily, Aiden, who really enjoyed food, would have reveled in the tender meat and hot baked potato smothered in sour cream. But tonight he was too preoccupied to do more than eat it, methodically taking bite after bite, barely aware of the flavor. His mind was on the conversation at the nearby table. The continuity of the words was interrupted by a myriad of so many other sounds that their discussion turned into gibberish by the time it reached his ears.

Aiden realized how extremely tired he felt. He felt let down, as though he had suffered some great disappointment. He felt empty, and for the first time in years, he felt lonely. He lingered over the last of his dinner, trying to decide whether to have a cup of strong coffee. He was not looking forward to the night ahead. First, there would be a long telephone conversation with his father. Then he would have to amend his proposal and call his father back for another long conversation. Perhaps a strong cup of coffee was in order. He was looking for his server when Jordan abruptly stood up. She reached for her purse hanging on the back of her chair and dropped it. Fenton stood, picked it up, and handed it to her. Aiden was shocked to see her waiver slightly, as though she was unsteady on her feet.

Now Aiden could hear their conversation. Fenton said, "Are you all right?"

"Yes, yes," said Jordan. "I just need to go to the ladies room. I'll be right back."

"I'll be here," said Fenton with a little laugh.

Aiden studied Jordan as she walked slowly out of the dining room. He had the distinct feeling that something was wrong. She walked like a person who'd had too much to drink and was trying not to show it. She must have changed her drink to something stronger at some point during the meal, he reflected. The server returned to his table. "Can I get you anything else, sir?"

Aiden never took his eyes off the dining room door. "Bring me a cup of strong coffee, please," he said. "Cream and sugar."

"Right away."

By the time the server had returned with his coffee, and he had stirred the cream and sugar into it, Jordan was coming back into the dining room. There was no mistaking it now, she was listing slightly, and her face had a determined look as she tried to keep her balance. Aiden was alarmed. He could have sworn she had ordered only ginger ale, but he'd obviously missed something.

He watched surreptitiously as she sat down heavily in her chair and spoke to her dinner companion. "Mr. Fenton, this has been… this has been a pro-productive meeting, but I'm not feeling very well right now. I think I'd better call it a night and go home."

"Are you all right?" asked Fenton in a concerned voice. "Would you like me to drive you home?"

Jordan laughed. "Oh, no, I just live up the street a short distance. I'll be fine. I'm just not feeling—well, I'm just not feeling right. We'll talk again in the morning. Thank you for the lovely dinner. I'm encouraged about the transition of ChatDotCom." She stood again, and Fenton stood with her.

"I have a feeling we're closing in on this and we can wrap it up tomorrow to everyone's satisfaction," he said.

"I'm sure we will," said Jordan, but Aiden sensed it was an automatic response just to be polite. It was obvious she was feeling awful. He watched as she wrapped her pashmina around her shoulders, picked up her bag, and headed for the door. Her walk seemed even shakier than before.

Aiden pulled out his wallet and put down fifteen dollars for a tip for the server. Then he signed the check with his name and room number. He made up his mind he would at least follow Jordan out to the parking lot, just to make sure she was all right. He was about to stand when Fenton's voice caught in his ear. He was talking softly into his phone.

"Yes, police?"

Aiden froze in his chair and listened.

"Yes, I'm eating dinner at the Inn here in town, and a young woman has just left the dining room. Yes. Yes. Obviously inebriated. Yes. She could hardly walk. I heard her say she was driving home. She said she was fine to people who offered to drive her, but trust me, she's not. Yes, that would be prudent. Oh, she's wearing a dark green dress. Has a shawl over her shoulders. Red hair. Or dark red, yes. Thank you. Yes, I'm just concerned, that's all. Don't want anyone to get hurt. Yes. You're welcome." Then he slipped the phone back into his breast pocket.

Aiden's mouth was dry. Everything hit him in the same instance. Fenton was setting Jordan up for some nefarious plan of his own. He must have put something into her drink when she wasn't paying attention. Hurriedly, Aiden stood and walked quickly from the dining room. Hopefully, he would not be too late. If she got behind the wheel, she would be breaking the law as well as endangering herself and whoever she might meet on the drive home.

Once through the big front door, Aiden broke into a run, jogging down the row of cars parked on the street outside the Inn. He didn't even know what kind of car she drove. Desperately he craned his neck, trying to see through the half-darkness. Then he saw movement at the end of the line of cars: Jordan. She was leaning on a black Jeep Grand Cherokee, repeatedly pushing the lock mechanism. Aiden could see the lights flashing on and off. He saw her open the door and ran as fast as he could, calling out to her. "Jordan! Jordan! Stop!"

He reached her just as she got behind the wheel, the ignition key in her hand. He took her forcefully by the arms and lifted her out of the car.

"What the hell! Hey!" she shouted at him. "What are you doing? Get your hands off me! Let go of me!"

"You can't drive," Aiden started to explain. He was breathing hard, but not from physical exertion.

"Get away from me or I'll start screaming!" She began to rummage in her purse. "I'm calling the police right now!"

It was then that Aiden saw the flashing blue lights of the police cruiser. "Somebody saved you a call," he said wryly.

The cruiser pulled up close behind Jordan's car, blocking any movement. A big uniformed officer got out, flashlight in hand.

"Jordan!" the officer exclaimed, recognizing her.

"John...John," she stammered, unable to finish her sentence.

"What's going on here?" said the officer.

Aiden spoke up, "We were having dinner, officer. She didn't feel well, and we came out here to lock up her car. I'm going to give her a ride home."

The big man turned to Jordan. "Is this true, Jordan?"

Aiden held his breath. He watched as Jordan blinked hard and leaned back against the vehicle.

"Y-Y-Yes," she said weakly, "that's right. I wasn't...I-I don't feel very good."

Aiden exhaled and unclenched his hands. The police officer turned to him. "I'm John Giamo, Clark's Corners Chief of Police," he said. "I've known Jordan since she was a child. She babysat for my kids. Just who might you be?"

Aiden cleared his throat and met the man's eyes. He noticed immediately that, although Giamo's general appearance was bland and ordinary, his eyes reflected an intelligence that was undeniable. They reminded Aiden of a hawk's eyes, missing nothing.

Aiden recovered his self-confidence. Jordan was going along with his ruse. "I'm Aiden Stewart," he said. "Ms. Fitzgerald and I were having a dinner meeting, a business meeting."

"Becky got a call at the station about an inebriated young woman in a dark green dress," the police chief said. "I couldn't believe it when I saw it was you. You sure you're okay?"

"Yes, yes, my stomach hurts and I feel dizzy," she replied, "but I'm not drunk. I just had ginger ale. I'm sure I'll be fine."

"Maybe you ate something bad," said Giamo. "Bill Noyes better check his kitchen. Say hi to your parents for me. Hope you're feeling better." He nodded at Jordan but then glared at Aiden sharply.

"I'll get her home safely," Aiden said, finally relaxing a little as the officer got back into his cruiser and drove away.

Aiden took a deep breath. The cool night air felt good in his nostrils. "Let me have the keys and I'll drive you home," he said gently.

Jordan put her hands up to her eyes. "What's going on?" she asked. "I didn't have anything, yet I feel like I drank a fifth of rot-gut whiskey. It must have been bad food."

"What did you have to eat?"

"Prime rib," she said weakly. "Don't talk to me about food."

"I had the same thing and I'm fine. I'll tell you what happened."

She looked up at him and suddenly her face went white.

"What's wrong?" Aiden asked urgently. "Are you going to faint?"

"Oh…oh," Jordan said softly. "I-I think I'm going to be sick. Get away. Get away from me." She waved her hand at him, turned, and slumped against the car. Aiden reached out and gripped her arms, holding her up.

"Maybe you need to go to the emergency room," he said. "I think Fenton put something in your drink."

"No! Don't take…don't take me anywhere. I can't go…go home like this. I can't let anybody see me like this. I'll be fine in a minute. Just let me lie down. I'll scream if you touch me."

Aiden ignored her. "Can you still walk? Here, lean on me." He slipped his arm around her waist and held her close to his body. "We're going up to my room."

He began to walk slowly back, half dragging the semi-conscious woman. He felt her sigh. Feeling the warmth of her body, he gripped her more tightly, protectively, as he guided her across the parking lot. He felt her shudder a little, and it seemed to Aiden that she was finally willing to surrender to his help as she slumped against him.

It was ten o'clock as they entered the lobby. Aiden was thankful that it was dimly lit and there was nobody behind the desk. He saw the stairway ahead and knew he would have to get her up to the safety of his room before they were seen. She was nearly dead weight now. He glanced around, and seeing no one, he carefully arranged her pashmina around her face to shield her from any surveillance cameras that might be there. Then he lifted her into his arms and made his way up the stairs.

Jordan nestled snug against his chest. For such a tall girl, she didn't feel particularly heavy or awkward to carry. Aiden climbed the stairs, holding her close. As he fumbled with his key in the door of his room, he could feel her heart beating next to his own.

Aiden carried Jordan to the bed and laid her down. She seemed to be sleeping now, and some of her color had returned. He positioned her head comfortably on the pillow, brushing her long hair back from her face. He paused a minute, feeling the softness of it, before pulling the comforter gently over her.

He turned and locked the door, thinking, *Now what?* Again he gazed at the woman asleep in his bed. Aiden ran his fingers through his hair. He had probably just blown the most important thing his father had ever entrusted him to do, but well, unforeseen circumstances had interfered with his carefully laid plans. He crossed the room and pulled down the blinds, shutting out the dim glow from the old-fashioned street light outside. He switched on the small lamp on the dresser. It was a three-way bulb, and he turned it to its lowest wattage. He paced the room for a minute or two, confused, glancing at Jordan repeatedly, watching for the rise and fall in the comforter that indicated she was still breathing evenly.

Finally, he blew through his lips in exasperation, and pulling off his shoes, he climbed up on the bed and sat beside her, propped up on pillows. He reached into his pocket, pulled out his phone, and began to play Angry Birds. Jordan was breathing regularly; it appeared any danger was probably past. Aiden would wait for her to sleep it off.

Chapter Five

The first sensation Jordan was aware of was one of being safe and warm. She stirred slightly under the soft comforter that covered her. As she pulled herself up into consciousness, she thought she must be in her own bed, her baby beside her. Something was vaguely different, though. She moved her hand, but there was no baby beneath it. Even before she was fully awake, panic began to set in. Where was she? Who was in bed with her? She moaned and opened her eyes. The realization hit her like a stone: she was not home, and she was not alone. Her eyes would not focus. The panic exploded in a rush of adrenaline. Jordan threw the comforter off and vaulted from the bed. In the half-light, she stumbled on something on the floor and cried out in pain.

A man shot up from the other side of the bed, and a cell phone clattered to the floor.

"What the hell!" yelled Jordan. "What the hell is going on? What am I doing here? Who are you?" A sudden dizziness set upon her, and she reeled.

In an instant, Jordan was caught in the man's arms as she sank to her knees. She mounted an effort to get away, and she stood again. "Get your hands off me!" she mumbled.

"It's me, Aiden. Aiden Stewart. Calm down. You'll wake the whole building."

"Let—go—of—me!" She struggled to break free of his grip.

Aiden dropped his arms and stepped away, his back to the door. "Calm down," he repeated. "Let me tell you what happened."

Jordan said nothing. She stood there, motionless, her hands clenched, her hair in a wild halo around her head and shoulders. And despite the pain in her stomach, her eyes widened in anger.

Aiden cleared his throat. "I think Fenton drugged your drink. He set you up, Jordan."

Jordan blinked. This couldn't be happening. "You're lying," she said in a deadly voice, but Aiden shook his head.

"I'm telling you the truth," he said. He was beginning to relax. His voice slowed, and he talked more confidently. "Will you please listen to me?"

The room was beginning to spin again. Jordan sat back down on the edge of the bed and stared at the floor. *I might as well hear what he has to say*, she thought. "Go ahead."

"How much do you remember?" When Jordan didn't answer, Aiden went on. "I was at dinner, seated just a couple of tables away from you, when you came in with Fenton. You didn't see me, and he doesn't know me. I could hear pieces of your conversation. I knew you were talking about Chat. Then, when you got up to go to the ladies' room, I could see something had happened. I knew you didn't feel well. At first I thought you drank too much."

Jordan made a sarcastic sound. "I just had ginger ale," she said emphatically.

Aiden continued, gaining confidence. "By the time you got back, I could see you were sick. When you left to go home, I overheard Fenton calling the police, reporting an inebriated woman in a green dress leaving the Inn."

Jordan lifted her head and looked at Aiden. Her eyes had adjusted to the partially lighted room, and she could make out his features now. She could see his concern. Her heart, which had been pounding in her chest, began to slow. "Fenton called the police?" she asked slowly.

Aiden nodded. "Yes," he said. "He wanted them to pick you up. He must have put something in your drink to mimic intoxication, to impair you. Do you remember anything about what happened?"

Jordan looked down at her hands, folded in her lap. "Are you making this up? Are you lying to me?" She still could not wrap her mind around such an incredulous scenario.

Aiden spoke sharply. "Jordan, this is serious! I'm telling you the truth. Now what do you remember?"

Jordan flexed her shoulders and brushed her unruly hair back from her face. Her stomach still hurt, and she felt weak and queasy. She tried to concentrate.

"I remember dinner, of course," she said slowly, not looking up from her hands. "I remember dinner and then, and then —" Jordan looked up and found Aiden's eyes, full of compassion and concern. She smiled ever so slightly. "And then I remember you. I remember you running toward me. I was only trying to get into my car and drive home. I was feeling so sick. You were yelling at me. You scared me."

"Sorry."

Jordan's smile deepened. "That's okay. Oh, and I remember John showed up."

"Who?"

"John Giamo, our police chief."

"Yes. He was there. He'll tell you they got a call about a young woman driving drunk."

Jordan put her hands up to her face. "I can't believe this!"

"Believe it," muttered Aiden. "Can I turn on a stronger light?"

Jordan nodded. Aiden switched on the bedside lamp, and Jordan glanced at the red numbers on the digital clock. It was two a.m.

"I've got to get home," she said.

"I'll drive you," said Aiden. "It still wouldn't be safe for you to drive."

"You're right." She sighed as she bent down to pick up her shoes from the floor. "I don't even think I can walk in these heels right now. I'm still dizzy."

"Oh, so you want me to carry you down, too?"

She looked at him, noticing a playful smile on his lips. "Did you carry me up here?"

"I did," he said. "I wanted you to be safe."

She was silent for a moment and then she said, "Well, thank you, Aiden. Thank you for that."

Aiden coughed in embarrassment. "It's okay," he said softly. "Any time."

Jordan stood up shakily. "I better go home. They'll be wondering where the hell I am."

Aiden stuck his neck out with his next question. "They?"

Jordan fumbled with her hair, trying to wind it back into a bun. "I live with my parents," she said simply.

"Is Grace your mother?"

Jordan looked up sharply. "Why do you ask?"

"You mumbled something about Grace while you were sleeping."

"Oh. Oh, well, yes. Grace is my mother. Look, I have to try to put myself back together. Excuse me." She went into the bathroom and closed the narrow door behind her.

"Crap!" she said with a groan. "I look a fright!"

"You don't," came reassurance from the other side of the door. "You look fine."

"Thanks for lying to me," she said as she opened the bathroom door. She was barefoot, and her hair was pulled back from her face except for a few tendrils that curved over her forehead. She was suddenly aware that Aiden was watching her with something in his eyes that made her pulse quicken.

"Let's go." Her tone was urgent. "I don't want anybody to see me here like this with you. Rumors spread like wildfire in a town like this."

Aiden led the way down the creaky old stairway. They crossed the lobby silently, and when they got outside, Jordan stopped for a moment. "Would you lend me your arm, please? I want to put my shoes on now."

Aiden offered his arm without hesitation as she lifted her legs up, one by one, and slipped her shoes on. Her dress hiked nearly to her hip, and she hurriedly yanked it down as she caught a glance out of the corner of her eye. "There," she said. "I'm ready. Where's your car?"

Aiden led the way to his BMW. He followed her directions and headed out of town on a side street. She had the strange feeling she was in high school again, sneaking home in the wee hours of the morning. It was good to drive over the back roads with a cute guy next to her. Aiden reached down to shift gears in the sports car as she gave directions, and his hand grazed the exposed skin of her thigh. He didn't seem to notice, but Jordan's heart leaped. Suddenly, it wasn't business anymore. It was personal.

"Here. Right here. Turn right," Jordan spoke up and pointed. A colonial style lamppost lighted the end of the driveway. Aiden turned in and pulled up to the garage door. The ride was over way too soon. Reality came crashing down.

"Thank you so much, really," Jordan said hurriedly as she opened the door, but as she turned her body to get out, Aiden laid his hand on her arm. She paused and looked back at him.

"Will we still be having a meeting tomorrow?" he asked.

"Of course," she answered stiffly. She paused, then continued, "Look, I really appreciate what you did for me—"

"You said that. You're welcome."

"What I mean is, you have to tell me what you think happened with Fenton."

"I told you what I *know* happened."

"I want to hear it again, in detail. This has changed everything. This is criminal. Can you meet me at nine in my office?"

"You won't get much sleep."

"I never get much sleep. I run a business, and I—" She paused and pushed the car door open.

"You what?"

Jordan gave a little laugh. "I get tired," she replied. "Good night, Aiden, and thank you again. We'll talk tomorrow. Or, rather, later this morning." She got out of the car.

"Good night."

It seemed he might have wanted to say more, but she needed to leave, to go inside and get the rest her body needed. Jordan closed the car door and walked away without looking back. From the front window of her parents' house, she peered out discretely, noticing that Aiden had waited until she'd gone inside before turning the car around and heading back down the road.

She tipped toed across the kitchen floor, trying to get to her bedroom without waking anyone, but it was too late. Her mother stood in the hallway in her nightgown and bathrobe.

"Jordan!" she admonished in a stage whisper. "Why are you so late? I was getting worried."

"Oh, Mom, I'm sorry. I—I had to go back to the office after the dinner and do some changes on the proposal. Did I wake Grace?"

Her mother shook her head. "She fell asleep between Dad and me. I just moved her into her crib a few minutes ago. You look a wreck. Are you all right?"

Jordan brushed at her hair with her hand. "Oh, I fell asleep in my chair while I was working."

"Well, get into bed as quickly as you can. You can still get a couple hours of good sleep."

"Thank you, Mom," Jordan said, and she bent forward and kissed her mother on the cheek.

"I'll just be happy when you get this behind you and you can work regular hours again and have more time with Grace."

"Me, too," agreed Jordan. She walked quietly down the hall and into Grace's room, closing the door softly behind her.

Grace lay asleep in her crib. Jordan gazed at her baby as the nightlight illuminated the innocent, rosy-cheeked face. She drew the blanket up tenderly over the baby's shoulders and watched her for a few more minutes. Nothing had ever been so perfect. Soft as a butterfly kiss, she touched Grace's cheek. Then she crossed the hall to her own room where she undressed and pulled on her old, comfortable pajamas. Exhaustion was setting in for real as she walked into her own small bathroom which her father had made for her out of part of her closet. She managed to wash her face and brush her teeth, but she crawled into bed without even trying to put a brush through her tangled hair.

The cloying, sick feeling was beginning to fade now. Jordan closed her eyes and willed herself to relax so that sleep might come, but her thoughts were slow to stop swirling. She was horrified by the events of the evening. Now all her plans for the business were in a tailspin. She couldn't even think about what to do until morning. She squeezed her eyes in an effort to banish the worry. As she drifted toward rest, she found herself thinking about Aiden. How did he happen to materialize just when she needed help? And why was he so maddeningly attractive? Jordan's thoughts stopped as she recalled her feelings at the accidental brush of his hand against her naked thigh when he'd shifted gears in the car.

That touch had made her stomach leap and her heart pound. She'd pretended she hadn't noticed, but the spot where his hand had touched her felt enflamed and hot. That heat had spread through her entire body, awakening feelings she had not felt since before Grace was born. Feelings she thought were gone for her forever.

Tears of exhaustion, confusion, and self-pity welled up in Jordan's eyes, but she blinked them back and buried her head deeper into her pillow. There was no room in her life for outbursts of feelings, emotional or physical. There was certainly no room for self-pity. The only thing that mattered now was that little person with the riotous red curls who lay sleeping in the room across from hers. She focused on thoughts of her baby and finally drifted into a fitful sleep.

Chapter Six

Even though Aiden's head didn't touch the pillow until three thirty in the morning, he was wide awake three hours later. He stretched and yawned, only to discover his mouth felt like the inside of a Dumpster. A shower was the first priority. He got out of bed, went into the bathroom, and cranked the faucet firmly toward "Hot." The little room filled with steam, occluding his reflection in the mirror as he brushed his teeth. *Just as well,* he thought. *I don't look so great this morning.* He pulled back the curtain and stepped under the cascading water.

Twenty minutes later, showered and shaved and dressed in jeans, a blue striped shirt, and a leather jacket, Aiden went downstairs to the breakfast buffet. Despite the weird drama of the night before, he was hungry. He took a plate, helped himself to blueberry pancakes and coffee, and revisited his little table from the night before, now empty and made up fresh for the morning with a spotless white tablecloth and a bud vase with a daisy in it. Flatware and a snowy napkin were already laid on the table. Aiden sat down to eat and ruminate on the events of the previous night.

His meeting with Jordan was at nine, and he wondered how she would act. He wondered whether it was prudent to bring up what had happened last night. Personally, he thought she should report the whole incident to the police and take Fenton to the mat. The man was ruthless to a dangerous degree—to the degree that he would actually play with peoples' physical well-being to get what he wanted.

His cell phone vibrated in his pocket. Aiden pulled it out and saw his father's number. He stared at the screen for a few seconds and then made a command decision, touching "Ignore." Aiden had not spoken to his father since the previous afternoon, before these unbelievable incidents had taken place. Now, until he managed to unravel this mess, he decided not to. There would be plenty of time to hash it out with the old Yankee. Whether he closed the deal or failed didn't seem so important to Aiden anymore. It was suddenly perfectly clear: what was important was Jordan Fitzgerald. From the start, she had affected him in a way he'd not been prepared for. He found himself thinking about her constantly—and not in a business sense. Now, Aiden wanted to know what this enigmatic young woman thought about him, if she thought about him at all. There was only one way to find out and that was to ask her. He gulped down the last of his coffee, pulled on his jacket, and walked outside.

The morning was cool and bright. Birds were twittering, and again there was an underlying scent of lilacs in the air. Aiden stood on the porch and breathed in the fresh air. The world of Clark's Corner was just beginning to wake. An empty school bus drove by, followed by a couple of pickup trucks. Otherwise, everything was quiet. The offices of ChatDotCom were only about three miles away. Aiden glanced at his watch; he had plenty of time and decided to walk there. As he walked, he looked around.

Clark's Corner was centered around the pretty little green, bordered on one side by the Inn and other side by the main route that ran through town. A quaint gazebo, reminiscent of the turn of the century, adorned the green at one end, its six-sided railing decorated with green planter boxes full of pansies. On the other side of the main street was a brick-walled cemetery. Aiden could see the old crypt, built into a rise in the ground and covered over with grass, as though it was part of the natural turf. He read the date, 1726, above the bolted steel door. In those days, when the ground was too frozen to dig a proper grave during the winter months, people were laid to rest in the crypt until warm weather in the spring allowed for burial. It was a peaceful, cozy cemetery with lilacs, old hydrangeas, and huge maples growing in between the old slate stones and the newer granite ones.

Most of the houses along the main street were the old Victorian style with their pretty gingerbread trim and their turret rooms. Many of these had been turned into businesses. There was a dress shop and a dentist's office in one, a real estate office in another, and then there was the one that housed MacTavish's Pub. As Aiden reached the end of the main street, the houses changed, reflecting the older Federal and Georgian designs. These had undoubtedly been built by the first wealthy farmers and merchants in the area. The Victorians would have followed later, when the factories were built along the river, on the other side of the railroad tracks.

Aiden walked along until the sidewalk ended. Then he crossed the main street and proceeded east toward the railroad tracks. The houses here were smaller, more tightly packed. They had been built by the first laborers who had saved enough money to build their own homes. In amongst these houses were nestled Rick's Garage, a plumbing and heating business, and a hardware store. The farther he walked, the more Aiden saw of the town's history, laid out before him like an open book. How many generations had struggled here in this sleepy place, building homes, businesses, building lives? How many people had been born here, labored here, and finally rested in the walled cemetery?

Aiden crossed the still active railroad tracks and proceeded along the road until he could see the offices of ChatDotCom. Despite its sleepy appearance, the town had a vibrancy that couldn't be denied. There was the school, a hospital, and Gene Palmer had stepped in, bought the deserted factory building and started his communications company. You couldn't get more current than Internet involvement and employment for four hundred people.

The renovated factory loomed ahead of him. Instead of walking across the new cement bridge to the parking lot, Aiden took the old footbridge across the canal, another relic of a time when all the employees walked to work. He pulled open the big front doors. It seemed light years since he had first entered this building, but incredibly, it had only been the day before. And in that one day, his outlook on a lot of things had changed dramatically.

Ashley was sitting at the curved, marble-topped desk. When she saw Aiden, she stood up quickly, a big smile on her face.

"Aiden!" she said spontaneously, then her hand flew to her lips. "Oh," she gasped. "I'm sorry. I meant, good morning, Mr. Stewart."

Aiden smiled back at her. "No problem. My name is Aiden. Is Jordan in yet?"

His use of Jordan's first name was not lost on Ashley. "Yes," she said, her smile returning. "She just came in a minute ago. Shall I tell her you're here?"

"Please."

Ashley opened the office door and slipped in. A moment later, she returned, much as she had done on that first day when he thought he was meeting with a cranky old man. "You can go in now."

Aiden walked into the office and closed the door behind him. Jordan was standing behind her desk, studying a document she held in her hand. Her appearance did not betray the events of the night before. She was once again the consummate professional, dressed in a form-fitting beige suit with a high-necked, white shirt. Her hair, so uninhibited just a few hours ago, had been swept into submission, wound into a tight bun at the back of her neck. She wore gold hoops in her ears.

"Hi," said Aiden.

"Good morning," she replied, not looking up.

Aiden's brow furrowed. He approached the desk. "How are you feeling?"

Jordan looked up. "I'm fine," she said. "Maybe a little tired, but otherwise fine. Thank you for asking. Now, shall we get started and discuss this Trade Winds offer?"

If she had slapped him across his face, Aiden could not have been more shocked. What the hell was wrong with this woman? "What do you mean?" he asked, speaking carefully.

"I mean, let's talk about what Trade Winds has to offer ChatDot-Com." Jordan held on to the edge of her desk, as if to anchor herself. "I have to make a decision."

Aiden threw caution to the wind. Let Fenton take over the company. Let him find holes in her contract and fire her. Let him break up ChatDotCom. If that was her decision, he wasn't going to fight it, no matter what his father thought. Trade Winds could survive without Chat, no matter what scheme Fenton pulled, but Aiden was not going to walk away without finding out once and for all what made M. Jordan Fitzgerald tick.

He crossed the room and leaned over her desk, looking straight at her. "Before I go one step further, we're going to hash out what happened last night. I got involved. I got involved because I felt myself caring what happened to you and your company, being played by a scumbag like Chris Fenton, and I stuck my neck out to make sure you didn't get a DUI like Fenton had planned. He put something in your drink, Jordan. He tried to set you up."

Jordan raised her head slightly and fixed her large blue eyes on him. "Well, just to satisfy your curiosity, I called Fenton this morning because we were supposed to meet today. I told him I was busy all day and would contact him later. He wasn't too pleased, but I held him off. And I do really appreciate your efforts on my behalf," she said, her grip on the desk tightening noticeably, "but I have to keep this on a professional level. I — "

Aiden brought his fist down on the desk so hard Jordan jumped back. "Stop it! Stop this bullshit now! I'm not curious. I'm concerned. And I'm not talking about anything professional until we get the personal side sorted out. Now just listen to me. Let me speak." He stopped to catch his breath.

Jordan blinked and said softly, "Go ahead. I'm listening."

Aiden took a deep breath and ran his fingers through his hair. "I'm sorry. I'm sorry for the outburst, but you got to me, Jordan. You got to me, and I'm not afraid to say it. The truth is, I think you're very brave. I see what you're going through. I see how young you are. You haven't had a lot of time to meet people like Fenton, but unfortunately, they're out there. Sometimes, a person is just born bad, and that's Fenton. I really didn't think he'd go as far as he did, but now that I've seen it with my own eyes, that's my opinion."

He turned away and began to pace back and forth in front of the desk. "I think you should file a police report. I think he should be confronted on this. You could have been killed or you could have killed someone else. My suggestion to you is that you file that police report today, and then you consider Trade Winds' offer of a merger with Chat. I promise you, I will work with you on the merger details to make it as advantageous to both of us as possible. I won't lie to you; Trade Winds wants its foot in this door pretty damn bad. We'll agree to a lot of things just for that position. I think we can give Gene Palmer what he wants and make you look good too. Work with me here. I'm your friend, Jordan. I'm on your side." Aiden was talked out. He slumped into one of the wing chairs and looked at her, waiting.

Jordan came out from behind her desk, her hands visibly trembling. She walked over to the other wing chair and sat down, clasping her hands in her lap, but Aiden noticed they were shaking.

"Aiden," she said, "you helped me. When you came running down the street, I couldn't believe it. I wanted to cry, but I was so — so impaired, I wasn't thinking clearly. Then, when I woke up later in your room, I didn't know what to think. I couldn't remember how I got there. I thought something might have, you know, something might have happened between us." She looked down into her lap and twisted her fingers. "I'm sorry. I shouldn't have said that, but I was so confused. I'm sorry you saw me like that. It doesn't mean I can't control myself. It doesn't mean I'm not a serious businesswoman. Mr. Palmer has put a lot of faith in me, and I don't want to let him down." Her voice gained strength. "I will continue to do the best for ChatDotCom that I can. As for Christopher Fenton, I don't want to file a police report. And before you make a comment, I'll tell you why. I couldn't pin anything on him. Whatever he used on me has left my system by now anyway, so I wouldn't be able to show that he'd drugged me. On top of that, if I chose to pursue it, the case would become the focus of more energy than I want to spend on Fenton. It would take away from what I have to do, from my duty to Mr. Palmer and the employees of Chat. I prefer to tell him in no uncertain terms that I will not accept his offer. I'm not even going to bring up the incident. I'm going to let him think it just didn't work."

Before Aiden could respond, Jordan's office door opened. Aiden turned to see a pleasant looking, gray-haired woman dressed in jeans and a light spring parka standing in the doorway holding a small child with curly red hair. He politely stood as Jordan leaped up from her chair. "Mom!" She was clearly surprised. "What are you doing here?"

"Mm-mm-mama," shrilled the little girl, holding out her arms. Aiden watched as Jordan took the child and cuddled her on her hip. "Baby, baby, baby," she crooned.

"Oh, I'm sorry, Jordan," said the older woman. "We were just in the neighborhood and decided to stop in. Ashley wasn't at her desk. It's lunch time. Can you go to lunch with us?"

"Oh, Mom, no, not today. I'm sorry." Jordan shot a few glances at Aiden as she held the girl. She looked uncomfortable, nervous. Aiden remained quiet, hoping to put her at ease, while questions exploded in his head. She turned to Aiden, gesturing to her mother. "Aiden Stewart, this is my mother, Sharon Fitzgerald. Mom, this is Aiden Stewart. He represents a company looking to merge with Chat."

Aiden extended his hand, and Sharon Fitzgerald took it in a firm handshake. "How nice to meet you, Mr. Stewart."

"Same here," Aiden said with a smile. Then he turned to Jordan, still smiling. "And who is this?"

Jordan kissed the baby on the cheek. "This is my daughter, Grace," she said firmly.

"Well," said Sharon, reaching out to take Grace back from Jordan, "we will be on our way, then, and let you two get back to your negotiations. Nice to meet you, Mr. Stewart."

"And you as well," Aiden replied.

"Bye, Mom. See you tonight."

The baby kicked her little feet and made fussing noises as her grandmother carried her out of the room.

Jordan closed the door behind them. She let out a quick sigh as she turned back to Aiden. "Let's get going, then. I'm all ears. What've you got?"

"So Grace is not your mother. You didn't tell me you had a baby."

"Why would I?" Jordan's demeanor had become nonchalant.

"I didn't know you were married."

"I'm not."

Aiden blinked. "Oh. What happened? Divorced?"

"No. I never had a husband. I don't have a boyfriend. I have Grace." Jordan's lips were tight as she spoke. "You're getting awfully close to going somewhere I don't think it's necessary to go. Why don't we just stick to business?"

Aiden gave in, putting up his hands in surrender. "Okay, okay. I apologize. She's a cute little girl, though."

Jordan relaxed and smiled at him. "Yes. She's the cutest."

"I was just trying to get to know you better," said Aiden, defending himself.

Jordan flashed him an enigmatic smile. "You don't need to know me any better than you do."

They retired back to the wing chairs and huddled over the low table, scrutinizing both proposals point by point.

As they worked, Aiden could see Jordan become more relaxed. He could certainly understand her desire to keep personal lives out of business associations. Aiden remained professional throughout their meeting. He didn't criticize her ideas, but took them all seriously and worked to fit them to the proposal in the most beneficial way. She listened to him as though trying to soak up all the business knowledge she could. But more was happening here; Aiden could feel it. More than once, he caught her watching him as he bent over the low table, eyeing the definition of the muscles in his exposed forearms. As he bent forward, her gaze lingered on his chest. Sometimes, as they worked, he would point out a specific paragraph or line, and she would lean in close to follow his pen on the paper. The warmth coming from their bodies—their awareness of each other—was obvious, and he sensed her heartbeat was quickening just as his was.

At last, Aiden straightened up and looked at his watch, breaking the sexual tension that had invaded the room. It was two o'clock. "I think this is coming together pretty well," he said. "I want to call my father and run some of these details by him. I think it's together enough for you to take it to Gene Palmer. What do you think?"

Jordan stood up and walked to the big windows to stretch her legs. She turned around, and Aiden looked up at her with a sudden smile. She couldn't suppress the need to smile back. They'd accomplished a lot in this meeting, most importantly, Aiden thought, establishing Jordan's willingness to trust Aiden.

"I'd like to take it to Mr. Palmer this afternoon," she said, "before he gets too tired and has to stress himself to concentrate. He's in the middle of a chemotherapy session again and it just exhausts him."

Aiden shook his head and said, "I'm very sorry that he is sick. I've never met him, but from what my father says, he's been a real force in the industry. And my father doesn't hand out compliments easily. It's too bad."

"I appreciate that, Aiden," she said, softening. "Mr. Palmer means the world to me. He gave me a chance when I didn't think I had one."

"I'd say you were capable of getting a good position wherever you wanted," said Aiden. "Where did you go to school?"

"I went to the University of Vermont for two years," Jordan said as she faced the span of windows.

"Then where?" Aiden said to her back.

"Then nowhere," she answered without turning around.

This girl was more of a mystery than he'd thought. "Well, how did you come to work for ChatDotCom?"

"Do we have to go there?"

"Not if you don't want to. All I asked was a simple question. What's all the intrigue?"

Aiden saw Jordan's shoulders drop as she turned around to face him. "There's no intrigue, okay? I came home to do an internship the summer of my sophomore year. At Chat. My job was working as Mr. Palmer's assistant. Actually, Ashley started that same year, as a receptionist. I loved it. I loved my job. Mr. Palmer was pleased with my enthusiasm, and he taught me even more than I learned acting as an intern. He sent me to conventions and special training sessions. He said I had a real head for business."

"I agree," Aiden offered. He leaned back in his chair, listening intently.

Jordan paced in front of the windows, looking down at the floor.

"That summer was wonderful. I really knew what I wanted to do. I went back to school in the fall, but I always came home every chance I got, for every vacation, to work with Mr. Palmer as much as I could. Then, when I went back to school after Christmas break and started the spring semester, things started to happen." She paused and sighed.

"Things?" prompted Aiden.

Jordan looked agitated, hesitant to share her past with him, but she continued. "Yes. My father lost his job. My mother was working part time at the town office, but it wasn't enough to support all our expenses. My father looked for work everywhere. He ended up getting a lot of temporary carpentry jobs, and he also mowed lawns and plowed snow for people. It's how they managed to barely stay afloat. I started to feel real guilty about my tuition bills. I borrowed all I could, and I did have some scholarships, but it wasn't enough. My parents borrowed money, too. And then…and then I got pregnant." Jordan stopped short, and Aiden thought she was done talking. He waited. Finally, she sighed again. "I got pregnant," she repeated, "so I didn't go back to school. I knew right away I wanted that baby—Grace—and my parents said we'd manage somehow. Then I went to Mr. Palmer and told him what had happened. I thought…I thought he might blow up at me, but he didn't. I remember the look on his face. He was shocked, I guess, at first, but he came around. Then he said he had an opening for an assistant and asked if I wanted the job. I almost cried with relief, and the salary was substantial. I could take some of the pressure off my parents. I would be able to support my baby. I took the job, and, well, here I am." She paused and looked straight at Aiden. Her eyes shimmered with gathering tears, but she blinked them back. "And then…that's when Mr. Palmer got sick and everything changed."

Aiden responded quietly, "I admire you. And as for change, sometimes we can't avoid that. It just happens."

"Well, I don't like it!" exclaimed Jordan passionately. "Change hasn't been good for me. It's swept the rug out from under me, and it's made things difficult. I do the best I can, and I keep things running smoothly."

"It seems as though you do," Aiden commented. He wanted to stand and wrap his arms around her. He wanted to kiss her.

A soft knock at the door interrupted them, and Ashley came into the room. "You two have been shut up in here for so long," she said. "You've got to have something to eat or take a break or something. Shall I order a pizza? It's almost three o'clock."

"Oh, thank you, Ashley," said Jordan. "We were just talking about taking a break. Actually, I want to take this to Mr. Palmer this afternoon."

Aiden stood and picked up his jacket. "I want to get back to the Inn and call my father to fill him in."

"Then no pizza?" asked Ashley.

Jordan gave a little laugh. "No, thanks," she said. "And you know what? By the time I get done at Mr. Palmer's, it'll be getting late. I'll just go home from there."

Aiden immediately saw an opportunity and took it. "Why don't you meet me at the Inn for dinner? We can discuss what Palmer and my father said then."

Jordan laughed so loudly Ashley jumped. "No thanks! I think I'll be skipping dinners at the Inn for a while. I'll just eat at home tonight."

"Well, why don't we meet after—" Judiciously, he decided to rephrase his question. "Can you meet after your little girl goes to bed? That way we can probably wrap up all the loose ends tonight."

Jordan pondered his offer. "Where?"

Aiden shrugged. "Anywhere you want," he said agreeably.

She took another moment, seeming to consider her options. "Why don't we just meet back here at my office at, like, eight o'clock?"

Aiden slipped his arms into his jacket and settled it around his shoulders. "Sounds good to me," he said as he walked out the door. "See you then."

Chapter Seven

Aiden walked briskly back to the Inn, following the same route he had taken that morning. It felt good to get out and stretch his muscles. The afternoon was sunny and warm. His mind drifted to thoughts of Jordan Fitzgerald. He wished vehemently, angrily even, that he had met her under different circumstances. He wished he had met her at a friend's house, or a party, or hell, even in the check-out line in the grocery store. She would have perceived him differently. He could have made her laugh. He could have learned more about her, more about what interested her. How did she see him, he wondered. She gave very little of herself away, and it both intrigued and frustrated him. Since he had first laid eyes on her, he had been desperate to crack that mystique, to break through that force field she surrounded herself with. Aiden knew there was depth and feeling to Jordan. He knew by the way she'd held her child. He knew by the passionate way she spoke about the business and Gene Palmer. No one with that much energy and drive didn't burn hot. She was so young to be in her circumstances, and yet she was more intelligent than any woman he had ever been with. He was hobbled by those circumstances now, and it was messing with his mind.

And then there was last night, when she lay sleeping in his bed, that glorious hair spilling over the pillows, her bare legs curled gracefully, and her feet peeking out from under the comforter. She had such pretty feet, Aiden thought, smiling at the memory of the long, delicately arched feet with the blush-painted nails. The ride to her house had nearly driven him crazy. Even sick, she was beautiful. All he had wanted to do was touch her. He ran his fingers through his hair and skipped up the front steps.

Susan Noyes looked up from the front desk as he hurried by. "Good afternoon," she said cordially.

Aiden managed a smile. "Hi," he said, and he climbed the stairs to his room. Once in, with the door locked behind him, Aiden lay on the bed, propped himself up against the pillows, and brooded. He wasn't allowed this reverie for long, though. His cell phone jangled, jarring him, and he knew who it was before he looked at the screen.

"Hello," he groaned.

"Aiden! Where the hell have you been?" his father roared. "I called. No answer. I left messages. No return call. What the hell! What the hell, Aiden!"

"Are you done, Dad?" Aiden retorted.

"Tell me what's going on? Did you make the deal?"

"One more meeting tonight, and I think it's a wrap."

"Ha ha!" crowed the old man. "Good job, son! Good job!"

"Well, save the celebrations for now. It's not a done deal yet."

"Give me the details."

For the next forty-five minutes, Aiden read the proposal to his father, going over the salient points. The elder Stewart picked and prodded at some of the more lenient concessions, but in the end, he was satisfied with the document.

"Good job," he said again, and Aiden breathed a sigh of relief. "Now, get this thing signed and sealed tonight. We don't want them pulling some fast one tomorrow. Any fuss from Fenton might start a corporate war we'll wish we weren't part of. We can't give a chance for rebuttal."

"I'll do it, Dad. We'll get it finalized this evening."

"Call as soon as you're finished."

"I will. Talk to you later."

Aiden clicked off before his father could launch into another tirade. Then he fell back against his pillows. He sighed deeply, closed his eyes, and was soon fast asleep.

He awoke two hours later with a start, his heart beating. The room was nearly dark. He glanced at the clock; he was to meet Jordan at her office in an hour, and he was starving. Reaching for the phone next to the bed, he punched "1" for the front desk. It would be a miracle if anyone answered, he thought, but he immediately heard Susan's voice on the other end of the line. "Front desk. May I help you?"

"Yes, I have a meeting at eight," Aiden replied. "Is there a place to order a pizza around here?"

"There is, Mr. Stewart," she said. "You can call Stoned Pizza. They're right on your way to ChatDotCom."

Aiden eyes widened. How Jordan could remain so mysterious in a town like this was astounding. Or maybe they just looked after their own here. Susan supplied the restaurant's number, and Aiden thanked her.

"You're welcome," Susan said and hung up.

Aiden punched the number into his cell phone.

"Stoned Pizza," a female voice said.

"I'd like to order a large pizza. I'll pick it up in about forty-five minutes. Onions, mushrooms, sausage."

"Thanks. Name?"

Aiden gave his name and number and clicked off.

A shower was in order. He was feeling stiff and disoriented after the unaccustomed nap. He stripped and stepped into the small shower stall, letting the hot water revive him. Half an hour later, he was in his car, dressed in jeans, a black T-shirt, and Nike trainers, pulling into the ChatDotCom parking lot, the still-hot pizza and a six-pack of Long Trail Lager on the seat beside him. He parked next to Jordan's Jeep Grand Cherokee, gathered up the pizza and beer, and went to the back entrance.

ChatDotCom worked round the clock, but after seven in the evening it was only a skeleton crew of a few technicians, a customer service supporter, and Dayton Phillips, the janitor and self-proclaimed night watchman. The steel door was locked, and Aiden pounded rather firmly on it, hoping someone would hear him before the pizza got cold and the beer got warm.

A minute later, he heard the clicking of locks being released and the door opened. He had expected to see the green-clad custodian, but it was Jordan who stood there, in a white v-neck T-shirt, jeans, and gold-colored flats. She was smiling.

"Come on in," she said. "Oh, you brought sustenance! Here, I'll help you." She reached out and took the pizza box. "Follow me. I saw you drive in, so I let you in myself. Let me just make sure this is all locked up correctly." She held the pizza with one hand and threw the dead bolts with the other. Then she flashed him another smile and walked past him down the hall toward her office. Aiden followed obediently.

He watched her from behind; her walk was graceful in the flat shoes. He was aware of her square shoulders and her small, trim waist. She was obviously active, athletic even, but ample and curvy where she should be, as revealed by her slim-fitting jeans. Aiden thought it was a good thing he was carrying the beer because he had the over-powering feeling he wanted to reach out and hold her. He ached to feel those smooth hips move under his hands. He swallowed hard.

They went into Jordan's office. She shut the door behind her and locked it. The office seemed different at night; heavy beige drapes had been drawn across the big windows, and the overhead lights were off. None of the daily noise of doing business filtered through the big door. Lamps on the desk and the small table near the chairs lit the room dimly. Jordan set the pizza down on the low table in front of the chairs. "Have a seat," she said.

Aiden sat down and took a beer from the six-pack. "Help yourself to the pizza," he said. "Do you want a beer? I'm starving. I haven't eaten since early this morning."

Jordan let out an awkward laugh. "Thanks," she said. "I had that meeting with Mr. Palmer, and by the time I got home, I had just enough time to sit down with Grace and share her sweet potato puree and prune pudding! I had a glass of milk, but I'll gladly have a beer now."

Aiden hadn't touched the beer he opened so he handed it to her and cracked himself another one. "Cheers." He lifted his bottle, and she reciprocated.

"Now, let's get down to business," said Jordan, leaning forward and opening her portfolio. "What did your father think of our agreement?"

Before answering, Aiden took another swallow of beer. The grainy goodness of it lingered in his mouth, bolstering his confidence. "He liked it, all in all." He opened his copy and flipped through the pages of the proposal. "There were a couple of things he wanted to go over. How about Palmer?"

Jordan was intently looking at the papers. "He was about the same," she replied. "There are a couple of things he wants clarified." Aiden hardly heard her, conscious as he was of the way her neck curved and the exquisite little hollow at the base of her throat. There were random delicate curls around her forehead and ears, as though her hair, confined by the large hair clip at the nape of her neck, was struggling to free itself.

They worked for a while, sipping their beers, compromising on the salient points. Then Aiden finally tossed down his packet. "Damn, I'm starving! I'm going to eat."

Jordan laughed as he tore into the pizza box and lifted out a generous piece.

"Want some?"

"Actually, yes, I do," she said and reached for the pizza. Aiden handed it over to her. A few mushrooms fell from the slice she'd selected, but she scooped them up and popped them in her mouth with a childish grin. He watched, mesmerized, as she licked her fingers clean.

"It's probably a little cool now," he said.

"Oh, I love cold pizza anyway. I give the crusts to Grace to chew."

"Ha! I remember when my sister used to give my nephew a bagel to keep him quiet, and he would sit there, sucking it, the snot running out of his nose right over the bagel. Then my sister would wipe his nose, without taking the bagel away or anything, and the kid would just go on gumming it. I guess that's a mother for you!"

Jordan laughed. "That's so funny!" she exclaimed. "I do the same thing with Grace! I take it you don't have any children?"

It was a bold question, as personal a question as she had asked him. Aiden looked up, taken by surprise. "No," he answered, "not yet."

"Grace is my parents' first grandchild. They take care of her during the day. It makes it easier for me to work, not having to worry about her."

"That's a good arrangement," agreed Aiden. He was sobered. The new, young mother, having to work more than full time for a man who called for her full dedication. His mother and both his sisters had been able to stay home with their children. It was a luxury he hadn't realized before this. "Her father doesn't participate?"

Was it the dim light or had he actually seen her face blanch a little? "No," she said softly. "No, he doesn't." She looked away. Aiden dropped the subject and searched for a new topic of conversation.

"Do you know," he started, struggling, "that when I asked the Inn owner where to get the pizza, she actually knew I was coming here with it? Doesn't it infringe on your privacy to have somebody know your every move?"

Jordan took a sip of her beer. "On the contrary. It's kind of comforting in a way. Everybody knows everybody. Families are intermarried, and it strengthens the fabric of the community. You know who somebody really is. You know their history. You know when somebody is competent in the job they're being asked to do. You know who to depend on. There's a network."

Aiden snorted. "Seems like it compromises the privacy of an individual to me."

"Well, not really," Jordan explained. "Nobody really knows the details about what goes on behind closed doors, but the general feeling of camaraderie is there. Don't get me wrong; people still have their problems. There's divorce and disagreements and situations that arise, but by and large, everybody in town is his brother's keeper, even when it's only the tiniest bit. It makes a difference."

Aiden watched her; he liked how open she'd become with him. She'd become relaxed, more comfortable, and seemed to now trust him. Their eyes met, but the spell was broken as her cell phone rang. She answered it quickly, and Aiden wondered if he should excuse himself from the room. He leaned forward to stand, but she smiled and gestured with a wave of her hand that he could stay seated.

"Hello?"

"Jordan?" Aiden could hear Fenton's voice booming through her phone. Jordan's demeanor changed in an instant. She caught Aiden's eyes, and the look on her face was not lost on him. She held the phone away from her ear, allowing Aiden to listen in.

"This is Jordan. Mr. Fenton?" She watched as Aiden shook his head slowly back and forth.

"Sorry to call so late. I hope you're feeling better. I was wondering when we might get together and finalize our agreement?"

"I'm feeling better," said Jordan tersely. "Thank you for asking. As far as the agreement goes, I think ChatDotCom and Fenton Enterprises are too far apart for any finalization. I'm sorry, Mr. Fenton. I should have called you earlier. You shouldn't waste your company's time trying to acquire Chat any longer. I have a number of merger offers from smaller companies that I feel are more suited to Chat than Fenton."

"I'm rather shocked to hear that," the man replied dryly. "I thought you were a smarter girl than that. You're too young, I guess, to recognize the opportunity I'm providing. I'm sorry you don't think it's a good fit, but I'm not giving up. I'll send you another proposal tomorrow. Let me know what you think. You won't be able to turn this one down. And keep in mind, I can and will go directly to Gene Palmer."

"Do what you think you must." Jordan's response was light, almost aloof. "Thank you for calling." She clicked off.

"Fenton!" breathed Aiden, pushing down his anger.

"Yes." Jordan sat back down, her phone still in her hands. "You heard how he basically insulted me?" She reached for another piece of pizza and nibbled at it.

"What an asshole," said Aiden bluntly.

"I hope he doesn't cause any more trouble." Despite Jordan's effort to appear unaffected, Aiden could tell the man's manner upset her, and the whole conversation brought back memories of the night before. "He said he would go directly to Mr. Palmer."

"Let him."

"Then I'll have to tell Mr. Palmer the truth about why I refused what appears to be a more lucrative agreement."

"Maybe that's not the worst thing." Aiden leaned back in the chair, studying the woman across from him. "How old are you, Jordan?"

"I'm twenty-five, last month."

Aiden smiled. "You are young, but you're also smart. And you're the prettiest CEO I've ever had to negotiate with."

He hadn't meant to say it, but it was said and it was heard. It seemed she realized his sincerity, and he hid his enjoyment at seeing her cheeks flush. Her hand shook slightly, and she dropped her pizza face down on the carpet.

"Damn!" she said, swooping down to pick up the greasy mess just as Aiden bent to accomplish the same task. Their foreheads cracked together.

"Ow!" she cried out before she could help it. She stood up, her hand to her head.

"That hurt!" Aiden stood as well, rubbing his brow, and they both began to laugh. "You're pretty, you're smart, and you've got a head like a football helmet!"

They looked at each other, and Jordan smiled. "Thank you for that."

"Hey, you've got a mark." Aiden instinctively reached out and brushed her forehead gently with his fingertips. "Does it hurt?"

"Not now," she answered. They were standing so close to each other, he could feel the warmth of her body and see the rise and fall of her chest through her shirt. Then, before either of them was quite sure of what was happening, Aiden's lips were on hers. Jordan's body drew up to meet him, her lips parting instinctively, inviting him in. A veil seemed to fall over everything as he increased the pressure of his kiss The relief it brought was overwhelming and her warm, earthy taste fanned his smoldering desires to flames. It was as though he had been awakened from a spell he had not realized he was under. He felt her skin grow warm beneath his fingertips. She lifted her face to his, and he let his lips travel lightly down the curve of her neck until they lingered in the hollow of her throat. His hair brushed her chin, and she uttered a small passionate murmur.

Her delicate gasp resonated through Aiden, overwhelming him with an excitement he had not experienced before. He wrapped his arms around her, holding her as close to him as he could. He felt her capitulate; he felt her firm shape melding into him, surrendering to him, urging him on. Her hands gripped him at the waist and moved upward, until she held his face in her fingertips. This time it was Jordan who initiated the most tender of kisses. Aiden savored her sugary taste. He felt himself transported by her touch, and passion rose in him. He slipped his hand down her back, over the soft swell of her buttock, and down her thigh.

Everything after that happened instinctively. Jordan lifted her leg to his hip, and he curled his hand up under her, supporting her against him. He backed up two steps and sank into the wing chair, hoisting her onto his lap. She straddled him, and his hands went up under her t-shirt. The softness of her skin intoxicated him. Their lips explored each other, seeking fulfillment, seeking completion.

Heat was growing in Aiden's groin. He shifted under her and felt her thighs tighten around him. She lifted herself ever so slightly and brushed back down on him. A groan of ecstasy escaped him. His hands went to her breasts, pushing up under her bra. He felt her taut nipples and took them in his fingertips, squeezing gently, then harder. Jordan lifted her lips from his, flinging her head back with an audible cry as her hips moved instinctively.

Then, just as quickly as their passion had escalated, Jordan wrenched herself out of Aiden's arms. She stood up, struggling to quiet her rapid breathing, her hand to her heart.

"I—I—I can't," she gasped. "I can't! Right now I can't." She looked at Aiden's face in the dim light of the lamp. "Don't look like that, Aiden. It's just that…it's just been so long. And—and—oh, I'm so sorry. I'm sorry." She brought her hands to her face.

Aiden was shaking. He stood and ran both hands through his hair. He struggled for a moment to grasp the situation, to stifle his physical innervation. He felt his ecstasy turn to pain, and he exhaled loudly. Jordan lifted her eyes to his, but Aiden didn't move a muscle.

"Please," she whispered. "Please understand. Aiden, it's not you. I'm so, so attracted to you. I just can't right now. It's me."

In a second, he was in front of her, his arms around her. "Shh," he murmured into her fragrant hair. "Jordan, it's all right. We can take this slow. We can."

Her face was buried in his chest, and he felt the warmth of her breath. "The business," she continued. "Mr. Palmer is depending on me. My child, my family, they depend on me." She shook her head back and forth. "How are we going to do business now?"

Aiden took her by the arms and held her out from him. For her sake, he forced a smile. "We're bigger people than that," he said. "We'll get this done. Look—" he paused to take a deep sigh "—I'm going back to the Inn now. I can't do any more business tonight. We'll sign this in the morning." He let her go and stood, his arms at his side. He was completely deflated; all his energy was drained. He had never felt so lost.

She looked up at him, her eyes shimmering with unshed tears. He saw her hands tremble. "Okay," she said softly. "Okay. I—"

Aiden held up his hand. His smile was kind but determined. "We'll continue this another time." Then he turned to leave.

Jordan's reply was barely audible. "I can't promise anything," she said.

Aiden looked back at her, every nerve in his body on edge. "I'm not giving up on us, Jordan," he said simply. "I'm not. I don't care what happens to Chat or Trade Winds. I don't care what happens with my father or Gene Palmer. I don't care what people think of us. I won't give up."

Jordan turned away as Aiden walked out the door and shut it behind him.

Silent tears overflowed Jordan's eyes and trickled down her cheeks. She clenched her fists as a sob escaped from her lips. She stayed there, leaning on her desk, until she was sure Aiden had left. Then she gave a shuddering sigh, pulled on her jacket, grabbed her bag, and left her office.

She was shivering as she pulled out of the parking lot, but it was not from the evening chill. Tears still occluded her vision. She just wanted to get home, to get into her own bed and hold her baby close. She pulled out into the street.

The angry blast of a vehicle horn shocked her, and she slammed on the brakes. Panicked, Jordan blinked her eyes against the glare of headlights. She had pulled right out in front of an oncoming truck. The pickup had stopped about a foot from her car door.

"What the hell!" Jordan heard the angry voice of the driver as he jumped out of the truck. "What are you doing? You got your head up your ass?"

Then, the passenger door opened, and Jordan heard Ashley's familiar voice. "Jordan!"

The young driver glanced at his wife and then back at Jordan, who was getting out of her vehicle.

"Jordan! Is that you? What's the matter?" said Kyle. "Are you all right?"

Ashley rushed up to her, pulling her into a quick embrace. "Jordan, what's the matter?"

"I'm okay. I'm okay," insisted Jordan. "We didn't collide." She saw Ashley and Kyle exchange looks.

"You're shaking," Ashley said. "Get over to the passenger side. I'm getting in." Then she turned to her husband. "Kyle, you go home. I'll call you to come pick me up later. I'm going to make sure she's okay."

Jordan overheard Kyle say softly, "Has she been drinking?"

Ashley shook her head as she climbed in behind the wheel. "I doubt it, but something's going on. I'll see you later, hon."

"Call me," he said as he gave his wife a quick kiss. He got back in his truck and drove away slowly.

Ashley put the Jeep in reverse, guiding it back into the parking lot. Then she threw the shift into park and turned to her friend. "You don't look so good, Jordan. Have you been drinking?"

"I had a beer."

"Well, that doesn't seem like a lot, but you were sure in a fog. Good thing we weren't going fast."

"What are you doing out at ten o'clock at night?"

"Picking up Kyle from a volunteer firefighter's meeting."

"Oh." Jordan paused and took a deep breath. "I'm glad it was you."

"You've been under a lot of stress lately, what with this buyout or merger or whatever it is. Have you even seen Grace in the last three days?"

Jordan held her head in her hands. "Hardly," she muttered.

"Did something happen? You weren't there with Fenton, were you? I didn't like that guy and after what Vanessa said Larry Sample said—"

"It wasn't Fenton," said Jordan, staring straight ahead. "I'm trying to close the deal with Aiden Stewart. We were hammering out the details."

"We? Then he was here with you?"

Jordan nodded.

"Jordan, what happened? Did he back out?"

"No." Jordan's voice was deadpan. "You might say I did."

"You?" gasped her friend. "I'm not understanding this. Jordan, tell me what happened. You're obviously upset about something. Get it out." Ashley began to tap her foot nervously.

Jordan turned and for the first time since Ashley got into the car, she looked directly at her.

"Ashley, I'm falling in love with Aiden Stewart." Then she buried her face in her hands. "What am I going to do? What am I doing!"

There was a long enough silence to prompt Jordan to look up. Ashley was staring at her, but suddenly a smile appeared on the girl's face and she laughed. "Oh, wow!" she exclaimed. "That's wonderful! That's just what you need! And he's adorable!" She clapped her hands.

Jordan was annoyed. "That's not what I need at all! Ashley, you don't understand. I have to go home."

Ashley completely ignored her. She stopped her chuckling and looked directly at her friend. "Tell me everything that happened. Did he kiss you?"

Jordan nodded, and then haltingly, slowly, she found herself telling Ashley the whole story. "And then he said…he said he wouldn't give up on us. Then he left."

They sat in silence for a minute or two. Finally, Ashley spoke. "Well, I can't tell you what to do with the business, but I can tell you what to do with a man." She settled back in the seat and propped her hands on the steering wheel. "Listen to me, Jordan. Falling in love is good. Believe me; it's a good thing. You know, I've been telling you for nearly two years that that's what you need. And yet, you ignore me. Now it's come for you. It's caught up with you. You're not superhuman, Jordan. You're not an exception. You need love like the rest of us. Stop trying to avoid it. Aiden Stewart is single. He's cute. And I know in my heart that he's a good man. His eyes are honest. If he's interested in you, it's coming from his heart."

"How do I know that, Ashley? How do I know, and what does that mean for me and the business and Mr. Palmer?"

"I'm only thinking what it means for you," answered Ashley. "And it means letting go. It means sharing yourself with another person who cares about you. It means somebody to kiss good morning and somebody to kiss good night."

"I can't weaken like this. I can't give in. I've got more important things to think about."

"The most important thing you need to think about is yourself. If you're all screwed up, you're compromised. You won't be able to function, and then you'll fail. You'll fail Chat and Mr. Palmer. You'll fail yourself."

"Oh, Ashley!"

"Look, I'm sorry. You've got to hear me out and listen to me. Falling in love with somebody isn't being weak. It's being strong. It makes you stronger. Yes, you can get along just fine on your own, but you can accomplish twice as much with somebody you love. Kyle and I have. Where would I be without him? Where would he be without me? We're a team. A strong team. Do you think your parents are weak for being married to each other? Do you think they'd be stronger if they separated? Think about it, Jordan. They get through bad times because they have each other. They have good times because they have each other. Support. It's all about support. You get strength from each other, not weakness. Love makes you strong."

"I have Grace to love."

Ashley made a frustrated snort. "You know that's not what I mean. Grace is your child. You have no right to put her into a position like that. She needs you as her mother. You can't tie her down by hanging onto her like an anchor. It's not healthy." The young woman paused. When she continued, her voice took on a gentler, quieter tone. "Do you reject love because of Grace? Do you feel guilty that it wasn't all open and above board? Jordan, you didn't know. Do you feel guilty for that? Is that what's scaring you? That an unintended affair caused an unintended pregnancy?"

The tears flowed down Jordan's cheeks unchecked. "I didn't know! I never thought, Ashley!" she sobbed. "I never thought I'd get pregnant! I was shocked when I found out. Now I have a double responsibility to Grace." She bowed her head and let the tears come. Ashley reached out gently and rubbed her back. "From the first day I realized it, I knew my life had changed forever. I knew for the rest of my life I had to make it up to this — this wonderful baby. I wanted her so badly, Ashley. I feel as though I've failed her. No father she can call her own. Goddam! It's not fair! It's not fair!"

"I'm so sorry for that, Jordan," Ashley said quietly. "I really am. You can't bear that guilt, though. You did the right thing. Grace is here. She's your daughter, come what may. She's here to be her own person. That's a legacy. You can't change what happened, but now you have Grace, your beautiful little daughter. Yes, you need to take responsibility for that choice, but you need to take care of yourself as well — your emotional as well as your physical self. You're young and alive, Jordan. You're alive, and you deserve to live. Live, Jordan, please. It's the best thing you can do for Grace — and for yourself." Now there were tears in Ashley's eyes, and she leaned over and held her sobbing friend in a warm hug.

After a while, Jordan raised her head and smiled at Ashley. "Thanks for being here for me."

"That's my job, isn't it? At work, at play, in the parking lot!"

They both managed a little laugh. "Now I'll tell you what we're going to do." Ashley's demeanor became more serious. "We're going to go back into your office. You're going to wash your face and re-do your makeup. Then you're going to go to the Inn and apologize to Aiden Stewart for giving him what I'm sure was an iron-clad hard-on that you proceeded to back out on. That's just cruel. You can buy him a drink. It's still not too late."

Jordan wiped futilely at her smeared mascara. "I don't even have any makeup here."

"Oh, my friend," chuckled Ashley, "you don't know me very well." She reached into her tote-sized purse beside her on the seat and withdrew a smaller, blue clutch. She waggled it in front of Jordan's nose. "Everything you need, baby. Everything you need."

Chapter Eight

J ordan steadied herself and took a deep breath before knocking on
Aiden's door. She hoped Ashley was right, that Aiden wouldn't be
angry with her about her sudden reaction earlier or her showing up
now. All she needed to do was apologize, explain her confusion at the
evening's events, maybe go downstairs to the bar and have a drink,
but then she'd leave. She heard some shuffling inside the room and
backed up a step in anticipation of the door opening.

"Who is it?"

"It's Jordan," she croaked nervously and cleared her throat. "May
I come in? Please?"

Aiden opened the door, his mouth agape. She'd obviously surprised him. "Come in," he said, backing up so she could enter.

Jordan stepped into the room and noticed Aiden's phone in his
hand. "Am I interrupting? I can go —"

He looked down at the open phone, clapped it shut, and tossed
it onto the bedside table. "No, don't. My father…" He pursed his
lips. "He wants an update, but I'll call him in the morning."

She looked up at him and hesitated before speaking, twisting her
fingers together. "I'm sorry," she said quietly. "I'm sorry I behaved
like that." She paused, and Aiden waited. "Do you want to go down
for a drink?" she asked. "We could talk for a minute."

"No," he answered huskily.

"Well, then," she stumbled with her words and turned to go. "Well—I don't blame you. I just wanted to say I was sorry and I—Don't worry. The deal's still on. We can sign in the morning."

Aiden reached out and closed the door behind her. He took her by both arms and turned her until they were face to face. "I don't want a drink," he said. "I want you." He pulled her in to him and held her against his chest. She laid her cheek on the soft cotton of his shirt. The song of his beating heart sounded in her ear. "Please stay," he said, bending his head to hers.

Jordan answered with her lips, lifting her face to his, seeking his mouth with hers. Their lips pressed together, parting slightly to let the tips of their tongues touch. Jordan could feel the urgency in his fingertips as they played lightly over her face, tracing down her throat. His lips followed, leaving a trail of burning kisses from her ear, down her neck to the top of her cleavage where he was stopped by her T-shirt. Deftly, he slipped his hands down her torso, took the hem of the garment, and in one sure movement, slipped it up and over her head. Jordan gave her arms a little shake, and it fell unnoticed to the floor.

Aiden cupped both of her breasts, sheathed in the white lace of her bra, in his hands. "You are so beautiful," he breathed. He reached up and unclasped the clip that held her hair in check. The auburn mane cascaded around her shoulders as he bent to smother her breasts in kisses. The day's growth of beard on his face prickled her soft skin, sending ecstatic sensations through her whole body. She buried her fingers in his thick brown hair until he lifted his face again to hers. Their eyes locked in a mutual silent exchange of questions and answers. *Do you want me? Yes! I want you more than I've ever wanted anyone else. Then love me now as you have never loved anyone else.*

Jordan released him, and without breaking the bond their eyes continued to hold, she reached down and unzipped her jeans. Aiden stepped back to watch as they, too, were left in a heap on the floor. Jordan stood before him, a smile playing on her lips. She stepped coquettishly around him and climbed up onto the bed, stretching out her long legs, and propped her head up on her elbow. "What are you waiting for?" she asked.

Aiden made no reply as he pulled at his shirt. Jordan lay there, watching him undress. As he bared his chest, her stomach gave a delicious little leap. His muscles were knit together over his taut, flat stomach; his arms were strong and lean. Her eyes fell on his muscled abs and the vee that flexed slightly as he unbuckled his belt. Feelings awakened in her that she could hardly comprehend. Feelings of desire and physical need. Feelings that smothered any other emotion she might have entertained earlier that evening. Now, the outside world seemed not to exist. All there was in the vast, infinite universe was this room and Aiden and herself.

Aiden stepped out of his jeans. He stood for a moment beside the bed; the subtle virility she had always sensed in him was now overt and overpowering. Then he sank down beside her, his arms encircling her, his fingers lighting little fires wherever they touched her. Jordan closed her eyes and let the elation of the moment awaken the blaze of desire within. She let her own hands play sensually over his back. Such contrasts, she thought. His skin was so soft and smooth, and underneath the muscles were so hard, so alive.

Aiden reached behind her and unclasped her bra, slipping it gently off her arms. The moonlight had begun to flood the room with a silver wash. Jordan heard him catch his breath as he caressed both breasts in turn and bent his head to pay homage to them with his kisses. She groaned with unabashed passion as his tongue slowly circled her nipples and his teeth caught them in playful tender bites. She thought she might lose her mind with the suspense of unfulfilled longing, and she arched her body up and into his in an effort to be even closer.

Aiden's mouth found hers again, and this time their kisses were unapologetically wanton as they sought to quench their yearning for each other. Jordan drank in the taste of his tongue on hers, feeling the heat of him flooding her body and pulsing now, in the very heart of her female self. She moved her hips and felt him, hard and male, against her. She reached down, and almost tenuously, stroked him. She heard him gasp. It emboldened her, and she took his hardened shaft in her hand, caressing, squeezing, teasing. He pressed firmly against her, burying his face in the curve of her neck, half kissing, half licking. His fingertips played around her navel, exploring, tickling. She moaned softly, and he stroked her at the top of her panties. Instinctively, she opened her thighs. *Please, please*, her mind screamed with desire. He squeezed her gently through the fabric, making her writhe with anticipation.

His hand seemed everywhere at once, except in that place she desired it most. He caressed her buttocks, and then, before she was quite aware, he had slipped the panties down, over her thighs, over her knees. She gave a little kick with one leg, and she was free of them. Her legs opened.

His fingers found her then, lightly probing between her folds of her, searching for that spot that would ignite her. She cried out in glorious frustration, spreading her thighs. He bent his head down, kissing her navel, kissing the swell between her legs, adorned with a strip of russet curls. He explored her with his tongue, first skimming the surface, then pushing deeper and deeper. He covered her with little licks and nibbles until she arched up against his mouth and cried out again.

She thought she might die of ecstasy as she felt his fingers devling inside her, rhythmically moving them, until she moaned and twisted. Then, Aiden raised himself up. He took her soft thighs in his hands, kneeling between them, looking down at her. Jordan opened her eyes. He was smiling at her in the moonlight. She reached out and took his erection in both hands, guiding him to her entrance. He pressed into her, hard and fast. The relief was overwhelming, intoxicating. He began his thrusts, slowly at first, then faster. She lifted her hips to meet him, grinding into him, meeting him stroke for stroke.

Their passion became almost frantic, even fierce, as though they were struggling to keep out anything except the physical sensation that washed over them both. Aiden's breath came faster and faster. His hands gripped her hips as she wrapped her legs around him. He lay his full length on her, pushing hard into her deep, sweet wetness. Their hands clasped together. Jordan felt him swell within her as his thrusts became stronger still. The motion transported her. She felt herself reaching a pinnacle of physical exhilaration she had never felt, and suddenly, that exhilaration crashed over her, drenching her in rapture, like crystalline waves on a faraway shore. She felt Aiden shudder, felt his breath catch as he matched her euphoria with the climax of his own passion.

The room was still and silent, glowing with the silvery blue luminosity of the moonlight. Aiden lay there with his face against Jordan's soft cheek. She felt the weight of him on her, comforting and strong. His hand was still clasped in her own. The warmth that coursed through her body filled her with a pleasure that deepened with every breath. She wondered at the heights of passion she had just experienced. She had not thought it possible. She had not thought herself capable of this fulfillment that reached to her core. And yet, she mused, lying there still tingling with the compilation of the sensations she had just experienced, the fulfillment didn't *reach* her core, it *started* there. She sighed contentedly.

As Jordan moved, Aiden rolled slightly to one side, both of them loath to disturb their physical connection. He gave a sharp exhale as he separated from her. Reaching out, he pulled the down comforter over them, drawing her into his body so they lay face to face, cuddling close under the blanket.

Jordan spoke first. "Are you all right?"

"I've never felt more content in my life," Aiden said softly.

Jordan whispered into his chest. "I needed to be here. Like this. I needed you. That's why I came to your room."

Aiden kissed the top of her head and buried his face in her hair. "Thank you for that. Thank you for coming. I needed you too. I was wild when I left your office. I thought I might never see you again and I didn't know what I was going to do. I needed *us*."

At that moment, there was nothing left to say. Aiden wrapped his arms around her. Jordan curled as close to him as it was possible for her to get. The warmth from him enveloped her, and she closed her eyes and slept.

When she opened them, the room was dark. *The moon must have set*, she thought. Morning would be coming soon. Morning meant the sun would shine its bright light on their world, exposing every nook and cranny in their souls.

Jordan felt Aiden stir. She heard him let out a contended little sigh and felt his arm tighten possessively around her. He was ready again. Silently, they gave themselves over to their physical desires. Jordan slowly moved her legs until she embraced him between her thighs. He slipped easily into her, arousing her sensibilities once again, lighting the fires of passion from the night before that still burned under the surface of her heart. She lifted her face to his, and Aiden covered her eyelids, her forehead, her cheeks, and her lips with kisses. He began rocking into her, transporting her to the same dizzy height of the night before. She teetered on the brink of sensation, then toppled into that abyss of ecstasy as the impact of her climax surged through her. She felt him match her passion, heard him gasp and felt his body shudder with the undulating rhythm of his own orgasm.

They lay in each other's arms quietly, each afraid to be the one to break the bubble of enchantment that isolated the two of them from the outside world. The world of responsibility, duties, and commitments to which they both must return.

"The sky is getting light," whispered Aiden, forcing himself to open his eyes.

Jordan answered without moving her face from the hollow of his neck. "I should be going. I told my mother I would have to work late at the office and might not be home until morning, but I better get home for at least a little while."

"We have work ahead of us, Jordan," he said as he propped himself on one elbow, playing with her hair on the pillow.

"I know," she sighed, stroking his chest, reveling in the feel of those muscles that flexed and tightened under her touch, like a wild animal's, tamed only for her sake. Could it be true she really had this power over him? Could she trust that he really felt about her as he said he did? A cold pain, like being stabbed with an icicle, suddenly pierced her. What if this had been a ploy? What if she had fallen into some sort of plot that this man had concocted simply to gain control of all she had labored to build? A tremor coursed through her.

Aiden felt it. "What's wrong?" he whispered urgently.

"Nothing," she said. "Don't worry."

"Something's wrong," he insisted, looking down on her anxiously. "I know you now. What were you thinking?"

Jordan sighed and shook her head. "It's okay," she reassured him. "I was just thinking about all the things I have to do today and how much I just want to lie here, in this bed, with you."

Aiden folded his arms around her. "I was thinking about us," he said. "We can't let this go."

"We can sign it today."

Aiden sat straight up in the bed, staring down at her. "What are you talking about?"

Jordan's blue eyes widened. "The contract. The merger."

"Is that what you thought I meant? You thought I was talking about the merger?"

"Weren't you?"

Aiden's voice went quiet and somber. "No." He ran his hand through his hair and took a deep breath. "I was talking about us, Jordan. *Us*. You and me. Together." He exhaled. "We can't let this go," he repeated. "The merger isn't a problem. We'll make it work. It's us we've got to think about. Unless you don't want it."

Jordan sat up, pulling the sheet around her. "I want to believe you, Aiden. I do. There—there's just so much to sort out. And I have so much baggage."

"What baggage!" scoffed Aiden, but he wouldn't allow her to answer. "What baggage would that be? A baby? I'm not bothered by that. My mother had three babies. My sisters have children. They used to be babies."

Jordan gave a little smile at his attempt at humor.

"Jordan, I want a future for you and me, no matter what."

Their eyes locked, and there was no denying the feelings that passed between them. Jordan's voice was now barely above a whisper. "I want that, too, Aiden, but I'm afraid of the future."

Aiden reached out and caught her once again in his arms, drawing her close. "Don't worry," he reassured her. "We'll work it out. We will. You've been working too hard. You're supporting your family. Your mentor is sick. You've got the responsibility for this merger. And you have a baby daughter. You're tired. You can count on me. I'll help you. I will."

Jordan drew back and gave him a wry little smile. "That might be the testosterone talking."

Aiden shook his head. "You sure are hard to convince. It's me talking. The man you made love to."

"Hey! One night doesn't mean you can just stake your claim!"

"Watch me," he warned, and he smiled and kissed her. "I think you like my stake."

"Oh, really!" Now she was laughing. "Let me go. I have to go home, get cleaned up, and see my baby. I'll be back at the office later, and I'll call you. We'll take this to Mr. Palmer this afternoon and finalize it."

"We're going to see Palmer?"

"Of course. He owns Chat exclusively. He has to sign."

"Interesting. I'm interested to meet him."

"He's a wonderful man. Now let me go."

He reluctantly released her, and she climbed out of the bed and dressed. When she was ready, he got up and, still naked, kissed her one more time as she turned to go. "I can't get enough of you," he admitted.

She laughed and returned his kiss. "I'll call you about what time to meet me at Chat. I'll drive us to Mr. Palmer's house if he's feeling well enough to see us today." She gave a final little wave as she slipped out the door.

Chapter Nine

Jordan spent the morning at home with Grace. They were alone in the house; her father and mother had gone grocery shopping and to a dentist appointment. Jordan fed Grace her breakfast and then took her outside to play in the sunshine on the lawn for a while. She called Ashley as she watched her baby delight in the feel of the grass in her fat little fingers.

"ChatDotCom. May I help you?"

"Hi, Ashley. It's me."

"Well?"

"Well, what?"

"How did it go?"

"It went fine. It really did. I — I, well, I'll tell you about it some-time. Anyway, thank you for being there for me. You helped me a lot."

"You're welcome," said Ashley. "Everybody needs support at times like this, and it just happens to be my particular area of expertise."

"Oh, Ashley, you've only had one man your whole life!"

"See what I mean?"

"Ouch. Touché!" Jordan laughed. "Grace, honey, don't put the dandelion in your mouth."

"Oh, you're home?"

"Yes." Jordan balanced the phone between her ear and shoulder as she tried to take possession of the dandelion head that Grace had squashed in her fist. "I just got home a couple of hours ago."

"You did! Really?"

Jordan winced. She hadn't meant to say that. She hadn't meant to reveal her feelings, even to Ashley. "Sorry, sorry," she said. "I meant—"

"I know what you meant." Ashley chuckled. "That's okay, Jordan. You deserve not to deny yourself. The important thing is, did you have fun? Did you like him?"

"Yes," admitted Jordan. "I did have a good time. I laughed."

"And did you like him?"

Ashley was not going to let this go. Jordan gave in. "Yes, yes, I do like him, Ashley, but there's just so much in the way right now."

She reached out and tickled her baby's nose with the dandelion head. Grace giggled. Jordan waited for Ashley's tirade, but none came. Instead, Ashley said cheerily, "That's okay, Jordan. Don't think about that now. You took the necessary first step. That's the important part. Everything else will fall into place."

"I wish I could be as sure about it as you are."

"Trust me. Now, are you coming in today?"

"Oh, yes. I'll be in about noon."

"I was going to meet Kyle for lunch at the diner, but I can stay so we can go over whatever…*business*…you guys got done last night."

"No, Ashley. You go to lunch with your husband. Just leave anything new that came up this morning on my desk, and we'll go over the merger agreement when I get back. I'm going to call Mr. Palmer. I'll go there this afternoon as long as he's up to it and finalize this. Oh, Ashley, I really hope this is the right thing to do."

"Of course it is," said Ashley firmly. "Trade Winds seems to be a focused company with the same principles as Chat. Fenton Industries, on the other hand, seems to be a holding company and who knows where Chat would end up being held. Besides, I don't trust that Christopher Fenton."

"I don't either." Jordan had never told Ashley about the dinner and how Fenton had drugged her. Aiden Stewart was the only other person who knew.

"Well, I'll see you after lunch, then," said Ashley. "Bye for now."

"Bye-bye," replied Jordan. She put the phone back in her pocket and turned to her baby.

The morning passed much too quickly for Jordan. She rarely got the chance to spend extended periods of time with Grace during the week, much less alone with her with nothing else to do. Jordan could not get over the wonder of her daughter. It was such fun to see this wondrous little girl of hers eat her Snack Puffs by herself, to join her on the kitchen floor as she played with the pots and pans, and to walk with her outside while she diligently picked the heads off the dandelions. Certainly there had never been such a delightful or beautiful baby!

By the time Jordan's parents had returned from their errands, Grace had eaten her lunch and was napping peacefully in her little room across the hall from Jordan's. Jordan showered and prepared for the afternoon ahead. She knew she was facing serious business negotiations, but she felt lighthearted and pretty all the same. The color rose in her cheeks as her mind flashed to the night before. The way Aiden had made her feel, the response he elicited from her. Nobody, she thought, had ever come close to uncovering the true depth of desire that lay beneath the veneer in which she carefully sheathed her personality. Before last night, she had been unaware she had possessed such a capacity for unbridled happiness. She stared at her reflection in the mirror as she put on her makeup. "Aiden," she breathed his name aloud.

The dress she chose reflected the mood she carried inside. It was vaguely retro, made of light cotton printed in pale yellows and greens and chocolate browns. It dipped just low enough at the décolletage to be feminine and still be demure. Short sleeves with small keyholes gave it a flirty look, and she chose a pair of summery yellow pumps for a pop of color. She finished with sterling hoops and several sterling bangles on her wrist.

The offices of Chat were quiet when Jordan arrived just after noon. Most of the staff was having lunch. Ashley's desk, always full of papers, water bottles, coffee mugs, and her company laptop when she was there, was barren and sterile, its marble top polished to a reflecting shine. It stood like the first line of defense against the outside world, awaiting her return. Ashley never left even the hint of a mess on her desk, whether she was going home for the day or stepping out for lunch. If she wasn't sitting there, it was hard to tell it was a desk.

Jordan's desk was a different story. As she stepped through the door to her own office, she made a wry face. Her office bore witness to the night before. There was an open pizza box with a couple of pieces of cold pizza in it, two or three empty beer bottles, and the unoepend remainder of the six-pack. Unfiled papers were strewn on the desktop, and the two portfolios lay on the small table between the wing chairs.

Jordan opened the heavy drapes, allowing the spring sunlight to flood in. Methodically she began to clean up the mess, stuffing the pizza box and leftover pizza into her waste basket. Then she walked across to the wing chairs to gather together the portfolios.

"It looks like somebody was working late last night," said a male voice.

Jordan gave a little yelp and spun around. In the open doorway of her office stood Christopher Fenton. Her stomach suddenly tightened, and she felt her mouth go dry.

"Mr. Fenton," she said, gathering her wits. "You should knock."

"The door was open. May I come in?"

Jordan hesitated. "Do we have something to discuss?"

Christopher Fenton took two steps into the room. "As a matter of fact, we do," he said. A slick smile spread across his face, but Jordan could see the malice behind his eyes. "You look lovely this morning. Ready to do business, I see."

Jordan ignored the remark. She wished Ashley would get back from lunch. She didn't enjoy being in the same room with a man who had purposely tried to bring about her demise.

"May I sit down?" His eyes traveled to the two wing chairs, but Jordan slipped behind her desk and gestured to the large Windsor chair across from her. She sat primly and upright, her back did not touch the back of her chair.

Fenton sat in the Windsor chair and leaned forward, his arms folded on the desk. "I want to talk to you about your decision to go with Trade Winds—or should I say Aiden Stewart—instead of Fenton Industries."

Jordan remained silent, trying not to look at the little clock on her desk. Where was Ashley?

"I just want you to be sure that this is the right decision for Gene Palmer's company," Fenton continued. "Something tells me he's not the kind to accept an offer of lesser cash value, to say nothing of the long-term benefits to the people he leaves behind when he…retires."

Instinctively, Jordan adopted a defensive body language. She leaned back comfortably and folded her hands across her lap, her elbows leaning on the arms of the chair. "I think it was the long-term issues of your offer that finally persuaded me to go with Trade Winds. I did my research, Mr. Fenton. You have a disturbing habit of chopping companies up. In fact, Trade Winds is a communications company, like Chat. Fenton Industries, on the other hand, is a holding company, and while you purport to be buying Chat for the purpose of expanding your interests in this area, your company history doesn't support that premise. Most of the companies you acquire are dead within two years. Chopped up, sold off, and relocated for the express benefit of Fenton Industries. Mr. Palmer has a keener sense of responsibility to his employees than that."

"Gene Palmer's final responsibility has always been to the bottom line. You know that. Have you discussed this decision with him?"

"Of course," Jordan lied. She would not betray Mr. Palmer's physical condition to the likes of this predator.

"How much have you told him about how you came to that decision?"

"Mr. Palmer and I discuss all aspects of the business freely, but that isn't any concern of yours, Mr. Fenton." Jordan was gaining confidence. Then, Fenton dropped a bomb.

"Does he know you're sleeping with Aiden Stewart?"

The color drained from Jordan's face.

"Yes, I know about that," said Fenton with a ghoulish smile. He lowered his voice. "I saw you go up to his room at the Inn the other night. You see, I'm staying there, too." He sat back and adopted a similar pose as Jordan's, his pale eyes gleaming with animosity. Jordan fought for control over her fear. Her palms were sweating. She wouldn't put anything past this man. Her throat seemed to be closing. After all, he had tried to poison her, to destroy her reputation in the eyes of her employer.

"I wonder how he would feel about that," murmured Fenton, suddenly interested in his own fingernails.

Jordan stood up, holding the edge of her desk to disguise her shaking hands. "Mr. Fenton," she said clearly and calmly, "my personal life is absolutely none of your business and absolutely off limits in any discussion you and I will ever have. I remain steadfast in my decision to merge with Trade Winds because Mr. Palmer and I believe it is the best thing for ChatDotCom. That's all you need to hear. Now, I must ask you to leave immediately."

Fenton stood up. He was still smiling his malicious smile. "Merge? Is that what you call it?" He gave a nasty short chuckle. "I'm not surprised, but I'd like to hear Palmer's take on it. What did he say when you told him?"

"Please leave now," said Jordan through gritted teeth. Suddenly, not thinking, she added, "Leave immediately, Mr. Fenton, or I will go to the police and tell them how you drugged my drink in an effort to sabotage my negotiations. Leave, Mr. Fenton."

Jordan saw a shadow cross Fenton's face. She had dealt a blow, but he was cool. In an instant his face had cleared. "Good-bye, Ms. Fitzgerald, but I'll warn you, you are a neophyte in the business world, and a little success in a tiny company does not make you competent to run with the big boys. We'll see how this all goes down." He turned and left, slamming the door behind him. Jordan fell back in her chair, tears of frustration and anger welling up in her eyes.

A moment later, Ashley came flying into the room. "What! What's going on here? I just passed Fenton in the hall. He didn't speak or look at me. What was that dirt bag doing here? Are you okay, Jordan? You look shaken."

Jordan hid her face in her hands for a minute and sighed. Then she looked up. "Sit down," she said. "I'll tell you."

Jordan told Ashley the whole story starting with her dinner with Fenton, the drugged ginger ale, Aiden's intervention that saved her from a certain DUI or worse, her feelings about Aiden, and her decision to accept Trade Winds' proposal for merger.

"Now all I have to do is tell Mr. Palmer," she said quietly, slumping back in her chair. She let out a deep breath between pursed lips.

"I knew that guy was bad news the minute I saw him! Fenton is a terrible person, Jordan," said Ashley, shaking her head in disbelief. "You are absolutely right to send him down the road. What a jerk!" Ashley walked to the big windows overlooking the river. "I just hope he doesn't find some other way of undermining your decision. He's a dangerous man with a lot of money. What's our next move?"

Jordan swung her chair around and followed Ashley's meditative gaze out over the lively river, its waves bounding and leaping over its banks with the spring run-off. The season's foliage had turned the bank into a palette of pastel colors, dotted with little white clouds of early cherry blossoms. "I want you to call Mr. Palmer," she said resolutely. "Tell him that I'd like to meet with him this afternoon. Tell him I've decided to go with Trade Winds and would like him to meet Aiden Stewart."

"You're going to bring Aiden with you?"

"Yes. Ashley, I don't know what's going to happen between Aiden and me, but I want Mr. Palmer to meet him. He has a real talent for nailing someone's core personality just by looking at them and talking to them. I want his opinion of Aiden."

"Then are you going to tell him about your personal relationship with Aiden?"

"I won't need to, Ashley. I won't need to."

Ashley turned away from the window and met Jordan's eyes. "I'll call him right away. I'll call Aiden, too, if you want."

"No, thanks anyway. I'll go to the Inn. He can come with me to Mr. Palmer's. When you call him, tell him we'll be there about three."

A few minutes later, Jordan was driving into town to find Aiden. She tried twice to call him. Each time, her call went straight to his voice mail. "This is Aiden Stewart. Please leave a message and a number where you can be reached. I'll call back."

After Jordan had left that morning, Aiden showered, dressed, and went downstairs for coffee. He didn't feel particularly hungry, so he took the coffee out onto the wide front porch. He found a quiet table, sat down, and called his father. The old man, Aiden knew, would be pacing back and forth in his office, fussing and fuming to himself because Aiden hadn't reported in for twenty-four hours.

"What the hell is going on there, son?" was Gordon Stewart's opening remark.

"A lot, Dad, a lot."

"Let me have it. Have you closed the deal? What's Fenton up to? Don't trust that jerk, Aiden. What's Palmer's condition? Have you met with him yet?"

"One question at a time, Dad," said Aiden firmly. He heard his father bluster and then silence. "You still there?"

"Of course I'm still here. I'm trying to give you a chance to tell me what's going on!"

"I'm meeting this afternoon with Gene Palmer and Jordan Fitzgerald. We're going to sign the contract."

"Have you spoken to Palmer?"

"No, not yet."

"Then you don't know for sure."

"Jordan Fitzgerald is in charge of the decision making process—"

"Just like you're in charge of the decision making process for Trade Winds, but I sign the papers. I give the final word."

Aiden sighed. "Yes, that's correct."

"Well, then, good work, Aiden. I hope it all goes through."

"I see no reason why it shouldn't."

"Well, you let me know as soon as you can and then get back here so I can finalize the whole thing."

"I will, Dad."

"Good luck." His father hung up without comment, as was his habit.

Aiden put his phone down on the table and bent his head to the daily newspaper that had been left there for customers to read as they lingered over coffee in the spring sunshine.

"Aiden Stewart?"

Aiden looked up to see Christopher Fenton and his cohort, dressed impeccably in three piece suits, standing in front of him. Aiden blinked. Of course, Fenton didn't know that Aiden knew who he was. He was cool in his response.

"That's right." Aiden offered nothing further.

Fenton sported an oily smile. "I'm Christopher Fenton of Fenton Industries. This is my CFO, Richard Tate. We were just finishing breakfast. I saw you sitting over here and recognized you from your picture on the Trade Winds website. I thought it would be interesting to meet the representative arm of Trade Winds. I understand we're after the same prize."

A million retorts flashed through Aiden's mind. He quieted them all with a sip of coffee and replied, "If you mean Trade Winds has a bid in for a merger with ChatDotCom, then you're correct. It's no secret."

The two men extended their hands across the table. Aiden shook them reluctantly.

"May I sit down?" Fenton didn't wait for Aiden's nod. He and Tate pulled out chairs and sat.

Aiden was silent. He was not going to initiate any discussion with Fenton. *Let him take the first step*, thought Aiden.

"Tate and I have been discussing the situation with ChatDotCom." Fenton paused, waiting for a reply, but Aiden remained silent, leaning back in his chair, watching the two men. Fenton cleared his throat and continued. "Yesterday, ChatDotCom turned down Fenton Industries' offer for a buyout. Ms. Fitzgerald, who, I'm sure you know, is heading the company in Gene Palmer's absence, informed me of her decision. I assume she is steering the company toward a deal with Trade Winds—a merger if you will. Is that true?"

Aiden set his coffee cup down carefully. Although people had often commented on how his features, as well as his calm personality, reflected the attributes of his mother, Aiden was his father's son, too. He would try to avoid a confrontation, but he would never back down from one. He looked hard at Christopher Fenton. "It's not my habit to discuss Trade Winds business with a competitor," he said.

Fenton leaned forward over the table, his pale eyes flashing. "That's what I'm talking about," he hissed at Aiden. "I'm suggesting we not be competitors. I'm suggesting we work together. Just listen to me." Aiden sat, silent, and Fenton continued. "Look, you've got the girl in your pocket. She wants to do the deal with Trade Winds. Fine. We'll let her. Go ahead and do the deal. What ChatDotCom won't know is that you and I, Trade Winds and Fenton Industries, have made a deal also. The second Palmer's signature is dry on the dotted line, I'll hand over ten million to Trade Winds. I've got an arrangement with a couple of the biggest communications and tech companies in the country to break up this territory. We'll sell a portion to each one, each portion for more than we'll pay for the whole company. Then Trade Winds and Fenton Industries will go sixty-forty, and we'll both win. The five year clause for Jordan Fitzgerald? Well, we can do something with that, too. We can put her somewhere for five years. Or not, and she can sue the offending party, if she can figure out who it is!" He laughed, reached into his breast pocket and pushed a folded sheet of paper across the table to Aiden. "I took the liberty of drawing this up. Read it; let me know what you think. You can reach me at the number at the bottom of the page."

It took Aiden only a moment to answer Fenton. "Not interested," he said, pushing the still-folded paper back across the table to Fenton.

"Didn't you hear what I said? You want to see more numbers? You want fifty-fifty? What do you say?"

Aiden cleared his throat in an effort to remain calm. "I say I'm not interested." He stood and turned away from the two men. He heard their chairs scrape the floor as they also got up from the table.

"I know you're screwing the girl," Fenton taunted. "That kid she's got is Palmer's. She didn't tell you that, did she? Think about it, Stewart, that's why all the funny business with the contract and the five-year thing. Palmer's bought her off so she can't sue the estate after he's dead. All I have to do is go to Palmer and let him know that she screwed him out of the best deal he'll ever get just because you're fucking her. You better watch yourself, or she'll have you on the five-year plan too. Stewart, this is crazy. You're a business man! Do business!" Then Aiden felt Fenton's hand on his arm.

Suddenly, the hot head that had made Gordon Stewart's reputation as a young man won out over the calm and careful demeanor Aiden's mother had tried so hard to instill in her son. Aiden whirled around, shaking free of Fenton's clammy grasp.

"Take your stinking hand off me!" He was seething. "Take your stinking hand off me, or you will regret the day you were born until the day you die!" He put a pointed finger in Fenton's face, causing the man to back up.

Neither Aiden nor Fenton saw where she came from, but Susan Noyes materialized, seemingly out of nowhere. Her normally friendly face was dark with anger. She spoke sharply, "Put an end to this, gentlemen. Right now." She held up her cell phone. "See this? I can press just one button, and John Giamo will be here in two minutes. Two minutes. John Giamo is our chief of police and my first cousin.

Don't push me to call him. This is not the Wild West; this is the twenty-first century. We may be a small town, but we're civilized, and I for one won't tolerate this behavior. Now go your separate ways." She glared at the three men.

Aiden stepped back from Fenton and his colleague, turned, and walked back inside. In a blind rage, he returned to his room. He slammed the door behind him, locked it, and sat down on the bed. Then he started to shake. He couldn't ever remember being that angry at somebody.

He ran his hands through his hair, recalling Fenton's parting shot. Palmer was the father of Jordan's child. No wonder she was so close-mouthed about it. Aiden felt sick. The range of emotions he was experiencing over these last few days was dizzying. Right now, he was having trouble keeping it together. He looked at the clock to see it was nearly one o'clock. Jordan would be at her office now, getting ready for their meeting with Gene Palmer. Aiden buried his head in his hands. As if it mattered who the father of her child was. It didn't change his feelings about her, his attraction to her. It didn't alter his memory of the night before, lying with her in his arms, her skin like silk against his, the intoxicating aroma of her hair.

It was time to talk to someone. It was time to talk to the two people he trusted most. He called his father's cell phone.

"Is the deal signed?" His father skipped the formalities of a greeting.

"Put the phone on speaker, Dad. I need to talk to both of you."

There must have been something in his voice, because Gordon said quietly, "Aiden, are you all right?"

"I'm fine, Dad."

"Nellie, how do you put this thing on speaker?" Aiden waited as they fumbled with the phone, and then he heard his mother's voice. "Are you okay?"

"Yes, Mom. I need to talk to both of you."

"Go ahead, Aiden," said his mother, "we can both hear you."

Aiden began to talk, generally at first, and then in more detail. Soon he was telling them everything, about the deal, about Jordan and the way he felt about her, and about his altercation with Fenton. "I'm going to Gene Palmer's house this afternoon with her to sign the papers," he concluded. "I've never felt like this about anybody before."

"Good job, son," said Gordon. "I like the way you handled Fenton! Left no room for misinterpretation."

"Dad, what am I going to do about Jordan? What's going on with me? What about the baby?"

Aiden heard his father make some sort of huffing and puffing noise, but it was his mother who spoke. "Aiden, you are an honest and good person. Just follow your heart. Whatever will happen between you and this young woman will happen. Does she care for you also?"

"I think so, but why doesn't she tell me about Palmer? Fenton said he was the father of her child."

"Think about this logically, Aiden. Fenton told you. Now I've never met the man, but according to you and your father, he's bad. Just plain bad. He's dishonest, an opportunist, and he sought to do that girl harm. Do you think he is a trustworthy source?"

"What do you mean?"

"I'm saying he might be lying."

"Why would he do that? How could he even think that up?"

"Oh, Aiden. He did it to pull the rug out from under you. He did it to manipulate you and throw you off course. And what if he's not lying? Think about what that might mean to you. Does that fact change the way you feel about her? Certainly the baby is not at fault. Don't forget, the truth will come out. You just tend to your business on the business side and follow your heart for your personal happiness. Things will work themselves out. And Aiden, this girl seems to mean a lot to you."

"She does."

"There can't be love where there isn't trust. They go hand in hand. As long as you feel this strongly about her, you'll just have to ask her outright."

Aiden sighed.

Gordon finally spoke. "Listen to your mother, son."

Aiden had to smile to himself. "Yes, Dad. Thanks, Mom. Thanks, Dad. Look, I've got to go. I'll call you right after the meeting."

Aiden paced the room, thinking about what his mother had said. Fenton could be lying, but what he said sounded perfectly logical. Was Jordan the person he thought, *he hoped*, she was? And what if she wasn't? What if what Fenton said was true and she had used the baby as a bargaining chip to trap Palmer into providing for her financial security? Aiden knew that everything his mother said was true. There couldn't be love where there wasn't trust.

As was his habit, he ran his hand through his hair. He would have to play this out, a step at a time, trusting his instincts all the way. He just wished he had as much faith in his instincts as his mother did.

Jordan drove straight to the Inn on the Green, not bothering to call ahead of time. She ran up the wide front steps. The lobby was deserted; the tourists weren't back from their afternoon soirees yet, and it was too early for the regular dinner crowd. Jordan crossed the large room quickly, passing an unattended front desk, and ran up the stairs. She hurried down the hall to Aiden's room and knocked on the door, longing to feel the comfort of his arms around her, to feel the pressure of his lips on hers.

Aiden opened the door and immediately took her hand, leading her into the room and then closing and bolting the door behind her. He wrapped his arms around her and kissed her upturned face. He kissed her eyelids, her forehead, her cheeks, but he lingered on her lips. She savored that sweet, almost imperceptible sugary taste, reveling in the softness of his kiss, remembering the night before when his lips had traveled down her body, kissing, caressing, exciting her until she was crazy with desire for him.

"I missed you," he whispered.

Jordan opened her eyes and smiled. "How could you miss me? I've only been gone a few hours."

"Too long," he said. He backed up, sweeping her along with him, and pulled her down onto the bed. They seemed to have a narcotic effect on each other, and there was nothing they could do about it. Fenton could wait. Palmer could wait. All the questions in the world could wait. Aiden's kisses told her that all he wanted now was to be with her.

Despite her own desire, Jordan knew they had to focus on business, not pleasure, and she gave a little laugh. "Let me go," she said. "I'll get all messed up!"

"I'm already messed up," he said. "Look what you do to me." He took her hand and guided it down his taught abdomen. She felt the buckle on his belt and then the bulge underneath. "I can't help myself," he said. She caressed him through his slacks, feeling the thrill as the embers of her passion leaped into flame at his touch. He rolled her gently over on her back and stood up. She started to stand, but Aiden held his finger to his lips and smiled, whispering, "Stay where you are."

She lay there and watched as he slipped out of his clothes. The sight of him was intoxicating. She reached out, but he shook his head.

"Don't move," he said. He bent over her and kissed her tenderly on the mouth, parting her lips with his tongue.

Then he put a hand on each of her hips and slid her down to the edge of the bed. Slowly he lifted her dress up around her waist, revealing her. He leaned down, kissing her belly, letting his tongue roll over her navel. She moaned and arched her hips as he kissed her along the top of her lacy panties. She felt his fingers pressing through the lace against that most sensual part of her. He straightened up again and slowly slid her panties down to her knees. She felt exposed, vulnerable, but her heart beat with longing and expectation. She strained against the offending panties, seeking to give him access to that hot, wet place that begged for him, but suddenly, he took both her legs in one strong arm and lifted them up, resting them on his shoulder. He reached underneath with his free hand, squeezing her round buttocks, while she twisted and moaned, wild for relief. He found the spot and slipped his fingers into her. She cried out with desire as he stroked the secret folds between her legs. She struggled again to open her legs, but he held her tight, teasing, tantalizing until she thought she might burst with pent up emotion. She gripped the bedclothes, twisting them in her fingers.

"Please! Please!" she gasped.

He gave a quiet little laugh as he held her legs tight against his chest. He took a step forward and slipped into her so fast, so hard and sure, from underneath, that she lost her breath. He began his thrusts, and she thought she would die of the ecstasy. The fire spread throughout her whole body, burning in her brain until she had to clench her teeth to keep from crying out. She writhed and twisted, feeling his hardness fill the void in her. He thrust harder and faster, all the while bracing her against the raw strength of his chest and shoulders. He stroked her legs with his other hand, and reaching down, found her small pearl, hard with lust and slippery with desire.

He fondled it, gently squeezing, pinching, pressing, until she spun out of control, contorting her body against him as the waves of her climax crashed over her.

She was still reeling from the ripples of her orgasm when she felt Aiden reach his own pinnacle, sending him tumbling over the edge of desire, spinning them both into the ecstasy they shared. He gripped her long legs, slumping against them in the weakness that followed. His knees buckled, and he sank slowly onto the bed beside her. Neither spoke as they recovered their senses. Then Jordan began to laugh softly, or maybe she was crying. She could hardly tell.

"Oh," she whispered, "I don't believe what you do to me!"

Aiden kissed her neck. "Sorry for the quickie," he said. "I couldn't help myself."

Jordan laughed. "There's something thrilling about a well-timed quickie," she said, and Aiden laughed too.

"Ah, but now we have work to do." He turned her face to his and kissed her deeply. She gasped as he broke the contact and stood up, pulling her with him. They held each other a moment longer, extending the warmth that coursed through their veins.

Chapter Ten

Twenty minutes later, they were driving up the curved lane to Gene Palmer's home.

"Nice house," commented Aiden. He took in the grand scene in front of him. "I like the architecture. I would say this was built right around, or more likely immediately after, the Civil War. Probably that's when manufacturing really took off here."

"You're right," Jordan answered. "It was built in 1866. Beautiful, isn't it? What's your house like?"

"Ha! I have a condo on the wharf right in the middle of Portland. I can see our offices from my balcony! I don't spend much on commuting. It's a good location and a nice place, but I guess it's my parents' house I still think of as home. The place where I grew up."

"Is that in Portland, too?"

"Well, Cape Elizabeth, to be specific. It's part of the greater Portland area, but it's right out into the bay. The house is on the coast. On a cliff, actually. The waves crashing on the rocks lulled me to sleep when I was young. It's about two hundred fifty years old and has a widow's walk. It was a terrible mess when my parents bought it, but it's beautiful now."

"It sounds romantic. I love the ocean but don't get there much. I probably haven't been there since I was a teenager."

"I can take care of that!" Aiden gave her a devilish wink.

Jordan answered with a smile. She pulled up to the front of the garage and turned off the car. "Are you ready?"

"I'm okay," Aiden assured her. "I think any reasonable man would like what we've drawn up."

"Let's see," said Jordan.

Aiden leaned in to give her a quick kiss, but she slipped casually out of the car just short of his lips reaching hers. He was taken aback, but quickly buried his anxiety and followed her to the atrium door.

A petite woman in her late sixties met them at the door. "Jordan, come in. Gene's in the den waiting for you." She stood on tiptoe and kissed the tall girl on the cheek, then she looked by her and smiled at Aiden. "And this must be Aiden Stewart of Trade Winds. Welcome, Mr. Stewart. I'm Marie Palmer. My husband is eager to meet you." She extended her hand, and Aiden took it gently in his.

"Very nice to meet you, Mrs. Palmer. Thank you for inviting us into your home for a business meeting."

Marie Palmer led them through the large, bright kitchen. "Gene likes to stay home as much as possible these days. He's comfortable here."

They walked through the front foyer that faced the large front door, down a short hallway, and into a small, wood-paneled room lined with bookcases and hung with an eclectic collection of oils, watercolors, and prints. Two windows looked out over the wide front lawn, and a single glass door opened onto a quaint stone terrace. The heavy urns that decorated the terrace were as yet unplanted, but the hedge of lilacs that ringed the low stone wall was in bloom. Their fragrance filtered into the room.

Gene Palmer was sitting in a large club chair, gazing out the two front windows. His wife ushered them through the door. "Jordan and Mr. Stewart are here, dear."

The old man picked up the cane that lay on the floor next to his chair and stood, slowly but steadily. "Jordan," he said, smiling, "come in, come in. And this is Aiden Stewart." He reached his hand out. "Gene Palmer. Very pleased, and interested, to meet you." Aiden took the hand and was surprised at the strength still evident in the ravaged body. *A truly strong man,* Aiden thought.

"Please, sit down. I'll sit here because this chair is comfortable for me. You two sit right there on the sofa."

Aiden and Jordan sat down, and Jordan pulled out the finalized copy of the proposal. "What did you think, Mr. Palmer?" she asked.

Gene Palmer took his copy from a small table beside the chair. "Thanks for sending Ashley up with a copy. I've read through it. I like it. I like it. I think you've both done a good job trying to do the best for your respective companies. You restore my faith in the upcoming generation." He turned and spoke directly to Aiden. "I know your father, you know, Mr. Stewart. He's a fine man and one tough business man. He's worked hard. I'm glad to see his son is worthy of his father's work."

Aiden smiled, somewhat self-consciously. "Thank you for that compliment, Mr. Palmer. My father speaks highly of you also."

Gene Palmer smiled at his protégé. "Jordan, you've done an exemplary job. I'm proud of you. This merger preserves the autonomy of Chat while benefiting Trade Winds and giving them access to new territories. You've forged a progressive partnership. I don't think I could have trusted this to anyone else."

Jordan blushed. "Thank you, Mr. Palmer. We tried hard."

"Now to the topic of Fenton Industries," continued Palmer, folding his hands in his lap. "Christopher Fenton showed up here today."

Jordan straightened her back as though she'd received an electric shock. "Here?" she exclaimed. "At your home!"

"Yes, indeed. He claimed he had information that would make me change my mind about accepting Trade Winds' proposal."

"Did you speak to him?" Jordan asked. Aiden could see her hands shaking and wished he could put his own over them.

"I did. I asked Marie to let him in, although she fought me on that. I had to speak to him. The man needed to be put in his place. I told him I didn't want to hear what he had to say. I told him I had no time for gossip or hearsay. I reminded him that before he formed Fenton Industries, he was nearly brought up on charges of blackmail and corporate spying, and I had no interest in being involved with anybody with that kind of background."

"Is that true?" Aiden leaned forward in disbelief. "Blackmail and corporate espionage?"

"It is true," answered Palmer. "I remember it distinctly. He was an up and coming young executive, and he actually tried to set two power service companies against each other. He worked for one of them. Too bad you can't shoot people for corporate treason. I'm sure there would have been volunteers for the firing squad!"

"What else did he say to you?" Jordan shifted uncomfortably.

"Nothing of any importance. In fact, I didn't let him say much. He left here spouting threats. I actually rather enjoyed cutting him off at the knees. Kind of limbered me up!" He gave a big smile.

The man has a lot of courage, thought Aiden with admiration. *No wonder Jordan thinks so highly of him. No wonder*—but he wouldn't let his thoughts go any further.

"However—" and this time Palmer's voice took a very serious tone "—I caution you not to underestimate this man. He has a criminal mind. He's unstable. Don't turn your back on him, and be sure to keep all your ducks in a row all the time. If he thinks he's losing ground, there's no telling what he'll do."

"I can do that," Jordan said. Aiden could sense that, although Jordan seemed to have become accustomed to seeing Gene Palmer during his illness, it always upset her. It was obvious she wanted so much for him to be well and would dread losing him, his mentorship, and his faith in her.

"Well, let's get this done." Gene Palmer perked up, rubbing his hands together. "Jordan, would you please find Marie and ask her to come in here? I want her to be here. She was as much a part of developing ChatDotCom as anybody. I couldn't have done it without her."

"Of course," said Jordan. "I'll get her right away." She stood and left the room.

Aiden watched the old man carefully, sitting with his head bowed. Was he tired? Was he thinking? Then Palmer raised his head and looked directly into Aiden's eyes.

"I'm old now," he said quietly. "I'm old and sick, but I wasn't always this way. I was a young man once. Young and strong, and I remember how that felt. I remember it as clear as day." He paused and Aiden waited, caught in the strength of the old man's glare. "If you think I don't know what's going on here, you are greatly mistaken."

Aiden started to speak, but Palmer held up his hand. He gave a little smile. "Don't worry. I don't disapprove. I like you, Stewart. I always liked your father. You're a pleasant surprise. I thought you might be a spoiled rich kid. Must be your mother's influence." He laughed at his own joke. "I do want to make sure you understand one thing, though. I was always a little disappointed that none of my kids wanted the business, even though I'm fortunate they're all doing well and they're good people." He paused for a reminiscent smile, but then trained his eyes back on Aiden's. "Then Jordan came along. Whatever happens, you should know that Jordan Fitzgerald means a lot to me. I've asked a lot from her, and she's given all that I asked and more. She'll do that for people she loves. Don't ever let me hear that you misused or took advantage of her in any way. And don't listen to gossip. I don't. Neither should you." He looked up then, past Aiden, to the doorway. Aiden turned and followed his gaze. Jordan and Marie Palmer were coming into the room.

Mrs. Palmer crossed the room to her husband's side. He reached out and wrapped his arm around her waist as she sat on the arm of the chair. "I was just telling Aiden that, believe it or not, I was a young man once. And here's the woman who keeps it fresh in my mind every day."

Palmer, Jordan, and Aiden signed the merger contract, and Aiden shook the Palmers' hands. Mrs. Palmer disappeared and returned a minute later with a bottle of champagne and four flutes. Aiden did the honors, popping the cork and pouring. Jordan passed the flutes. "Here's to the next generation," said Gene Palmer, raising his glass. Aiden thought he saw the old man's eyes glistening with unshed tears, but his voice didn't falter as he spoke. "You've inherited a difficult world to manage, but we wish you the best. You can do it."

Half an hour later, Jordan and Aiden sat quietly in her car. She reached for the key. "Where do you want to go?" she asked him. "It's five thirty."

"I've got to call my father. He'll want to know everything was finalized except for his own signature. We better go back to the Inn."

"I'm afraid to go to the Inn with you," Jordan said with a giggle. "We'd better go to my office."

"Oh, sure, let's go there. Those chairs are pretty comfortable."

"Aiden!" She laughed, but then she became somber as she started the car and turned down the sweeping drive.

"Are you sad?" asked Aiden.

Jordan nodded. "A little," she admitted. "It's kind of the end of an era. And I hate to see him sick. I hate it, Aiden."

Her eyes filled with tears. One trickled down her cheek, and Aiden reached over, brushing it gently away. "He means that much to you?" It was a cautious question.

Jordan threw him a glance and then fixed her eyes on the road. "Yes, he means that much to me. He just about saved me! He gave me a way to support Grace. He gave me a way to help my family. Times have been hard for my mother and father lately. I support most of the expenses of the household. Don't get me wrong, I'm glad to do it, but I wouldn't be able to if Mr. Palmer hadn't given me the responsibility and the position he did."

"Do you think he did it just to be a nice guy?"

"What do you mean?" Jordan's voice was icy.

"I mean, do you think he would have done that—given you the position and the responsibility it requires—if he didn't know you could do the job? No. He knew your potential, Jordan. He knows what you're capable of. You just need to be aware of it, too. The company is basically yours now."

They drove the rest of the way to Jordan's office in silence. Jordan punched in her code, and they entered through the back door. Ashley's desk, as usual, stood like a sleek, marble fort above the shiny hemlock floor. As Jordan turned the key in her office door, Aiden took her hand and led her to one of the chairs. He sat down and pulled her into his lap.

"Sit with me," he said. "I want to hold you."

She sighed contentedly. It felt so good to have his arms around her. In this moment, she wished nothing existed outside the confines of the chair and Aiden's arms.

"I wish I could sit here," she said, pressing her lips to his forehead. "I wish I could sit here just like this until I feel strong enough to move on."

"You can sit here as long as you want." Aiden laid his head against her breast and held her tightly. The unchecked passion that had fueled their wild, glorious lovemaking the night before burned softly and steadily now, filling them both with a mutual courage neither had known before.

"I'm scared I won't be able to do the job," whispered Jordan, suddenly aware of her new position. "I'm scared I won't be able to do it without Mr. Palmer."

Aiden drew back and looked at her. "You've got me. This is a merger. You are every bit as capable with Palmer as without him. Jordan, that man would never have set things up like this unless he had complete trust in your abilities."

Jordan turned her head and gazing out the window. "I feel so alone right now." She stood and wandered to the big windows, staring out onto the river. The sun had set and evening was closing in. It was always a lonely time of day for her, a time of day when her mind wandered to things she would rather leave behind. All she wanted was to be home with her baby.

Aiden remained seated, watching her, waiting. She was glad that for the moment Aiden didn't say anything, ask her anything. Jordan kept her back to him, unable to look at him for fear her emotions would once again make her feel vulnerable. "I want to go home, Aiden. I want to go home and be with my child. I'll give you a ride back to the Inn."

She heard Aiden get up from the chair. "Thanks," he said, "but I'll walk in. I could use the exercise." He came up behind her and put his arms around her, turning her so she faced him. "Look at me," he said softly. She lifted her face to his, and he kissed her lightly on the mouth. "Palmer has faith in you. I have faith in you. I have faith in us. Jordan, I said it once and I'm saying it again. I'm not giving up on us." He kissed her harder, and she surrendered under the pressure of his lips. Her own lips parted and she kissed him deeply, wrapping her arms around him. They stood, locked in that embrace, feeling their hearts beating together.

At last Jordan broke gently away. "I have to go," she whispered.

Aiden brushed a curl back from her face. "I'll call you tomorrow," he said. "Don't worry. We'll work everything out." He kissed her quickly once more, and before she could respond, he smiled and left the room.

Aiden walked into town without noticing anything around him. His mind was turned completely inward and his thoughts were swirling like the eddies in the boisterous river that swept past Jordan's office. He knew he should be elated at the acquisition of ChatDotCom. It was a real victory for Trade Winds, a way to expand into what was becoming one of the fastest growing markets in the country. He knew his father would be proud and pleased that he had been able to handle the matter and see it through to the desired end, but business was the farthest thing from his mind. Instead, his thoughts were crowded with pictures of the bits and pieces of the last few days. The shock of seeing Jordan for the first time: a pretty girl, almost painfully young, standing behind a huge desk in a huge office where he had expected to meet a graying veteran executive ready to do battle down to the last penny. The smell of her hair. The shape of her hips as she walked down the hall in front of him. And the touch of her, of her lips and her skin, and the deep, hot recesses of her. His stomach constricted and, unbidden, his loins tightened with desire.

When Aiden reached his room, it was nearly dark. He didn't turn on a light, but kicked off his shoes and lay down on the bed, staring at the ceiling. Then he turned his head. The last of the day's light filtered in through the western-facing windows and softly illuminated the picture of the couple of long ago, hand-in-hand in the apple orchard. Aiden's mind continued on, thinking the thoughts that only occur to lovers. He hadn't meant to fall in love, but he knew he had. He knew it was real. He couldn't be mistaken about that. His feelings were so different, so completely foreign from any feelings he had ever had for a woman before. Now an awful dread filled him, stabbing him to his core. What if she didn't love him? Or refused to let herself love him? What if she was overwhelmed with the responsibilities of running a company under new management, helping her family, and raising a daughter? What if she couldn't bring herself to take on a relationship, to give herself up to love? Women were capable of such things, he reflected. They could throw their own wants and needs into the sacrificial fire at a moment's notice and never look back. Aiden had seen his mother do it and even his sisters. They would give up something he knew was important to them, just for the sake of somebody else's comfort. He rubbed his hands over his face. *I won't let her do it,* he thought, *I know she loves me. I won't let her throw us away.*

Suddenly, he remembered he had not called his father. He picked up the cell phone and entered the familiar numbers.

"Is the deal done?" barked Gordon Stewart into the phone.

"It is, Dad," replied Aiden. "It's signed, at least from this end. You'll have to give the final signature."

"You get in your car and get up here. I'll sign it, and you can return a copy tomorrow."

"Hold on!" exclaimed Aiden. "I'm exhausted. I'm not going anywhere tonight. I'll get on the road tomorrow."

"Exhausted!" the old man barked. "Exhausted at your age? When I was your age, well, I won't even tell you what I did on a daily basis. You wouldn't believe it! Stay there, then. Your mother's shushing me from this end, too. Just get on the road as soon as you can in the morning. And, Aiden?"

"Yes?"

"Good job."

"Thanks, Dad."

Aiden put the phone down on the bed beside him and resumed staring at the ceiling. Thoughts of Jordan high-jacked his mind once again. He would call her in the morning, to tell her he was going to Maine. He would be back the following day, probably with a couple of members of the Trade Winds board of directors to discuss upcoming strategies for the two companies working together. Then what? Where was this leading, and how were they going to get there?

The memory of the sensation of making love to her washed over him, tying his stomach in knots, making sweat break out on his forehead. He groaned aloud and heaved himself to his feet. He felt as though he was walking through waist-deep water as he went into the bathroom, stripped, and stepped into the shower. The water felt comforting, running down the back of his neck, soothing his tense body, relieving the pain of the separation he felt.

As his muscles loosened, an idea occurred to him: Jordan could come with him, to Maine. She could meet his father, his mother. It would be business. After all, he had met Palmer. The three-hour ride would give them time to be together, to talk it out, to formulate a plan. Aiden's heart leaped. He felt encouraged. He stepped out of the shower, toweled off, and climbed into the bed. Now that there was a plan, at least the start of a plan, maybe he could relax a little. He flicked on the television to catch the late news.

An hour or so later, he woke up from a fitful sleep. He turned the television off and lay on his back, once again wide awake. He tossed and turned for another hour until, finally, he grabbed his phone from the bedside table and texted Jordan.

Can't sleep. Call if you're awake. Miss you.

Thirty seconds later, his phone buzzed. "Hello?" he said.

"I couldn't sleep either."

"I miss you. You should be here in my bed."

"I miss you, too, Aiden, but Grace is sleeping in my bed right now. That's why I'm whispering." She gave a little laugh.

"Don't wake the baby. I talked to my father. I've got to leave tomorrow morning and take the contract back for him to read and sign."

"Oh. Well, then..."

Aiden put his plan into words. "I want you to come with me. I want you to meet my father, the owner of Trade Winds. I went with you to meet Palmer, and I want you to come with me."

"Oh, Aiden, I—I don't know."

"Why not? Don't you want to? We'd have three and a half hours to ourselves. And three and a half hours the next day on the way back. There's no cell phone reception across most of New Hampshire so nobody would be bothering us. We could talk about how we're going to handle our—our situation."

"Aiden, I'd love to go with you. I really would. It's just that I don't like to leave Grace."

"Can't your parents watch her?"

Jordan laughed a little. "I can tell you're not a parent yet! Of course they would watch her, but I don't get much of a chance to be with her, and my evenings and nights with her are precious to me."

"I understand," said Aiden a little sulkily. Then it hit him. "Hey! Bring her."

"What?"

"Bring her. Why not? We're going to my parents' home. They're used to babies. My sisters had babies all over the place there for a while."

"Oh, Aiden, I don't know. Besides, your car has two seats."

"We'll take your Jeep."

"Well, oh well...I guess that would be okay. I could go with you. Grace is a good traveler."

"Settled. I'll pick you up at ten tomorrow morning. Is that enough time for you to get ready? If we wait too much later, my father's head will explode."

Jordan laughed out loud. "Oh, I have to be quiet," she said quickly in a whisper. "Don't make me laugh!"

"I'll see you at ten, but I still think you should be here in my bed."

"Good night, Aiden."

"Good night," he sighed contentedly and clicked off the phone.

Chapter Eleven

In the morning, Jordan was ready at nine thirty. She angsted over what to wear and finally settled on a conservative, sporty khaki skirt, a scoop-necked white cotton T, and camel-colored flats. She carried a blazer of deep forest green. Grace was fed, bathed, and dressed in ruffled overalls and a yellow striped shirt. The diaper bag was packed with bottles, wipes, diapers, extra clothes, teethers, pacifiers, baby blankets, and baby food. Jordan stood, coffee mug in hand, staring out the front window. Grace played, cooing and squealing, in her playpen.

"Jordan," said her mother, picking up Grace and going to stand beside her daughter. "Stop fidgeting. You don't have to go with this person if you don't want to, you know. Is he a reliable man?"

"I want to go, Mom," said Jordan, not taking her eyes away from the window. "It's just good business. It's very nice of him to let me take Grace. We'll take my car, because it's got the car seat in it. I told him he could just leave his here."

"Where are you staying?"

"We're going to Portland. We're going to meet with his father, who owns Trade Winds, at their home. I imagine I'll get a room in one of the hotels there in town. Aid — Mr. Stewart will see to it, I'm sure. Don't worry; I'll let you know what's happening along the way."

"Are you sure you just don't want to leave Grace here at home?"

"Oh, Mom, I work all the time. I can take her. I don't like to spend any more time away from her than I have to."

"Well, I understand. I guess this man does too."

"It's a family company. I suppose that's why."

"Does this man have children as well?"

"No, he's not married."

"Is this the man I met a few days ago at your office?"

"Yes, yes it is," said Jordan.

"Oh my," said her mother in a different tone of voice. "Not married..."

"What?" asked Jordan. "What do you mean by that, Mom?"

At that moment, Aiden arrived and parked the car at the edge of the lawn. He got out of the car and proceeded up the walk to the front door.

Jordan's mother said, "Are you going to answer the door?"

"Yes, yes..." Jordan was flustered, wondering whether this was such a good idea after all. She set her mug down on the counter and went to open the door.

"Hi," said Aiden.

"Hi." Jordan smiled shyly at him.

They stood for a moment in the door.

"Can I come in?"

"Oh, of course," said Jordan. "This is so silly! I feel like a high school girl on a first date. Please, come in."

He reached out for her, but she eluded his touch as she led the way into the kitchen. He was only able to brush her hand instead. She glanced back over her shoulder and flashed him a smile.

"Good to see you again, Mr. Stewart," said Jordan's mother.

"Nice to see you, too, Mrs. Fitzgerald."

"I'm glad you were able to reach an agreement with my daughter about ChatDotCom. Is this the final step, then?"

Aiden nodded. "Yes, it is. We're very happy to merge with Chat. Jordan handled it like a pro."

"She is a pro," said Mrs. Fitzgerald with a mother's pride.

"We'll be meeting with my father. His is the last signature needed. It's a long drive for a day trip, so we'll start back tomorrow morning. Jordan and her daughter are staying the night at my parents' home."

"Really!" Jordan's mother gasped in surprise, and Jordan shot Aiden a startled look.

"I spoke to my mother this morning. She insists. Make no mistake about it; she's used to doing this, with all the business associates my father's brought home over the years!"

"Are you sure she's prepared for a baby?"

"Mom…" protested Jordan, but her mother looked straight at Aiden.

Aiden laughed. "I told her about Grace. She's looking forward to it."

"I see," said the older woman. "Well, please drive safely. Call me when you get there, Jordan."

"I will." Jordan picked up Grace's bag and her own. Then she took her daughter and kissed her mother on the cheek. "Don't worry."

"This all seems rather unconventional to me," her mother muttered.

"I'm ready," Jordan said. Aiden gently slipped the bags off her arm and hoisted them onto his shoulder. "I'll call later, Mom."

"Nice to see you again," said Aiden, and they were out the door.

Jordan handed him the keys as she got into the passenger seat. "You drive," she said, "then I'll be free to tend to Grace if she gets fussy on the trip."

Once in the car, with Grace safely in her seat, Jordan let out a deep sigh. Aiden laughed as he turned the key in the ignition. "Your mother knows something's going on."

"Just drive." Jordan, suddenly feeling awkward, stared straight ahead. The whole scene was so surreal. Heading out on the road, to a business meeting, with her baby. With a man she knew very little about — though she'd slept with him — and who continued to elicit wild emotional responses from her. It was all very confusing.

"You're quiet," said Aiden after a while. "What are you thinking about?"

Honesty was the only way to go, thought Jordan. She turned in her seat to look at him, his handsome profile, his strong hands relaxed as they rested on the steering wheel. It was his hands that caused her heart to leap just then. Looking at them, she could almost feel how they had traveled over her body, caressing, exploring, raising her to emotional and physical levels she had never gone before. A delicious tremor shivered through her, but she quelled it and tried to speak rationally and logically. "I look at you," she said, starting slowly, "and I wonder, where did this man come from? Who is he and what is he doing in my life? When we're together, it seems like I know you inside and out. It seems like you're part of me—a really important part. But then I think of the reality, and the reality is that we've only known each other a few days. A few days, Aiden. It's almost absurd. And it's all tied up in the business, too. We hammered out a complex, multimillion-dollar business deal. Did we get caught up in the romance of it? Is that what this is? It's so complicated."

Aiden glanced over at her. He didn't laugh or try to trivialize her concern. "I know there are a lot of unresolved issues we face, Jordan, but the one thing I am sure of is how I feel about you—about us. I know what you mean. I look at you and think, where did this woman come from? Was it chance? Was it fate? I feel like it was meant to be. Otherwise, it wouldn't be so sure in my mind. I think the best way to handle it is to not over analyze. We can't afford to panic. Let's just enjoy this…this time." He reached across the console and put his hand over hers. "Please, don't panic. Don't think too far ahead. Trust me."

Jordan smiled bravely and lifted his hand, pressing it to her lips.

The trip went fast. Grace fell asleep soon after they were on the road. Jordan and Aiden talked about many things, from politics and their personal beliefs to silly trivia. Their laughter came easily and for most of the trip, Aiden drove with his left hand and held onto Jordan's hand with his right.

Jordan's heart beat faster as they neared the city of Portland. As Aiden talked about his childhood, sailing on Casco Bay, catching his own lobster, and spending summers camping with his friends on wild little islands, her mind wandered. She didn't know exactly what to expect. They were making the trip, theoretically she knew, in order to sign the papers that would finalize the merger between ChatDotCom and Trade Winds. That merger would make her, Jordan Fitzgerald, CEO of the northern branch of the bigger company Trade Winds would become after the acquisition was complete. She looked forward to meeting Gordon Stewart, notable and foresighted businessman and founder and CEO of Trade Winds.

Yet, deep within her soul, Jordan knew there was another reason for the trip to Portland. A more personal reason. Aiden was bringing her home to meet his mother and father. While Gordon Stewart was indeed founder and CEO of Trade Winds and he'd just bought ChatDotCom from Gene Palmer, her boss and mentor, he was also Aiden Stewart's father, and this was, to Jordan, the more important of his roles. She stared ahead as they drove, feeling Aiden's fingers lightly caressing her own. Her mother had always said she would know when the right one came along. *You always know,* she had said. *Well,* Jordan thought, *the right one has come along. I know it.* A sudden, intense memory flashed in her mind's eye and she saw herself lying in his arms, warm from his warmth, passionate with his passion, her skin against his skin, even their breathing synchronized. She wanted with all her heart to shout it out to all who would hear that she loved this man and he loved her. Yet there was a cloud over her happiness. Jordan knew that honesty was the cornerstone of love. It was the foundation that would support love through all kinds of trials and tribulations. And though she had not been dishonest with Aiden, she had not told him the whole truth about everything. For so long, she had maintained that the identity of Grace's father was her business and her business only, but now she had met a man with whom she wanted to share everything forever. Now, her conscience told her, it was his business, too.

They drove over a bridge. As Jordan looked out her window, she could see the huge oil and fuel tanks along the shore of the bay.

"Have you ever been to Portland before?" asked Aiden as they proceeded along the highway that ran parallel to the water.

"No," admitted Jordan. "I haven't been north of Ogunquit."

"Well, this is Commercial Street, where Trade Winds' headquarters are. This was the wharf area, and from the late seventeen hundreds on, it was a bustling shipping hub for the whole Northeast. There's still business that goes on here now, especially fishing and lobster wharves, federal and state buildings, a lot of retail, and some private companies like legal firms and Trade Winds. We recently bought one of the old warehouses and renovated it. Renovations were finished last summer, and we moved in just before winter. There it is. See? You can see it straight ahead. The tall brick building with the balcony overlooking the water."

Jordan let her gaze follow the direction of his pointing finger. She saw the large, solid brick building rising up over the working wharfs on either side. Large white letters attached high up on the street side of the building read "Trade Winds." The roofline dropped a story on the bay side of the building. The lower roof was ringed with a wrought iron railing, and Jordan could see chairs and umbrellaed tables.

"I'll just drive down to the ferry at the end of the street so you can get a feel for the area. This is called the Old Port, and it's a real tourist place. Kind of high end with a lot of good restaurants and retail. Portland is famous as a foodie town," explained Aiden as he drove along the bustling street. "And see there, just next to the lobster wharf? See those long blue buildings? That's Chandler's Wharf. That's where I live."

"You do?" Jordan craned her neck to get a good look as they drove by. "I can see why you said you have a cheap commute! And short, too."

Aiden swung the car around in the parking lot at the end of the street. "Ready to meet my father and put this thing to bed?" he asked her. He lifted her hand to his lips and kissed it.

Jordan let out a big sigh. She squeezed his hand. "Yes, I'm ready. I am. Let's go." It was all overwhelming, she thought. Suddenly, she felt more like a pawn than a player in this game, this merger between two powerful New England families. Where did she fit in, anyway? She looked across the console at Aiden. He drove on, his noble, patrician profile intent on the busy main street. It was confusing, she thought as she looked at him. Sometimes she felt so close to this man, as though she could trust him with her life, so sure of their love that she would follow him anywhere. And then, in the blink of an eye, she could feel so alone, so detached, so forgotten. He was an owner, after all; she would be an employee. Well, she would just play this out. Right now, it was okay. Right now she would bury any doubt that threatened to rise up in her mind and quell her happiness. She would bury the doubt and play along, do her job, provide for her daughter and her family. Things would become clear as time went on. She hoped.

Aiden turned left into the large parking lot, cut diagonally across, and pulled into a parking space marked by a little sign that bore his name.

"Here we are," he said. From the back seat Grace let out a high pitched squeal as she felt the car come to a stop.

Jordan laughed. "And not a moment too soon!" she said, opening her door.

The salt air washed over her like a soothing balm. She took a deep breath, savoring the scent of the ocean. Seagulls circled the working lobster docks on either side, calling and scolding. She had not been seaside in so long, she had forgotten how charming and calming it was.

"This is beautiful," she said sincerely.

"It is," agreed Aiden. He opened the back door of the Jeep, and Jordan reached in, freeing Grace from her confinement in the car seat. Cradling the baby against her hip, she rummaged in the diaper bag and located a bottle. Grace took it eagerly.

"I'm not exactly dressed for a business meeting," she said.

"You look, ah, good enough to eat to me." Aiden winked at her as he wrapped her and her baby in his strong arms and kissed her on the mouth. "I know you're nervous," he said. "Don't be. Everything is fine. My father huffs and puffs, but he's a good man, and besides, the hard part is done."

She smiled at him. "Lead the way!" she said bravely. Aiden smiled and ran his fingers through his hair. Here, in his own element, with the sea breeze playing with his wayward hair, his eyes seemed to sparkle. He was sexier than ever. Jordan felt her stomach leap, and her heart fluttered in her chest as she followed him into the building.

There was a small desk, behind which sat a heavy-set, uniformed guard who stood as they came through the door.

"Good morning, Mr. Stewart," said the guard.

"Hey, Ray," Aiden greeted him, smiling, then glanced at his watch. "Is my father back from lunch yet?"

"I don't think he went out today. He's expecting you. He's called down here about six times!"

Aiden laughed. "Give him a call and tell him we're on our way up."

"Will do." The guard grinned as he picked up the phone.

Aiden guided Jordan, still carrying Grace on her hip, to the elevator. Once inside, he set them on their way to the third floor. "Hm," he said, "I've always fantasized about elevators, but you seem to have an appendage."

Jordan laughed. The elevator stopped, and the door slid silently open. They stepped out into an ante-office. A trim, gray-haired woman sat behind a desk in front of a bank of windows that looked out onto the wharves. When she saw them, she stood, walking forward to greet them.

"Aiden! You're back!"

"Hi, Mrs. Barnes. Yes, I'm back. And may I introduce the CEO of our new partner in northern New England, Jordan Fitzgerald. Oh, and I can't forget Grace."

"How lovely to meet you, Ms. Fitzgerald." Mrs. Barnes held out a finger to Grace, who wrapped her tiny fingers around it. "And you, too, Miss Grace. What an adorable child!"

"Oh, thank you," said Jordan politely. "It's a pleasure to meet you also."

"Is my father in?" asked Aiden.

"He's in his office," said Mrs. Barnes. "I'll get him."

They heard a door open behind them. "No, I'm not! I'm not in my office," boomed the old man, striding forward. "I'm right here." He made straight for Jordan with his hand extended. She was struck by how his energy reminded her so much of Gene Palmer before he became ill. She gripped Grace extra tight, for moral support, and put out her hand.

"My father, Gordon Stewart," said Aiden. "Dad, this is Jordan Fitzgerald, our new partner."

Gordon took her small hand in his big one in a firm clasp. "Pleased to have you on board," he said, smiling widely. "I've been looking forward to meeting you. Gene Palmer is an old friend and adversary of mine. You have to be pretty special to have his trust."

"I'm very pleased to meet you," said Jordan sincerely. "I'm eager to work with Trade Winds, Mr. Stewart. I know our companies will be stronger together than they ever were separately."

"I think you're right," said the old man, putting his hand on her elbow. "Come along with me, Ms. Fitzgerald. We'll go into the office and sign this thing."

Jordan let him guide her into his office. She glanced back once, quickly, just to make sure Aiden was coming too. He winked at her, and it bolstered her courage.

"Here, here, have a seat on the sofa," said Gordon.

"Thank you," said Jordan, gratefully sitting down. Gordon Stewart acted as though all of his business cronies brought babies to their meetings. She was thankful for that. She settled Grace on her lap and waited. Gordon went to the door and spoke to Mrs. Barnes.

"I'd like to you bring in the documentation, if you would, Betsy," he said. He turned to Jordan. "The lawyers have been over it with a fine-toothed comb," he said. "They started nit-picking, but I put my foot down finally. We're ready to sign it. You know, the lawyers have to keep the dialogue and the conflict going or they don't make any money." He chuckled as he took the papers from Mrs. Barnes and sat next to Jordan on the sofa. He laid open the folder on the coffee table and took a gold pen from his pocket, handing it to Jordan. "Ladies first," he said. She smiled at him and, feeling strangely at ease, signed the document. She set the pen down. Gordon Stewart picked it up and signed his name under hers. The deed was done.

"Welcome aboard," he said, holding out his hand. "This is something to celebrate."

Jordan shook his hand. "I feel good about this," she said. "I do." She caught Aiden's eye across the room and smiled at him. Grace wiggled.

"Go ahead," said Gordon. "Set her down. When my grandchildren were that age, I had toys in here, but they're teenagers now!"

Jordan set Grace down on the carpeted floor. She teetered a bit, and then seeing Aiden smiling from across the room at her, she began her baby Frankenstein-ish walk toward him. Gordon turned to Jordan. "Tell me about Gene," he said seriously. "How's he doing?"

Jordan drew a deep breath. "You know, he's doing okay," she answered. "Emotionally, anyway. Physically, he's frail. He gets tired easily. I usually have a daily meeting with him, but sometimes he can't sit through it. I hate seeing him that way. When I think of the way he was when…when we first started to work together…" Her voice trailed off.

"I'm sorry," said Gordon sincerely. "I'm sorry about it, but you've done him proud. I'm sure it makes this whole situation easier for him. Congratulations on our merger."

It could have been his honest manner, or it could have been his perceptive assessment of how she felt, but two tears, beyond her control, slid down her cheeks. Flustered, she quickly brushed them away.

"I'm sorry," said Gordon. "I didn't mean to upset you."

"Oh no, no," Jordan tried to reassured him. "It's me. I guess I'm just being emotional. I'm usually a lot more hard-boiled than this, but this is an emotional time for everybody at Chat, and while we welcome this merger, it's the end of an era too." Aiden, Grace in his arms, crossed the room.

"Are you all right?" he asked.

"Please, please," said Jordan, embarrassed. "I'm fine. Just an overflow of emotion, I guess. Really, I apologize. I'm being such a girl right now."

Gordon laughed outright, lightening the mood. "There's nothing wrong with that." He chuckled. "Now, let's drive back to the house and have some lunch. Aiden can show you where he grew up. My wife, Nell, is expecting us."

Jordan reached out and took Grace from Aiden. Gordon motioned to the door, and the three of them walked into the elevator.

Once outside, Jordan turned and looked back at the building. "It's a beautiful old building," she said. "You know, Chat's offices are in a restored factory building as well."

"Too much good space to waste," said Gordon. "We got a good deal on it two years ago. Restoring and re-doing it to our specifications took a little time, but we moved in earlier this year. And it's a great commute for Aiden!"

Jordan laughed, "So he told me."

Gordon waved to them. "I'll see you at home." He crossed the parking lot and got behind the wheel of a big Mercedes. Jordan buckled Grace into her baby seat and then belted herself into the front passenger seat.

As Aiden followed his father out onto the road, Jordan's cell phone rang. It was her mother.

"Hello?"

"Jordan, are you there? You didn't call."

"Oh, I'm sorry, Mom. Yes. We've had our meeting, everything is signed, and we're going out to Mr. Stewart's house for a late lunch."

"How is Grace doing? Is she fussy?"

"Oh, no, Mom, she's doing great."

"Well, I have really good news."

"You do?"

"Yes. Your father's been hired by the Mountain to oversee the construction of a whole group of new condominiums!"

"Mom, that's wonderful! That's so wonderful!"

"He's thrilled, Jordan. He's thrilled because it means we won't have to tie you down anymore. The money is really good, and the work will be steady. He'll work as an independent contractor directly with Mountain. I guess they saw his work around town, and, you know, the Mountain was sold last year, and the guy who bought it is young and progressive. He liked your father."

"Mom, that's just the best, but you never tied me down. You're my mother and my father. I was pleased to help. You helped me, too. How else would I have managed with Grace?"

"Well, you enjoy your time there, honey. You deserve it. I'll talk to you soon."

"Bye, Mom. I love you." Jordan clicked off.

"What's so great?" asked Aiden.

"Oh, Aiden, my father got a job. A wonderful job. He's supervising the construction of new condos at the ski mountain. Some guy just bought it and is expanding it. It's amazing!"

"I'm happy for all of you," said Aiden. "Your family reminds me of mine. They stick together."

"We do," confirmed Jordan. Her mind began to wander as a surreal feeling settled around her. Such circumstances had occurred to bring her to this point! It all seemed a whirlwind now. Her mind drifted back in time to when she was a student at the University of Vermont. Her father had lost his job. She'd been desperate for tuition money. She remembered it as clearly as though it had happened yesterday how she went to her adviser, explaining the situation to her and asking for help. As it was, Jordan held a number of student loans, to be paid back after graduation. The adviser had taken the bureaucratically correct steps, applying for more financial aid, but troubles had run deeper in the family. The cost of just keeping the house up was astronomical enough when the only money coming in was a weekly paycheck her mother received from working part time at the town offices and an unemployment check to her father. Her father also managed to do some odd jobs around town, but these were not steady, and the price of gasoline he had to pay just to get to the job sometimes was more than the job paid. Fuel oil and electricity expenses continued, to say nothing of health insurance for the family.

Jordan's parents remained optimistic, at least to the outside world. "It'll turn around," said her mother confidently. "Don't worry. You just stay in school. We'll find a way. Derek has one more year of high school, and by the time he's at the University, we'll be back on our feet. Don't you worry."

Jordan did worry, though. At the end of the spring semester, she went to the dean of students and asked about a leave of absence from the fall term. Wisely, the dean tried to persuade her to return in the fall. If it turned out she couldn't stay, well, then they would cross that bridge when they came to it. Jordan didn't tell anyone about her talk with the dean. She spent the last warm days of school trying to behave as though nothing was wrong. She went to parties with her friends, crammed for finals, and tried to find comfort casually dating. At the end of the semester, she packed her things and returned home. The next day, she went looking for a job. For a week, she filled out applications in every available place of employment within commuting distance. Time was of the essence. Jordan needed to make the most of her time off from school. She needed to make money as quickly as possible in order to help her parents, in order to save for the fall semester which was a mere three months away.

She began revisiting the hospital, the restaurants, and one particularly depressing day, she revisited ChatDotCom. Ashley, whom she had known peripherally in high school, was sitting at the big marble desk in the foyer.

"Hi, Jordan," Ashley had said pleasantly as Jordan approached.

"Hi, Ashley." Jordan tried not to seem too desperate. "Is there any word on my résumé yet?" She had applied for a web manager position. She knew she was qualified, even over qualified for the job.

"No, I'm sorry, I haven't heard, but I could call into personnel and find out for you."

"Oh, please, could you do that?"

Ashley had nodded and picked up the phone. "Carol, this is Ashley at the desk. Jordan Fitzgerald is here. Have you reviewed her résumé yet?"

"Ask her if I can please just talk to her." Jordan leaned over the desk, whispering to Ashley.

"Oh, really? Oh, I'll tell her — "

"Please, Ashley, ask if I can talk to her."

"Oh, Carol, she's asking if she might speak with you. Oh, okay. Fine, I'll tell her." Ashley hung up the phone. "She says she doesn't have time today."

Jordan would never forget her reaction to the news. She slammed her hand down on the marble. It made a loud slapping sound and bruised her fingers. "Damn!" she said, louder than she should have.

"Damn! I have to get a job doing something somewhere. And I'm qualified for this job! I can do this!"

Ashley never lost her poise; she sat quietly looking straight at her with her heavily made up eyes. Suddenly, the big door behind Ashley opened, and a man peered out. "What's going on here, Ashley?"

It was Gene Palmer. Jordan recognized him. She had seen him around town and in the newspaper. Immediately, she regretted her outburst, but she kept her dignity. "I'm sorry I disturbed you, Mr. Palmer. I just lost my temper for a minute. I applied for a job, and nobody has reviewed my résumé yet."

"Really? What position did you apply for?"

"I applied for the web manager's position."

Gene Palmer walked out of his office and stood beside Ashley. "What's your name?"

"I'm Jordan Fitzgerald," she answered. She thought she detected something like a smile forming around the corner of his eyes.

He held out his hand. "I'm Gene Palmer," he said. "Why don't you come into my office. If Carol is too busy to see you, you can talk to me."

And that was it. She started the next day. She never understood what had caught his attention, but she never questioned it. She was too grateful.

Jordan recalled vividly how, as fall and her return to school approached, Mr. Palmer had taken her into his office, alone.

"I just want you to know that a job exists for you here at Chat, whenever you want it. I know you have to finish school, but I am very sorry to…to lose you. I wish I could make you sign a contract to come back, but you'll probably need to see the whole wide world before you return to our little company in Clark's Corner. I'll miss you, personally and professionally."

She was overcome at this admission of feeling from him, and she blushed. At that moment, Ashley walked into the room, a sheaf of paper in her hands. "Mr. Palmer," she began, but then intuitively felt the tension of the situation. She looked quickly from one to other and then said smoothly, "I have the insurance papers ready for your signature. Is this a good time?"

"Certainly," said Mr. Palmer, and the tension was broken. "Bring them over here, and I'll sign them now."

They didn't speak personally to each other again. The summer ended. Jordan had been able to pay enough of her tuition with the help of financial aid to return to school. She left a sizable sum of money for her parents to pay bills with while they continued to job hunt.

"Why so quiet?" Aiden's voice jolted her back to the present. "What are you thinking about?"

"Oh, nothing, really. Just looking around," she lied. She had been thinking about something. She had been thinking about that day in late September when she found out she was pregnant. She'd shut down then. She'd shut down and crept home. After she'd told her mother and father, she'd gone that same afternoon to see Gene Palmer. He'd acted toward her as he always had. "We can manage this," he'd said. "Welcome back to Chat."

Chapter Twelve

As Aiden and Jordan made their way along the old Route 1, Jordan watched the sunlight play on the white-capped waves. "It's pretty, isn't it?" Aiden said. "My parents' house is right around this bend here. It's on the cliff and overlooks the bay."

Jordan was sure it would be beautiful. This was such a different world. Her thoughts escaped her before she could stop them. "I'm feeling like I'm in some kind of haze right now," she said to Aiden. "I'm here with you, in this beautiful place, but I don't really know you, and I don't really know where I am or how I got here. I feel—I feel like I don't really know much at all." After she spoke, she felt like a fool. She shouldn't betray her vulnerability like this, even to Aiden. "That's not what I mean," she added hastily. "I'm perfectly competent and confident about the business…"

Aiden made a sharp turn into a side road and stopped the car. She looked at him questioningly. He turned in his seat and took both her hands in his. "Look at me," he said quietly. She looked up into his beautiful, bright eyes. There was a hint of a worry line between his brows. "Jordan, of course you're confident about the business deal. You orchestrated it. You wrote most of it. You risked your life doing it, what with Fenton's bullshit. Nobody doubts you as an exceptional business head." His breath caught for an instant. "That's part of the reason you're here, but there's another reason you're here, Jordan."

They looked into each other's eyes, each searching for the thing they wanted to see, the one thing they hoped to find there. "Jordan, I love you."

Jordan's eyes dilated. She moved her mouth as if to speak, but no words came. Instead, she felt an intense heat flush through her, and her stomach flipped. Finally, she whispered, "Aiden…"

"Shhh," he said softly. "You don't have to say anything. I want you to know how I feel. That's the other reason you're here. I want you to see who I am, who my people are. I know you have so many more responsibilities than I do, so right now, just know that I love you. I don't want to burden you with it; I just want you to know. We can go from there."

Slowly, Jordan pulled her hand free of his. She lifted it to his face, cupping his cheek. *Such a dear face*, she thought. She leaned in and kissed him tenderly on the mouth. She spoke barely above a whisper. "Aiden, that makes me very happy. I love you too."

Aiden put his hands on either side of her neck and rested his forehead against hers. Then he kissed her again, this time deeper, his tongue probing between her lips. His hand slipped down to her breast. With a sigh, he pulled back. "Circumstances prevent my going where I really would like to go." He grinned at her. "We better go up to the house. My father will think I kept on driving."

Jordan gave a little giggle to cover her nervousness. "I guess this is where I meet your parents, then," she said.

"Yes, it is."

They continued up the dirt road, which was actually the long driveway to the house. Jordan could smell the sea breeze through her open window. They swung up a gentle turn, and the house came into view.

"Oh, it's beautiful, Aiden," she said, charmed. It was a tall, two-story colonial, painted yellow with deep green shutters and white trim. A graceful porch swept down onto the front lawn where the drive widened out into parking places. Aiden pulled in beside his father's Mercedes.

"It didn't always look like this," said Aiden. "When my family moved in, I wasn't even born yet. There was no working central heat, and the roof leaked. My father bought it for the property alone. My mother made it beautiful."

"Well, you saw where I live. I bet you could fit our whole house in your living room!"

"Not quite," said Aiden. "It's got a nice view of Casco Bay. I'll take you down to the boathouse later. Let's go in."

Jordan unbuckled Grace from her car seat and shouldered the diaper bag. "I'm going to have to change Grace," she said. Aiden took her arm and led her across the graveled drive to the front door. It opened before they reached it. Jordan knew by family resemblance that the smiling woman standing before them had to be Nell Stewart.

"Welcome, welcome," she said. "Please, come in. What an adorable baby!" Grace stared at her with wide eyes.

"Mom, this is Jordan Fitzgerald and Grace. Jordan, this is my mother, Nell Stewart."

"I'm so happy to meet you, Jordan," said Nell. "And congratulations are in order, I hear. Gordon told me you cemented the merger this afternoon."

"It's nice to meet you, Mrs. Stewart," answered Jordan. "Yes, we finalized everything. I think I can say everybody is satisfied with the merger."

"Come in, please," said Nell, opening the door wider.

"Is there somewhere I can change Grace, Mrs. Stewart?" asked Jordan.

"Of course. Follow me."

Nell led the way through the foyer and down the hall to the kitchen. It was a long, sunny room with a bay window that looked out over cliffside gardens down to the water. At one end was a lovely fireplace with the original beehive oven built into the old bricks. A wood burning stove sat to the right of the oven. Jordan noticed it was similar to the one in her parents' home. In the bay window there was a window seat upholstered in spring green toile. From somewhere, the scent of lilacs was drifting into the room.

"Change her right there on the window seat," said Nell. "I'm just getting some tea ready. We'll have some out on the porch. It's so beautiful this afternoon."

"Thank you," said Jordan, settling Grace down to tend to her diaper. As she changed the baby, she watched Nell collecting the cups and teapot on a tray. The kitchen was modern, with granite countertops and stainless-steel appliances, and yet it was warm and inviting.

There was a stool at the island, an invitation for somebody to talk to the cook. The cabinets glowed with the subtle warm orange tone of cherry wood. A cozy seating arrangement was clustered around the fireplace, and the table was big enough to seat a large family.

"What a beautiful room," she commented.

"Well, it didn't always look like this." Nell laughed as she opened a drawer and took out spoons. "When we first moved in, there was a big hole in the floor over there near where you're sitting. I was so afraid one of the girls was going to drop right through it. Gordon nailed a piece of plywood over it. We spent most of our time in this room because the wood stove was here. It was the warmest place in the house. I used to have the wood stacked where the porch is now. It was just an overhang then, and close to the house. For a while, it was usually me, my two little girls, three dogs, and two cats penned up here together most of the day. Summers were fine, because we could be outside. Winters got a little tough, though. I felt like a pioneer woman."

Jordan lifted Grace up and sat her on her lap. The baby was quiet. It was nearly time for her afternoon nap. "It must have been hard at first," she said. "How long did it take to restore it?"

"Oh, it was a long, slow process. Gordon worked most of the time. I did what I could, like painting and things, but we couldn't afford to do the important things for quite a while. And then, whenever we had some money, we would have to choose how to spend it. We would sit at that table right there and weigh the pros and cons. Do we need to fix the roof, or will the patch hold for another season? Can we afford not to get storm windows? Things like that. Little by little, we did it. By the time Aiden was born, my girls were ten and twelve. That was a surprise, I'll tell you! It was that year, though, that Gordon really made some money and the ball started rolling. After that, it got easier. Looking back, I don't know how we did it, but, you know, we didn't even know how hard it was when we were going through it. It's only looking back that I just can't believe it!" She laughed her lyrical laugh again. There was something about her that reminded Jordan of her own mother. No matter what happened, they pushed through, hand-in-hand with their husbands. Could she and Aiden form a partnership like their parents? She shuddered, suddenly, and buried the thought. It wasn't good to speculate on assumptions.

Her shudder was not lost on Nell. "Are you cold, Jordan? Would you like a sweater?"

"Oh, no, thank you. I'm really quite comfortable."

"Let's go out on the porch, then. Gordon and Aiden will appear the second I bring these brownies out."

Jordan gathered up her daughter and followed the older woman out onto the screened-in porch. She sat down in one of the cushioned, wrought-iron chairs and cuddled Grace as the baby drank her bottle. It was a peaceful outdoor room, dotted here and there with pots of flowering plants. There was a view of the evening sun-lit bay across the sloping lawn. Lilacs, in full bloom, hugged the corners of the porch, their scent wafting through the screens.

"There they are," said Nell, pointing out over the lawn. "What did I tell you? Men will gather every time you put food out!"

Aiden and Gordon were walking back toward the house. Aiden opened the door and held it for his father. "We were just down inspecting the boathouse," said the old man, sitting down heavily in the chair next to Jordan. He reached for a brownie, carefully avoiding his wife's disapproving glare. "Aiden will have to take you down there," he said to Jordan.

"I would love to see it," said Jordan politely. The brownie smelled heavenly, and a cup of tea would be just what she needed now, but Grace had gone to sleep in her arms, and she was afraid to move. Aiden saw the sleeping child.

"She's asleep," he said. "She fell asleep!"

"Babies do that, dear," Nell replied.

Jordan laughed softly. "It's all the traveling and new faces. She's tired out."

"I'll get that playpen or whatever it is in the back of the car," said Aiden. "You can put her down in that."

"Thank you," said Jordan, smiling up at him. It was all too familiar, somehow. As he turned and went out the screen door, Jordan caught the glance between Gordon and Nell. This little interaction, so simple and yet so intimate, had just blown their cover. Nell and Gordon were his parents, after all. Jordan felt acutely awkward, but Nell said, smooth as silk, "How old is Grace, Jordan?"

"She turned one on April sixth," answered Jordan. "She's thirteen months old."

"That's when they start to be a handful. And she's walking already, too! She's such a good baby, though! Aiden walked when he was a year old. He started climbing things before we knew it. He was always trying to keep up with his sisters." Nell laughed at the memory. "He wore me out!"

"Are you talking about me? My ears are burning." Aiden came back, carrying the folded portable crib. "Where do you want this?" He addressed the question to Jordan. She looked at Nell.

"Let's take it right into the kitchen. We'll put it in the corner by the fireplace. I'll stay right there with her. You take this opportunity, Jordan, to take a walk around with Aiden. You can talk about the business and see the boathouse. Just relax. Grace will be perfectly safe with us."

As though she had known her all her life, Jordan felt she could trust Nell. "Well, okay, if—if you don't mind."

"We don't mind at all!"

Aiden set the crib up in the corner. Jordan laid the sleeping child down on a colorful quilt and pulled a light blanket over her. "Now, go. Go before she wakes up," whispered Nell, making shooing motions with her hands.

"Thank you so much," said Jordan.

"Thanks, Mom," Aiden added. He opened the screen door, and he and Jordan walked out onto the wide lawn ringed with colorful perennial beds.

Both of them distinctly heard Gordon say to his wife, "Like hell they're going to talk about business!"

"Gordon, keep quiet!" Nell scoffed. "They'll hear!"

Aiden stifled a laugh. He bent down and whispered to Jordan as they walked across the lawn, "My father couldn't keep quiet to save his life!"

Jordan laughed out loud. She was starting to feel relaxed, starting to cautiously enjoy herself and the company of this man with whom she suddenly found herself in love.

Aiden led Jordan down the slope of the far end of the lawn. As the lawn dropped away, he turned to take her hand and was unexpectedly electrified by her beauty. The spring breeze blowing off the bay had caught her coppery hair. It billowed softly around her face, alight with a burnished glow from the evening sun. Her modest clothing only accentuated her voluptuousness. Aiden felt his heart leap. He took her around the waist and swung her down to stand beside him on a wooden deck built out over the rocks. Wooden steps, supported by rebar drilled into the ledge and weathered and gray with age, led down over the rocks to the small beach, a tiny inlet within the bigger bay, protected between two small pine covered peninsulas. A small white clapboarded building sat over the water. A dock stretched out into the bay, and the *Nellie Bly*, the fifty foot sailing yacht, sat tranquilly in the dark water, rocking ever so slightly as the waves lapped at her sides with the eternal ebb and flow of the tide.

"It's beautiful, Aiden," said Jordan, leaning on the deck's railing and looking at the vista that stretched before her. "It's absolutely beautiful. It doesn't even look real!"

"It was always beautiful," agreed Aiden, following her gaze. "Even when the buildings and the property was a mess, this was always here, always beautiful. I remember looking down from my bedroom window when I was small and seeing my mother and father standing here together, just staring out to sea. It always made me feel safe." He laughed and pointed to one of the spits of land. "See that old, gnarled pine sticking out over the water? That rope hanging from it? We used to swing out over the water and drop right into the ocean. It's a wonder we never killed ourselves on the rocks!"

"Well, you saw where I live! It's not like this, but we had our adventures, too. The boys used to swim in the old canal that runs by the factory. Nobody ever drowned, but I don't know how!"

"I think our upbringings weren't as different as you might think."

"What? Your parents were rich; mine certainly weren't. We've always been a classic blue-collar family. Even now. My father is still a contractor. Neither of my parents went to college. They moved into that house when I was only a year old, and they've been there ever since."

"What I'm saying is the similarities outweigh the differences," said Aiden soberly, watching the glint of the sun on the waves. "Would you say your parents had a good relationship?"

"The best," said Jordan firmly. "They're best friends. They smile at each other every time one of them comes into the room. When I was growing up, I didn't think about it." She paused. "Now I do."

"That's what I'm saying," Aiden said emphatically. "I'm not sure I can remember my parents ever fighting. Of course I was born just as things started to get easier. My sisters can remember when it was harder." He turned to look at her and smiled. "And you're not a blue-collar family anymore. You're now officially management, my love!"

Jordan dipped her head with a little grin. "Maybe, but I remember where I came from."

"That's why you're so effective." Aiden took her hand again. "Come with me. We'll walk on the beach. I'll show you the boat."

Together they descended the stairs. The sun's rays stretched from the west out across the small beach, turning it golden. When they reached the sand, Jordan slipped off her shoes. Aiden stole glances at her as she allowed the cool sand to massage her feet as she walked close to the water. The gentle waves licked at her toes. "Wow!" she giggled, stepping back. "That water is cold!"

"It's Maine," said Aiden, smiling at her from where he perched on a seaweed-covered rock above the tidal pools.

"I remember," Jordan replied, standing her ground and letting the water numb her toes.

"Come on," beckoned Aiden, jumping down from the rock. "I'll show you the boat." He held his hand out to her, and she skipped across the beach to take it. She followed him up a wooden stairway to the dock that led out to the *Nellie Bly*.

"This is my father's one real indulgence," explained Aiden. "When he finally had enough money to consider purchases for pleasure, he bought horses for my sisters, and he and my mother bought this boat. They both love the water. They're both experienced sailors. They used to go pretty far up the coast, but they mainly stick close in now. They're getting older, I guess." Aiden stepped from the dock into the stern of the yacht. He held out his hand again, and Jordan hopped daintily in beside him.

She looked around her. "This is the first time I've ever been in any boat bigger than my cousin's outboard motorboat on Lake Champlain." She ran her hand over the rich, dark wood and lightly touched the brass that was shining in the sunlight. The boat's wheel and compass stood at the ready, flanked by padded seating and storage units. Steps led below deck. "It's a beautiful boat."

"Want to see below?" He had descended the three steps and raised up his arms to help her down.

"Do you have ulterior motives, sir?" Jordan teased as she stepped down into the hatchway with her bare feet.

Aiden laughed and wrapped his arms around her. She lifted her face to meet his lips with hers. They stood pressed together for a long moment, feeling their hearts beating together. Once again, Aiden was struck by the way this woman felt in his arms, compared to all the other women he had ever held, had ever kissed, had ever taken to bed.

"Come with me," he whispered urgently, and taking her by the hand, he led her through a small door in the bow end into the master berth. It was dim and cool. What light there was shone through two brass-rimmed portholes. The bed was large and covered with a thick duvet in a blue and white nautical print. Aiden lifted her and laid her back onto the soft mattress, then lowered himself over her.

He felt her arms go up around him, caressing his ear and the back of his neck. Her touch always started a fire in the very core of him, searing him with her sensual smell and taste until he could scarcely control the flames of desire that flared within him. He slipped his hand up under her skirt, feeling her silky skin under his fingertips. His hand followed the curve of her buttocks as she lifted her hips in response to his caress. He felt his passion rise as he pressed his body into hers. Her thighs opened gently. Now his passion became a burning need to possess her. He stood up, unbuckled his belt, and stepped out of his jeans. She lay still on the bed, gazing at him with a small smile on her lips. He got onto the bed beside her and lifted her skirt, exposing red lace panties. His breath quickened. He lowered his lips and kissed her through the panties. A small moan escaped her, fanning the embers of his desire to flames. Suddenly, he could wait no longer. The desire in his groin swelled up, filling him with an urgency he could barely control. He peeled the delicate panties down over her thighs and she lifted her legs free of them. Now he could see the place where he ached to be, the russet curls trimmed in submission to a narrow strip leading to the entrance of her secret heat.

He touched the place with his fingers, pushing between the folds. She moaned again, opening her thighs wider. And then her fingers were beside his, opening and spreading herself for him, inviting him in to fulfill her overwhelming need. He could wait no longer. He kneeled between her soft, open thighs and thrust into her.

Jordan cried out at the intensity of the relief it brought both of them, to satisfy their mutual desire to be this close, this intimate.

She gripped the duvet with both fists and lifted her hips up to meet him until their bodies ground together with the heat of their passion. Aiden gripped her hips, pulling her into him, raising his ardor to a fever pitch. He began his thrusts, slow and silken at first and then harder and faster. Aiden knew Jordan could sense his ecstasy growing, straining inside her, filling her with indescribable excitement until at last, her rapture exploded over her. Aiden mirrored her emotion, following her climax with his own. He groaned and shuddered, collapsing at last on top of her, his damp heat mingling with hers.

They lay together until their heartbeats slowed and they began to breath evenly again.

"I love you, Jordan," Aiden whispered in her ear. Jordan answered with her body, pressing against him, holding him tighter. Aiden lifted his head out of the hollow of her neck. He looked at her and smiled mischievously. "I waited to say that until after we made love," he said, "so you wouldn't think I said it just to get in your pants."

Jordan laughed out loud. "Well, how considerate of you, Mr. Stewart—" she giggled "—but I think we should go back to the house now. I'm afraid Grace will wake up and be upset if I'm not there."

Aiden stood up and buckled his jeans. Jordan smoothed her skirt and straightened her T-shirt. She peeked into the small mirror that hung on the wall.

"Oh dear!" she exclaimed, smoothing her hair. "I look like...I look like—"

"Like you've just had mad, passionate sex?"

"Well, if you put it that way, yes!"

Aiden laughed. "It was kind of a quickie, but I'll make it up to you later."

Together, they climbed out of the *Nellie Bly* and started up the stairway to the wide, green lawn.

As they walked toward the house, Jordan noticed another car parked beside her Jeep in the driveway. It was a sleek, red Mercedes roadster. Jordan had only ever seen one other; Gene Palmer's son who lived in North Carolina drove it. There was a lot of money around her, but Jordan felt herself only a witness to it. She wasn't part of it.

No matter how much money she made as CEO of Chat, she would never be able to spend like some of these people. For her, things had an intrinsic value, and past that value, she couldn't bring herself to spend. Even if she were able to afford it, she would never spend fifty thousand dollars on a sports car.

"Look," she said to Aiden, "somebody else is here. Is it someone from the company?"

"I don't know who that is," said Aiden, looking hard at the car. There were temporary plates on it. It was brand new. "Let's go find out." He made a move to take her hand, but she slipped it behind her back and arched her eyebrow at him. He had forgotten: their personal relationship had not yet been made public. He smiled and stepped playfully away from her.

They crossed the lawn and followed the flagstone walk up to the screened porch. Aiden held the door as Jordan walked up the steps into the shaded room. Nell was coming through the kitchen door, and Gordon was sitting on the wicker sofa. Beside him sat a tall, cool blond woman. She was young and wore a sleeveless summer dress that accented muscular, rather sinewy arms. Her skin was tan, and she wore her thick, straight hair down. She looked up and smiled as they walked in. Her eyes were very blue, and her smile was wide, with teeth a trifle too white and a trifle too large.

She rose and crossed the room, taking Aiden by the hands and kissing him on the cheek. "Aiden! I came to congratulate you as soon as I heard. You scored ChatDotCom! What a coup! And look, did you see my new car?"

Aiden appeared dumb struck, and Jordan wondered nervously who this woman was.

"Aiden! Did you hear me? I said congratulations!"

Aiden seemed to struggle inwardly to find his words. "Oh, thank you! It was really sort of a mutual merger." He tried to back away from her, but she wouldn't release his hands.

"My ass!" exclaimed the young woman. "You did it single-handedly!"

"Word travels fast," Aiden muttered, pulling his hands back until she was forced to let go.

"I heard from my father who heard from your father! Isn't that right, Gordon?" She turned and flashed a brilliant smile at Gordon. Jordan noticed Aiden cringe and wondered if this woman was assuming a familiarity that wasn't warranted. As close as Jordan was to Gene Palmer, she'd never called him by his first name, instead maintaining a respectful tone due him for his age, experience, and position in the company. She suspected Mr. Stewart would prefer the same.

"Jennifer," said Aiden. He spoke a little harshly to get her attention. "Jennifer, I'd like you to meet Jordan Fitzgerald, CEO of ChatDotCom."

Jordan conquered her surprise—and the unexpected hint of jealousy. She stepped forward and, with her smoothest professional manner, extended her hand.

"Jordan, this is Jennifer Webb," said Aiden, letting it go without an explanation.

"Oh, nice to meet you. I'm a friend of Aiden's," said Jennifer, peering closely at Jordan.

"We're happy to join Trade Winds," said Jordan. Her mind was spinning. Although she was anxious and curious to find out who this woman was and what she was to Aiden, foremost in her thoughts was Grace. She took a step toward the kitchen door, but Nell held a finger up to her lips to signify the baby was still asleep. Jordan smiled and relaxed. Nell came forward, and taking Jordan's arm, said pleasantly, "Let's all sit for a minute. Did Aiden show you the dock and the *Nellie Bly*?" She addressed the remark to Jordan, but Jennifer spoke up as she settled back into her spot on the sofa beside Gordon.

"Oh, did Aiden take you to see the boat? Beautiful, isn't she? Remember when we took her out to Long Island in the far end of the bay and we got stuck in that storm coming back in?" She tossed her hair and laughed heartily. "Do you sail?"

Jordan sensed open warfare, but she remained unruffled. "No," she said.

"Well, I guess that's not surprising. Vermont is landlocked, isn't it? What do you do there for fun?"

Aiden opened his mouth, but Jordan spoke first, sitting in the chair nearest the kitchen door so she could hear Grace. "We do have Lake Champlain. A lot of sailing goes on there. Interestingly enough, it's where the United States Navy began. And of course I ski. We're all born skiing in Vermont."

"Well, welcome to Maine," said Jennifer, leaning forward, "or, at least to one of Maine's premier companies. Do you intend to stay with Chat?"

"I do," said Jordan, choosing not to elaborate.

"Good for you! I'm sure you'll find these two gentlemen a pleasure to work for."

Now Aiden spoke up, "Jordan is working *with* us, Jennifer. She'll maintain her position as CEO of that branch. Chat will technically remain the same operation. We'll just expand on it."

Aiden's tone was not lost on anybody in the room. Everyone was a just a bit uncomfortable except for Gordon, who seemed to be enjoying himself, entertained by the emerging drama. It was then that they heard a small squeak from Grace.

"Excuse me," said Jordan, rising from her chair. "My daughter's waking up from her nap."

"There's a daughter?" Jennifer smiled, blinking her eyes in an exaggerated manner. "You're full of surprises!"

Jordan ignored her and went in to tend to Grace.

Jennifer stood up suddenly. "Well, I've got to get going. After-hours business at the bank." She raised her voice and called into the kitchen, "Nice to meet you, Jordan."

Jordan came to the door; a sleepy Grace, her head cuddled into her mother's shoulder, sat on her hip. "Pleased to meet you too. Hope to see you again," she lied politely.

"I'll walk you out to your car," said Aiden.

"Thank you, Aiden," said Jennifer. "Good-bye, Gordon, good-bye, Nell."

"Bye," echoed the two together.

Aiden hurried her along the walk to the driveway. As much as Jordan knew she shouldn't, she positioned herself near a window overlooking parking area. She watched as the two of them stood close to each other, deep in conversation. Aiden seemed agitated, but Jordan couldn't be sure. Then, the woman leaned forward and drew Aiden into a passionate kiss. Jordan gasped; this was not a casual kiss good-bye.

It appeared that Aiden pulled back in anger, but the woman laughed as she got into her car, spun the wheels, and raced out to the main road. Aiden stood for a moment and then glanced toward the house, a look of guilt on his face. Jordan quickly stepped away from the window, her heart aching at what she'd seen. She busied herself as Aiden rejoined his father on the porch, not sure what she should say or do. As she put shoes on Grace, she couldn't help but overhear the conversation between the men just outside.

"That was an unexpected visit, I take it," he said dryly to Aiden.

"I don't know what she was up to," Aiden replied.

"She likes to cause trouble. She's always been like that. Are you still seeing her?"

There was a pause before Aiden said, "No," he said simply. "No, I'm not seeing her anymore."

Nell came out onto the porch followed by Jordan who led Grace by the hand. "Aiden," she said, "why don't you and Jordan take Grace outside for a bit to play? Dinner will be ready in about ten minutes."

"That's okay, Aiden," Jordan said. "You don't have to come. I'm only going right out here so she can walk around for a few minutes."

Jordan didn't look at him as she spoke. She had seen the kiss Jennifer given him, had seen Aiden pull back. It was obvious they had, or at least used to have, a relationship of some kind. She struggled with her feelings as she led Grace down the steps onto the lush grass. Grace let go of her hand, plopped on her fat little bottom, and began to pick at the grass. Jordan's mind raced on. Of course, he must have had numerous relationships before theirs. Was he the kind of man who could juggle more than one at time? Did he pull back because he didn't want to kiss Jennifer, or because he didn't want Jordan to see him kiss her? Suddenly, she felt confused and lonely. She wanted to be home. She was a total stranger to these people, no matter how nice they appeared. They had a working relationship, and they were doing the polite business thing to do. And now she couldn't be sure of Aiden. Suddenly, she couldn't see their future path. How would it work out? How could it possibly work? She lived in Vermont; he lived here. They had businesses to run, responsibilities that had been in place long before they met. Panic began to seize her.

"What are you thinking about?" Aiden had approached silently and was now standing close behind her.

"I saw that kiss," she said, trying to sound light.

"You read my mind," he answered. "I hope it didn't upset you. She was just trying to make trouble."

"Are you dating that girl?"

Aiden stared at her. "No, Jordan. I love you."

"You did date her, though."

"Yes, I've dated her off and on for years. Since high school."

"That's a long time."

"Well, there were other women in between, and after all those years, our relationship hasn't progressed past a certain point. When I met you, I knew why."

"Why?" She knew she'd added a sarcastic edge to her voice.

"Because I didn't love her." He stepped toward her. "Jordan, I—I didn't invite her here. I haven't even thought about her." He paused. "What's bothering you? Is there something more going on than just a visit from an old girlfriend?"

"When did you sleep with her last?" Jordan hadn't meant to say it. It was a silly, immature thing to say, but it slipped out.

"I can't remember."

Jordan shot him a withering look, and he took a deep breath. If Jennifer had been in his life on and off for years, he'd certainly remember their last time together.

"Dinner is ready," called Nell from the porch door.

Aiden and Jordan looked at each other. Neither one spoke. Aiden scooped Grace up and started in to the house, and Jordan was glad her daughter felt so comfortable with him. She tried to relax her face, tried to banish the tension in her shoulders as she followed them.

Dinner was lovely, and Jordan wished she could have enjoyed it more. It was the perfect meal for the warm spring evening. There was lobster risotto with a fresh green salad and asparagus from Nell's garden. Dessert was a creamy cheesecake drizzled with mashed strawberries. Grace sat on Jordan's lap, tasting bits of the food and gurgling happily. Jordan made an extra effort to bury the fear and confusion building up within her and concentrated on feeding Grace her own dinner of sweet potato and chicken puree.

After dinner, Aiden helped his mother clear the dishes. Jordan could hear him in the far corner of the kitchen, his voice rising and falling, but she couldn't make out the words. As she sat holding her daughter, she turned her attention to Gordon, who sipped scotch from a snifter.

"One of the first things we'll do," he was saying, "is take a detailed census of the territory. Vermont is seeing that the whole state is set up for DSL and cable. We need to sort through the economic loopholes and figure out what to spend where and when."

"I totally agree," Jordan remarked, glad to have her attention on something so concrete and impersonal. "I was planning on calling a meeting with our board and our comptrollers when I get back for just that—"

"Excuse me." They both turned to look at Aiden, and Jordan sensed something different in his tone. She could see fire behind his normally tranquil deep brown eyes. There was more of a connection between the two of them than she had realized. She could read his look. It wasn't anger. It was more like he was asserting himself. More like resolve. She wondered, nervously, what it was he had to say. "I'd like to talk to Jordan for a few minutes, Dad. Jordan, can you leave the baby with my mother? We won't be too long. We're just going to take a walk while it's still warm."

Nell held out her arms for Grace. "Come with me, Gracie," she cooed. "I have a magnificent set of measuring cups I just know you'll be crazy about!"

Jordan followed Aiden out into the night to the end of the lawn again. They stood silently for a few minutes at the head of the stairs that led down the rocks to the beach, and they watched the lights twinkle far out over the water, illuminating the islands in Casco Bay.

"What is it, Aiden?" asked Jordan. The night air seemed to clear her mind and sweep her earlier anxiety away. She felt once more her own woman, and Aiden was the man she loved. She reached out and put her fingers lightly on his forearm.

"It's time for full disclosure," said Aiden quietly. Jordan said nothing at first, listening to the comforting sound of the waves slapping on the rocks below and the *whoosh* as they receded again. Over and over they would repeat this motion until the tide was in, and then the motion would take the tide out again and it would go on like this for eternity. *Who are we?* thought Jordan. *What do our lives mean? Are we meant to be together?*

Aiden took her hands and turned her until they were facing each other. "I'm going to tell you all about myself," he said. The moon had risen. It was not yet full, but bright none the less. It reflected off the sea and lit Aiden's face so that his noble cheekbones were highlighted and his eyes shone like pools of sweet water in the brown leaves of the forest floor after a rain. Jordan gave a little gasp. He captivated her so much in that moment, she forgot to breathe.

"I've had a lot of women. I always liked women. I always preferred to be in the company of a girl than getting drunk with a bunch of guys. Jennifer and I have known each other since high school. We dated pretty steadily until we each went off to college; then we saw different people. When we were both home at the same time, we'd get together. I guess it was just habit. She's got a bite to her, but she's not a bad person. I think everybody expected that we'd get married one day. I think she began to expect it herself, but I just kept thinking I wasn't ready. And I wasn't. What I didn't know was that I would never be ready...for her. I didn't love her. She's convenient, yes. I guess I'm guilty of that. I kept telling myself I loved her, but now I know I don't and never did. I confused familiarity with love. And I have slept with her recently. I slept with her last week. Before I met you." He paused. Jordan was looking down at their clasped hands.

"Jordan, look at me." She raised her eyes and he searched her face. "Jordan, in a little less than a week, my life has changed entirely. Last week, I had sex with Jennifer Webb on the couch of her apartment. It was just like the sex we used to have when we were teenagers. It was just sex. And to tell you the truth, I had a date the following evening with a woman from Boston. I was supposed to drive back here after I met with you. I couldn't wait to sleep with her because I hadn't before and I was hoping for something different and exciting. Except I met you. And then I couldn't even think about Jennifer or the girl from Boston or anything except you. You affected me. You changed me from the minute I met you. I could only think about touching you, kissing you, but it was different because it wasn't from a conquest standpoint, like all the others had been. It was...it was something else. It was a connection. Am I making sense? Are you listening to me?"

"I'm listening, Aiden," she whispered, squeezing his hands.

"So I asked myself, was it because it was all wrapped up in the business? Was it because you were so young and looked so vulnerable? I don't know. I only know how I felt when we first made love. As long as I live, I will never forget that feeling. It's the first time in my life I felt like that, and I feel like that every time I look at you. I love you, Jordan, but you're holding something back. You're not where I am. Do you love me? I knew right away I loved you. Maybe it doesn't work that way for you. I don't care. I'll wait. You've just got to be honest with me. I've told you everything. You've got to tell me. We can only make it if we're honest with each other. I don't want any secrets between us. Love can't be like that. What is it?"

Jordan sighed. She knew this day was coming. It had hung over her head for days now. The only time she didn't think about it was when Aiden's arms were around her, when he was filling her emptiness with himself. When they were joined as one. "Aiden, I'm a simple person. You know everything about me. I'm a single mother struggling to raise my daughter and help my family. I didn't count on falling in love with you. I didn't plan it. And I don't know how to handle it. I can't turn my back on my responsibilities."

"I'm not asking you to do that," said Aiden, exasperated now. "I'm asking you, do you love me? I'm asking you, what is holding you back?"

She dropped his hands and turned away from him, wandering up the grassy edge of the rocky drop-off. "I—I don't know. I have Grace. I—"

"So what? I love Grace, too. I know she comes with you. I'm willing—eager, even—to take that on!" Then he asked the question she'd been dreading, the question that must have been haunting him. "Jordan, tell me about Grace. Who is her father? I don't care, but I've got to know. Is it Gene Palmer, like Fenton said? Is that why you won't talk about it? Is it? Tell me, please!"

Jordan spun around viciously, tears in her eyes. "Is that what you think?" She fairly spat the words. "You're just like everybody else! You think, how could somebody like me get a job like that and a salary like that! It must be because I let the old man fuck me! Isn't that what you think, Aiden? Then I got pregnant. You think Grace is Mr. Palmer's daughter, don't you? Well, join the crowd, mister. Everybody thinks that. And I don't care! It's not Grace's fault. She deserves the best of everything I can give her. And I intend to see that she gets it. Nothing else matters. Nothing!"

She was really crying now, and she began to run along the bank. Aiden caught up to her in two strides and snaked out his hand to grab her arm. "Oh no," he said, his voice angry as he spun her around to face him. "Oh no, you don't. I'm not going to let you sabotage what we have because it's easier for you! This isn't just about you! Or Grace! This is about me, too. This is about us! You slept with me, too! You told me you loved me. You let me in, Jordan. You just can't cast me off because you're afraid of I don't even know what! Now, once and for all, if you love me, if you want to give us a fair chance, tell me you do and tell me about Grace. Tell me your story, Jordan. I deserve to know. I'm fighting you on this because I think we're worth fighting for!"

When he grabbed her, she tried to jerk away from him, but he held on and had his say. Now she looked up into his liquid brown eyes. Suddenly, she felt almost too tired to move. Every emotion seemed to have left her body. She sat down heavily on one of the rock outcroppings. Aiden waited.

Jordan spoke softly. "The fall I went back to school after working for Mr. Palmer all spring and summer, I was feeling pretty good about myself. Too good. Mr. Palmer had hinted that if I wanted to finish school at a later date, he would be pleased to have me on as a permanent employee. He outlined how my position within the company would grow and that he could teach me a lot that I could later use to my advantage in getting my degree. When I said I really wanted to return to school, he was fine with that, and he told me I would always have a place at Chat."

"So you went back to school," prompted Aiden.

"Yes. Yes, I went back. It was the end of August and everybody was settling in. There were parties on the Lake. I hung out with a group of party-loving girls, and we were invited to something almost every night. I just went on the weekends. My roommate went three or four times a week. I hardly saw her. Then one day she came in and said she had met this really cool guy. He was in the National Guard. He wanted to take her out that weekend and wanted her to find a date for his friend. She talked me into going." She looked up into Aiden's eyes, and he saw the anguish there.

"He was a nice guy, Aiden. He really was. His name was Mark McGuire. He was from a little town in the Northeast Kingdom, in Vermont. We started seeing each other. We didn't get much time together because he was in training and I was in school, but we saw each other when we could. I liked him. Then he found out his unit was being deployed to Afghanistan. They hardly gave them any notice at all, Aiden. He tried to see me as much as he could before he left near the end of September. We wrote and emailed back and forth quite a bit. You know, what we were doing and stuff like that. I — I guess I kind of thought the relationship would just dissolve after that. It didn't bother me because I wasn't that caught up in it. We'd had a good time and I liked him." Jordan stopped and wiped at her eyes.

"The next month, I found out I was pregnant. *Pregnant.* My world went into a tailspin. All kinds of thoughts went through my head. Finally, Thanksgiving break came and I went home. I packed my stuff up. I knew I wasn't coming back. I told my parents. They were pretty upset, but they stuck by me, Aiden. My father had just been laid off, and I know it must have been a terrible blow to them. I must have really let them down. The only friend I had whom I felt I could trust was Ashley, so I told her. She and Kyle had just bought Kyle's cousin Caleb's house in town. I remember going there and helping her move in, crying all the time, wondering how I was going to manage. Finally, she suggested that I go talk to Mr. Palmer. At first I refused. How could I face him? Ashley kept after me, though, and I went. I can't tell you how hard that was, to stand there and tell him that I was pregnant and that I needed a job."

Jordan looked up again and continued, "And, Aiden, he was so good to me. So nice. He didn't judge me. He asked how I was feeling. He asked if I thought I could take a forty-hour week. He asked when the baby was due. That's all. Then he outlined the maternity leave policy at the company and gave me my job back. Just like that. I can never, ever thank him enough for that. All I can do is do the best I can for Chat."

Aiden was silent for a moment. "What did Grace's father say when you told him?"

Jordan buried her face in her hands, then said softly, "I never told him. I never told him I was pregnant."

"You mean, this man doesn't know he has a daughter?" Aiden was shocked.

"It's worse than that," whispered Jordan. She began to sob. Aiden lifted her to her feet and held her close.

"Tell me," he whispered in her ear. "Tell me. We can work this out. I know we can."

She looked up at him, her cheeks wet with tears. "Aiden, he's dead. Matt McGuire is dead. He was killed in Afghanistan. I got the news just before Grace was born, from the girl who had been my roommate. He never knew. I am so awful! I was so selfish!" Her body racked with sobs again, and Aiden held her tight, smoothing her hair.

Finally he spoke, "Shhh, shhh. Tell me about it. Talk to me, Jordan."

Jordan gave a shuddering sigh. Then she spoke softly, not raising her head from Aiden's chest. "By the time I found out I was pregnant,

Matt had already been deployed. We weren't even communicating that often, and I assumed our relationship was winding down. So, when I realized I was pregnant, I sat up all one night thinking out different scenarios." She was silent for a while and Aiden waited.

"I finally decided what to do," Jordan continued, speaking barely above a whisper. "I decided that this baby, this new life, was my responsibility and my responsibility alone. I decided I didn't want anybody else's opinion about it. I didn't want anybody to try to tell me what I should do. This situation was mine to handle as I saw fit. So I went back to where I knew my decision would be supported no matter what. I went home. I said my father was sick and I couldn't stay in school. Matt emailed once after I came back, and I emailed him the same thing. Then I didn't hear from him anymore. Just before Grace was born, I got an email from the girl who had been my roommate telling me that Matt had been killed." She buried her face in Aiden's chest, her tears soaking through his T-shirt. He lifted her face and looked into her eyes.

"Jordan, you didn't do anything wrong. You did the best thing you could do under the circumstances as you saw them at the time."

"It's not good enough," muttered Jordan. "Maybe if I had just told him about Grace, if I had told him I was pregnant, everything would have been different. Maybe he wouldn't—"

"Stop!" said Aiden. "Stop beating yourself up. What's done is done."

Jordan looked up into his face. "I was afraid to tell him. I was afraid that he would be an influence in Grace's life. I was afraid he would try to marry me. I felt guilty that I didn't love him, that our relationship was just superficial yet it resulted in the least superficial thing that can happen. A new life. A new life based on what, Aiden? Is my daughter doomed because her life started on such egotistic, careless behavior by two people who were not even thinking of her? I have felt so guilty. It's almost like I stole something from him and he didn't even know it. How would you feel, Aiden, if you found out that a woman you slept with had your child and never even told you about it?"

Aiden sighed; Jordan knew her remark hit home.

"How can I forgive myself?"

Aiden wrapped her again in his arms. He spoke, his lips brushing against her fragrant hair. "It seems as though you've been carrying this burden a long time without sharing it with anybody. Does anybody else know?"

"Ashley knows. My parents know. Mr. Palmer knows. None of us ever talk about it."

"No wonder it's seemed to me you've been holding back, keeping yourself at bay somehow. You have. You've been denying yourself, punishing yourself. That's not healthy, Jordan. It's not healthy for you or for Grace. Or for us."

"Is there an 'us'?" Jordan asked weakly. "What does that mean? Where is the 'us'?"

"Right here," said Aiden determinedly. "We are right here, right now. This is us. Come on, Jordan. Now you have me. You have me to share your life with. You have me to talk things through with. And I have you. I don't care if I ever speak to Jennifer Webb again. I have you. All that random sex is over. I can see that it was only something to feed my own ego. It was nothing. It's us that counts. Right here. Right now."

He lifted her face and kissed her tear-streaked cheeks. His lips traveled down her face to her mouth, and she easily surrendered to him, opening her lips, letting his tongue in to press against hers.

"Yes, we do count, don't we," she whispered. "We do, but we'd better not make a show of it right here. It might be awkward."

He gave a little laugh, and they started back toward the house, hand in hand. Jordan smoothed her hair and hoped her eyes weren't too red from crying. The chill of the evening had settled with the setting sun. Jordan shivered a little, and Aiden put his arm around her shoulders. It was clear he was past caring who saw them.

When they entered the kitchen, Nell was watching Grace play on the kitchen floor with some pots and pans and wooden spoons.

"Mmmama," said the baby, smiling up Jordan. "Poon. Poon."

"Do you have a spoon, Grace?" cooed Jordan, bending down to kiss the child's upturned face.

"Poon," Grace confirmed and went back to banging the pots.

"Your phone went off a couple of times, Jordan," said Nell. "You might want to take a look at it. I brought it in from the porch. It's on the table. Don't worry; I'll keep an eye on Grace."

"Oh, thank you," said Jordan. "It's probably my mother." She reached for the phone and checked for missed calls. Ashley. How odd. Jordan punched the recall button and stepped politely out onto the porch.

"Oh, Ashley, no! Oh no!" Jordan cried out. "Oh, I'm on my way right now. Yes, now. I'll be fine. I'll call you along the way."

She came back into the room, and there were fresh tears in her eyes.

"What's wrong?"

Aiden's voice sounded hollow to Jordan. "Mr. Palmer!" she choked. "Oh, Aiden, Mr. Palmer died."

Nell was at her side in a second with a glass of water.

"Sit down, dear," she said, guiding her to a chair at the table. "Take a drink. What happened? I'm so very, very sorry."

Gordon came into the room from the back of the house. "What's going on?"

"Dad, Palmer's dead," said Aiden.

"What!"

"Shhh," said Nell, shooting him a look. "What happened, dear?" She addressed the remark to Jordan who lifted the glass of water to her lips with a shaking hand. She felt the cold liquid in her mouth and swallowed automatically.

"This is awful," she said. "I just saw him. He seemed like he was doing okay, actually a little better than he had been. Ashley said—" Her voice caught, and she struggled to keep back the sob. "Ashley said she had taken the summary of the day's business to him at home. She said he went over it with her, that he was weak because he had had chemo this morning, but that he seemed in good spirits. He said he gave her a pep talk about sticking with me, that things were going to get busy and I would need her help. When she got ready to leave, he said he was going up for his nap." Jordan stopped talking and wiped an errant tear from her face. Grace's babbling was the only sound in the room.

"Ashley said Mrs. Palmer called her about half an hour ago," Jordan continued. "Apparently he had gone for his nap, and when he didn't come down at his usual time, Mrs. Palmer went up to check on him. He had passed. Just like that."

"Who's with Marie?" asked Gordon.

"She told Ashley her children were on their way. The closest one lives about an hour away, so she must be there by now. She asked Ashley to call me. She didn't have my cell number." Jordan stood up and paced the room. "This is awful," she said. "I knew he was very ill, but, you know, I kept thinking he would make it one more day, and he would. I guess I thought it would just go on like that."

She bowed her head. Aiden stepped forward and put his arms around her. "We'll go tomorrow and find out what's to be done."

"No, no." Jordan shook her head. "No, I have to go home tonight. I have to be at the company in the morning, and I'll have to talk to Mrs. Palmer as soon as I can."

Nell spoke up. "You can't go tonight, dear. You're too tired. Just stay here. Aiden will go with you in the morning."

"Thank you so much," said Jordan. She began to gather her things together. "Thank you, but I have to leave tonight. Aiden, I'll let you know what transpires. I'll be fine, really. I wouldn't sleep all night now anyway. Grace will fall asleep. She's a good traveler, and her bedtime is creeping up."

"Jordan, please," started Aiden.

"Don't fight me on this, please." Jordan was firm. "I need this time alone. I'll call you. Please."

Gordon stepped forward. "Go, Jordan. We'll wait to hear from you. Call us if you run into any kind of trouble. Please let us know when you get there, no matter how late. We'll worry if you don't call."

Jordan gave him a grateful look. "Thank you. Thank you for your hospitality and your kindness."

Aiden stood still, saying nothing. Jordan stepped forward and shook first Nell's hand and then Gordon's. She turned to Aiden and said, "Thank you, Aiden. I'll call when I get home and then let you know what's happening tomorrow. I have to be there in the morning." Tears still brimmed on her thick lashes, but she was calm. Aiden nodded. Jordan picked up Grace.

"Aiden, help Jordan out to her car with her bags," Nell said. "Jordan, please drive carefully. Call us for anything. I'm a light sleeper." Jordan gave her a grateful smile as she left. Aiden followed her out the door.

A few minutes later, Aiden returned to the porch doorway as he watched the lights of the Jeep disappear down the drive. Nell came and stood beside him. "You must go after her," she said quietly. "You must follow her home. She'll need you, though she doesn't know it yet."

Gordon spoke up, blowing and blustering as was his habit. "What the hell is going on around here? Girls taking over the business. Girls showing up unannounced. Babies! Well, Palmer didn't time this quite right, did he? He and I should have cut this whole deal and set this girl to rights, so she knows what she's about. Then he could have died when we were done! You better do what your mother says, son. Get in your car and drive to Vermont. Who knows what kind of shape she'll be in in the morning."

"She's perfectly capable, Dad," said Aiden. "And don't forget, I drove here with her. My car is in Vermont."

Nell took his hand and put a set of car keys in them. "Take your father's car, dear. I think it has a full tank of gas."

"My car! What the hell, Nell! We'll have every car in the family in the backwoods of Vermont!"

"Shush, Gordon," said Nell firmly. There had only been a handful of times in his whole life that Aiden could recall his mother pulling rank on his father, but "shush" was her code word, and when she said it, Gordon obeyed.

He grumbled something, then said to Aiden, "I'm not sure exactly what's going on here, but I think I've got a pretty good idea. I'm only going to say one thing: Don't lose that girl, son. Don't lose her for the business's sake and, more importantly, don't lose her for your sake."

Aiden opened his mouth to speak, but Gordon waved him silent. "Don't explain. You don't need to. I can see, can't I? Now get going." Gordon smothered him in his customary bear hug. Aiden gave a little smile, hugged his mother, and kissed her on the cheek.

"Do you have clothes?" asked Nell, always practical.

"I'll have to stop at my place and repack," said Aiden. "It won't take long." Then he said, "Mom, how did you know you would marry Dad?"

"How could she pass up such a good deal?" snorted Gordon.

Nell ignored him and looked at Aiden. "The first time I met your father, I knew. I knew I had met my lifelong mate. It wasn't bells and whistles and fireworks."

"It wasn't?" Gordon sounded incredulous.

"No, Gordon." She laughed. "That came later. What I felt was a wonderful peace of spirit. That's how he made me feel. I felt there was nothing I couldn't say to this man. He is my best friend."

"That's the way I feel about Jordan. That's how I want her to feel about me."

Gordon coughed, but Nell said, "Jordan has other issues to work on, Aiden. You'll have to be patient with her. It's never simple when there is a child involved. And she's responsible for the business now, by herself. She's very bright, but she's also very young and without a lot of experience. It's obvious how she feels about you, but she's still trying to sort things out. Be there for her, but let her find her own path. It will lead back to you, dear." She reached up to her tall son and kissed his cheek.

Aiden smiled at her. "I'll let you know what goes on," he said. "Thanks, Mom."

"Hey, it's my car. You're taking *my car*. What about thanking me? I hate driving your mother's car."

Aiden hugged his father. "Thanks, Dad."

"Let us know about the funeral arrangements," said Gordon. "It would be black ingratitude and bad manners if we didn't show up."

"Okay, I'm off." With that, he sprinted to his father's big Mercedes and drove away.

It took him twenty minutes to reach the Wharf. He waved at the gate attendant and drove up the brick drive to his door. A turn of the key and he was inside. He climbed the stairs to the living area two steps at a time, and then went into his bedroom. He yanked out some clean clothes and a dark spring suit. It had been ages since he had worn a suit. He crammed the clothes in a duffel bag and zipped a garment bag over the suit. Hoisting them to his shoulder, he flew down the stairs, locked his door, and jumped into the car. In five minutes he was out of town, headed west.

The drive went smoothly. There was almost no traffic. The calm conditions of the road, however, were not reflected in his mind. He was anything but calm. He built and destroyed scenario after scenario in his head. How would his relationship with Jordan progress if they were two hundred miles apart? Could he induce her to move to Portland? Then who would run Chat in Vermont? Maybe Thatcher from the home office. No, that idea didn't fly. Thatcher was an idiot. Or at least, not to be let loose on his own. Could he, Aiden, take over the Vermont operation? That would be risky. Something told him Jordan would not want to be encroached upon. He wouldn't want her to feel as though he was trying to replace her, contract or no contract.

"You're too tired to think straight, man," he said out loud to himself. He decided to stop thinking about the whole situation. It was like his mother always said, morning was wiser than evening. He would be there tomorrow, assess the situation, and pick his path from there. He plugged his iPod into the car's stereo system and listened to his music, trying to rest his mind.

Chapter Thirteen

When Aiden pulled into town, he drove slowly down the main street. It was a little after midnight. The Inn was dark, except for the red glow of an exit sign he could see far back within the building. Three street lights illuminated the green with a misty glow, but there were no other lights on anywhere. The local Jiffy Mart, the only gas station in town, had closed at eleven. Nothing moved. He followed the street out and around and drove into the ChatDotCom parking lot. He pulled up under a security light, shut off the car, and listened to the silence. The building was quiet, but Aiden knew that Dayton Phillips, the night watchman, was in there somewhere. He would have to make his presence known soon or Phillips would wake up the town and Aiden would have to explain himself once again to John Giamo. They didn't care if he owned Chat now or not. Gene Palmer, even dead, had more sway over the townspeople than Aiden did.

He pulled out his phone and texted Jordan.

> In Chat parking lot. Can I sleep in your office?
> Sorry to wake you. ~Aiden

It was a minute or two before his phone buzzed. He read her reply.

> Wasn't asleep. What are you doing here? ~Jordan

Aiden was glad she was awake.

> Need to be here in the morning. Don't want you to have
> to face this alone. I love you. ~Aiden

> I will call Dayton. He will come out and let you in.
> Where are you? ~Jordan

> In parking lot under security light. Don't let him shoot me.
> ~Aiden

> Very funny. He doesn't carry a weapon.
> You can sleep on the sofa in my office.
> Blanket and pillow in the closet at far end of room. ~Jordan

> Thanks. I love you, Jordan. ~Aiden

> I'm glad you came. See you in the morning. ~Jordan

Was she just going to leave it like that? He came here to be closer to her in this difficult time. Then, his phone buzzed again.

> I love you, too, Aiden. ~Jordan

His breath caught. It was what he had wanted to hear. It was hard to know what would come next, how they would sort this all out, but she had said it. That was a good place to start.

The knock on his window made him jump. He looked up to see Dayton Phillips. "Mr. Stewart? Jordan Fitzgerald called me and told me to let you into her office. Follow me."

Aiden got out of the car, shouldered his bag, locked the car, and followed the heavy-set man. Apparently the tradition of the taciturn Vermonter was lost on Dayton; he babbled on and on as they walked to back of the building.

"Terrible about Mr. Palmer, huh?" he said over his shoulder as Aiden followed him into the building. "Yah, everybody thought he was doing good, you know? He'd even come into the office once in a while. Oh, you could see he was failing, but he kept going. Nothing else to do. Just keep going. Hope he didn't suffer much. Seemed quick, anyway."

Aiden was relieved when they reached Jordan's office. The watchman turned the key in the lock. "There you go, Mr. Stewart," he said with a chuckle. "Have a good night. We shut up early around here!"

"I'll sleep like a baby," said Aiden sarcastically, knowing Phillips would never get it. "Thanks for letting me in." He stepped through the door into the office.

"I'll be here till six in the morning, so you just call if you need anything."

"I will, thanks." Aiden finally succeeded in shutting the door. He stood still for a moment, listening to the watchman's footsteps as they disappeared down the hall. Then, he turned into the room and exhaled, his body giving in to exhaustion. Bending down, he pulled off his sneakers and walked to the closet at the end of the room. He was glad he had made the trip. He felt more at peace, somehow, here in her office. Closer to Jordan.

Aiden went to the big window and gazed out across the dark river. The moon was nearly full, shining through the high, scudding clouds. Silvery lights bounced from bank to bank only to disappear in the inky undergrowth. Suddenly, a dense shadow fell across the room. It moved like a living thing. Instantly, Aiden was on guard. He peered through the window, trying to determine where the shadow had come from. As suddenly as it had crossed the room, the shadow receded, almost as if it had sensed it had been seen.

As quickly and quietly as he could, his heartbeat racing, Aiden sprinted down the hall and opened the small, back door to the outside. There was silence. "Anybody there?" he called into the night, but the rushing river was the only sound he heard in answer.

"There a problem?" came a voice behind him, causing Aiden to jump.

"Dayton! You startled me! I was looking out the office window and I saw a shadow—a big shadow—move across the lot back here. It looked like a person's shadow."

"Hm," said Dayton, rubbing his chin. "You want me to take a look?"

"I'll go with you," said Aiden.

Together, the two men walked out into the back lot. Dayton shined his flashlight across the pavement. Two Dumpsters stood against the far back corner of the building. A light breeze ruffled the night air, but nothing moved.

"Don't see nothing," grunted Dayton, scanning one more time with the flashlight. "Probably just a raccoon or something."

"Probably," said Aiden dubiously. He followed Dayton back in the building, but he couldn't shake the uneasy feeling.

"You're just tired," said Dayton. "You get some sleep. I'll wake you up if I hear anything else."

"Thanks, Dayton." Aiden went back into Jordan's office and locked the door behind him.

He opened the closet door, pulled out the light down comforter and a pillow from the top shelf, and lay down, fully clothed, on the sofa. He sighed and closed his eyes.

To his surprise, when he opened them, morning light flooded the room and a gentle hand brushed the hair back from his forehead.

"Did you sleep well?" Jordan asked softly.

He smiled, took her hand in his, and kissed it. "What time is it? What are you doing here?"

Jordan kneeled down on the floor beside him. "If you remember, this is my office. Don't worry; it's only six o'clock. I brought us coffee and bagels from Jiffy Mart."

"Hmmm. I can smell it." He raised himself up on his elbow and kissed her. "You smell good too."

Jordan stood up and handed him a coffee and a bagel with cream cheese.

"I feel a little moldy," he said. "I'll take a shower when I get a room at the Inn." He reached out and touched Jordan's face as she sat back down, leaning against him. "How are you?"

Jordan sighed. "I'm okay," she said. "Sad, though."

"Did you speak to Mrs. Palmer?"

"Oh, yes. I stopped in last night to see her. We sat at the kitchen table until about midnight, just talking. Sandy, her youngest daughter, was there with us. We talked about a lot of stuff. You learn things."

"Like what?"

"Well," said Jordan, "I found out that one of the reasons none of Mr. Palmer's kids wanted the company was that they always felt they came second to it. They felt that all his energy went into the company, that they could never measure up somehow."

"Really?"

"Sandy said so. Oh, she said that the feelings dissipated as they matured and they realized that their father did love them, but by that time they had all made their own lives and the sale of the company was a more realistic solution for all of them. I was frankly kind of shocked."

"Well, it's family dynamics. All families have them. Don't you think?"

"I suppose," said Jordan. She stood and went to the window. Aiden flung the blanket off and walked across the room to stand closely behind her. She spoke without turning to face him. "I just grew up in the shadow of the Palmer family, you know. They were wealthy, with that beautiful old house overlooking the whole town. Their kids had everything. They were older than I was, but I saw them around town a lot, driving their foreign cars, dressed in clothes I only saw in magazines. And now, look. Look who's running the company. Me. It's so odd, Aiden. It's so peculiar." She turned, looking up into his face. "Maybe that's why I feel so responsible. Maybe that's why I just don't feel free, like my life is my own. I feel as though I almost infringed upon something that wasn't mine."

"That's not the case," said Aiden, putting his hands on her arms and drawing her closer. "You've earned everything you have. You deserve it. Palmer thought so. And his daughter said that none of his kids were interested in it. On the contrary, you are totally free. You run the company with Trade Winds now, and we reached a merger that allows us to do so. Happens all the time." He enfolded her in his arms, but she gently pushed away and paced across the room. He followed her only with his eyes.

"Now I feel completely on my own," she said. "I'm responsible for the company. I'm responsible for people's lives. And I'm responsible for Grace most of all." She turned to face him. "Aiden, sometimes I feel as though I stole Grace. It was the way I wanted it. I thought I was taking responsibility for a mistake I had made, that I wouldn't burden anyone else, that I would just go on with my life and let everybody else go on with theirs. Now, when I see how much Grace means to me, I feel as though I stole her. I had no right not to tell him. Before she was born, I could not even imagine loving something as much as I love Grace. That's what I stole from him, and now I don't even have the chance to amend it. He's dead, and I can't fix that."

Aiden's heart sank at that moment. He gripped the edge of the big desk as he felt his future slipping away from him. Once again, he didn't know how to read this girl. He was sure of his own emotions, but he wasn't sure of hers.

"I'm going to the Inn now, and getting a room," he said. "Please let me know when you find out the funeral arrangements."

"Do you want me to come with you?" Jordan asked, and Aiden heard something in her voice that he had not heard before. Was she asking for his help? Mentally, he shook it off. He had to be strong. She was so stubborn with herself, she would need to reach her own conclusions, make her own choices, or he could never be sure of her love.

Aiden held up his hand and smiled a little. "For the first time in my life, I've been honest with myself and I'm being honest with you now. I love you, Jordan. I love Grace. Why wouldn't I? She's part of you. I don't think you know who you love. I don't think you know what you want. You have to figure that out for yourself. That first night you came to the Inn, I realized what real love was. Did you feel the same? Or was it sex? Was it sex for comfort or to fill some biological need? Maybe everything happened too fast. Listen to me. I thought the girl was supposed to ask these questions, but I found myself in love with you. I love you so much; I want to be with you for the rest of my life. I know it's only been a week, but the way I see things has changed that fast.

"If you decide you don't want to be with me, if you decide you don't want to give us a chance, then I accept that. Even if it means walking away from here and never coming back. You can handle ChatDotCom with one hand tied behind your back. I'm not worried about that, but you have a lot of issues to resolve. Maybe you should think about taking care of them.

"Find Grace's family from her father's side. Find them and tell them about her. She's the only child of their dead son. Think about that. They need to know her. She needs to know them. Come outside of yourself, Jordan. You're shielding yourself with what you're calling your 'responsibilities.' You're hiding. Take real responsibility and include the people who love you in your life. I know you run Chat and its employees, and you take care of your brother's tuition and your parents' mortgage and everything under the sun for Grace, but you use that power of being able to do those things. You manipulate your situation and separate yourself from all those people. You don't work *with* anybody. You hold the reins; you control things. That's a safe place to be. Telling people what to do isn't hard. Cooperating is hard. Sharing is hard. It takes love, Jordan. I love you so much that if somebody told me I had to face the rest of my life alone, without you or any other woman ever, I could do that. I could live on this past week. I let you in, Jordan. Now I'm wondering if that was such a wise thing to do. That's what's happened to me this past week. What happened to you?"

He crossed the room and cupped her face in his hand. He kissed her lightly on the forehead, and set his jaw determinedly. "You let me know about the funeral arrangements. I'll be at the Inn. I always have my phone on me. You take your time. Think about what I said. I have to have all of you, Jordan, because you have all of me. That's only fair. Sharing a life means just that."

She was silent as he pulled open the door. Then, he paused and turned. "One more thing," he said. "My father told me something once, and it's stuck with me. He said, 'Do you think your mother and I got where we got by standing around gazing into each other's eyes? Hell no! We got where we got by looking together in the same direction, putting on the same harness, and plowing forward. That's love.' I think he paraphrased some poet, but he was right. That's what I want, Jordan. I'll see you later."

Without looking back, he walked out and shut the door quietly behind him.

Jordan stood, her body leaden. When she felt as though she could move, she turned away from the door and walked slowly back to the window. For a while she just stood, watching the river jump and splash and swirl into frothy little eddies. She wasn't sure what had just happened. Had their relationship taken a step back, or a step forward? Her mind roiled in chaos.

"I have to sort things out," she said aloud. "There are priorities." She looked down at her desk and tried to organize her spinning thoughts. Almost without knowing what she was doing, she picked up her phone and called Ashley.

"Hello?" said a groggy voice.

It was only then that Jordan realized that it was barely seven o'clock in the morning. "Oh, Ashley! I'm so sorry to wake you. I didn't think about what time it was."

"Jordan, is everything all right? Where are you?"

"I'm at my office. Look, I know it's Sunday morning, but if you can, could you come down and help me with a few things? Would Kyle mind?"

"Kyle? Ha!" snorted Ashley. "He's at some fireman's muster or something down at the firehouse. I think they're washing the trucks. He's oblivious to me today. I'll be right down."

"Thanks, Ashley."

Jordan sighed deeply. She would work this out. She would have to.

Jordan marveled when, twenty minutes later, Ashley walked into her office, neatly dressed in jeans, a white ruffled tunic, and bright red flats. Her raven hair was down, brushing her shoulders in a long pageboy. Not one hair was out of place. Ashley's makeup was as it was every day, far too much for Jordan's style, but impeccably applied. It was early on a Sunday morning and Ashley was camera ready.

Jordan shook her head.

"What's the matter?" asked Ashley.

"You look like you just stepped out of the pages of *Style Magazine*!"

Ashley laughed. "Well, I didn't even stop to get a coffee. I was hoping there was some here."

Jordan rolled her eyes and handed Ashley her own cup.

"I don't want to take yours," protested Ashley.

"Don't worry about it," said Jordan sarcastically. "I'll drink Aiden's."

"He was here?"

"He just left. After giving me a lecture."

Ashley sat down on the sofa. She took a sip of coffee, staring thoughtfully out the window. "I guess I just don't understand you two. Jordan, do you love him? Do you want to pursue the relationship? If you don't, then end it right now."

Jordan let out an audible groan. "Oh, but I do love him. I do. And how can I even say that? Maybe I only love the sex. Maybe I just caved in a weak moment. We haven't even dated, really. And how am I going to juggle everything? One minute, I want to spend the rest of my life with him, and the next minute, I'm seeing that it's just impossible."

"As long as you two love each other, anything is possible. That's the truth."

"Ashley, I told him about Grace. He thought Mr. Palmer was Grace's father, and that made me so mad I nearly swore I'd never speak to him again, but I had to tell him the truth."

"Well, that's a step in the right direction," said Ashley. "It had to come out sooner or later. It's nothing to keep hidden, for Grace's sake if nobody else's. How did he take it?"

"Like he takes everything. He's so logical and laid back. I feel hysterical in comparison most of the time."

Ashley gave a little laugh. "You have to learn to relax, Jordan. You're wound so tight, some days I expect to see you unravel right before my eyes."

"Is it that obvious?"

"Not to most people, but I know you pretty well. Where's Aiden now?"

"He went to get a room at the Inn. He's staying through to the funeral. After the funeral, he wants to meet the employees and make sure everybody knows him and knows that things are staying pretty much as they are."

"What have you heard about funeral arrangements?"

Jordan sat down next to her friend. "I expect the wake will be tomorrow night and the funeral will be Tuesday. I'll close the company except for essential personnel. Everybody should at least get a chance to pay their respects. Ashley, there's something Aiden said…" Her voice trailed off.

"What?"

Jordan sighed. "Aiden said that I should find Mark's parents and tell them about Grace."

Her friend paused before she commented. "I can't say that I disagree with that, Jordan. Grace is your daughter, but she doesn't belong to you. Grace is a person in her own right, and she has the right to know who her father was and the right to know his people."

"Why is everything so complicated!" Jordan stood up quickly and returned, agitated, back to the window.

"Life is complicated," snorted Ashley.

"It isn't for you," retorted Jordan. "You've got Kyle. You've got your job. You've got a pretty little house. Everything seems to go like clockwork for you. You never mess up."

Jordan was looking out onto the river as she spoke, her back to Ashley. When she made no reply to Jordan's comment, Jordan turned to look at her.

Ashley still sat on the sofa, but her face under the makeup was drained of color. Her jaw was set in a peculiar way, like she was trying not to cry. Surprised, Jordan said, "Ashley, did I say something? What is it?"

Ashley held up her hand. "I'm going to tell you some things. You haven't known me all my life, Jordan. You and I weren't close in high school. You were a couple of years ahead of me, and besides, I was one of those kids you wouldn't have hung out with."

"Ashley! I—"

"Just listen to me, Jordan. My mother was a drunk. She drank herself to death when I was twelve years old. My brothers were nine and ten. You know where we lived? We lived in that big house across from Chandler's Market that they cut up into low income housing units. My father got an apartment there. He had one bedroom, and my brothers and I shared the other one. There was one teeny bathroom. He was out of work a lot of the time. Sometimes he tended bar at MacTavish's or the Inn, and in the winter he always tried to get a job as a lift operator at the Mountain. We had nothing. I did the best I could taking care of my brothers. My father did the best he could, too, I guess, but to tell you the truth, I didn't see him much through my whole teenage years. Oh, he came home every night, and brought in groceries so I could feed my brothers, but he was always out working this job or that. Like I said, I think he did the best he could.

"And Kyle? Kyle's father knocked him and his mother around pretty good, and a lot when Kyle was little. If it hadn't been for his uncle Tom Cochran, Kyle said he doesn't know where he'd be now. He used to go to Tom's house and stay with Tom and his aunt and his cousins. That's why he's so close to them now. You think things just happened for Kyle and me? You think we just sing and dance through our lives? When Kyle and I got together in the seventh grade, we just had this bond. That was real special, and I don't really know why. We just clicked. We could trust each other, and we wanted the same things. Kyle and I worked real hard to get where we are, and we work hard to stay there.

"We want things, too, and we're working to get them. For instance, I want a baby, Jordan. I want a baby so bad, and so does Kyle, but we want to be able to afford the baby. I want to stay home with my baby, at least for a while. Sometimes, when I see you with Grace, I'm so envious. Such a beautiful little girl with those red curls! I think, how lucky is Jordan to have a baby like Grace? Then I get scared and think, what if I can't have a baby? So, Jordan, you can't get away from the complications. They're everywhere and everybody has them!" Ashley stopped and gave a shuddering sigh. "I'm sorry I went on a rant, but that's what I think."

Jordan opened her mouth to speak, but no words came out. She felt awful, as though she had hurt this gentle and loyal person who had waited on her, run interference for her, guarded her secrets, and become her friend. She crossed the room slowly. Finally she spoke.

"Ashley, I am so, so sorry. You're right. I don't know what I'm talking about. I've been selfish. Aiden said the same thing."

"You need to let Aiden know that you trust him, Jordan. You need to believe that you two can make it together. Otherwise, don't even bother. I'm not saying you have to be with Aiden. I'm only saying you have to be sure. And don't make the mistake of thinking you'll compromise yourself with a partner. No, that's not how it works. Love can only make you stronger. Kyle and I don't have a dependency, Jordan. We have a commitment. We've been married—married—since we were eighteen and nineteen. We know we can depend on our love for each other. Love makes everything easier. Even when Kyle and I lived in that three room apartment above MacTavish's, and we didn't know from month to month whether we'd be able to pay the rent, it was easier because I could reach out and touch him in the night. That's how you know you love somebody. We knew together we could do it. And we are doing it. Every day. We make it happen for each other. I never get tired of seeing his face, Jordan. If you don't feel that way about Aiden, then that's the reality. But if he lifts your heart, if you feel stronger with him than without him, then give in to that strength. Stop sabotaging yourself."

The two sat silently for a while. At last Jordan said, "I'm going to go to the Inn and see Aiden. I think I need to talk to him." She stood up.

Ashley looked up at her as she walked toward the door. "Did you hear what I said, Jordan?"

"I did." Jordan began to smile. "You're a dear friend, Ashley. Thank you for that."

"Go," said Ashley, returning Jordan's smile. She waved her hands, and Jordan closed the door behind her, walking with renewed energy out of the building.

Aiden drove to Inn, parked in front, and glanced at the car's clock. It was seven. The desk wouldn't open until eight, so Aiden got out and walked slowly down the green. It was a sunny morning, warm for May. The lilacs were in full bloom now and, as before, Aiden was reminded of the house where he grew up. Pansies made a splash of color in the railing boxes on the town gazebo, and lily of the valley grew along the stone wall of the old cemetery across the street. The earth was waking up, and suddenly Aiden felt lonely. He reflected on how his life had changed in just a few days. Nothing was the same or, for that matter, could ever be the same again. He was seized with panic. He knew he could never go back to the way he had been before. He could never be the cavalier young man he had been, sleeping indiscriminately with whomever caught his eye. He could never again go back to the carefree days of juggling one, two, three girls at a time, sending them flowers or calling just because of the ego boost it gave him to know how much they wanted his attention.

Aiden ran his hand through his hair. "Shit!" he said out loud. Could he have ever been that shallow? Now, he felt his future was on the line. He knew Jordan loved him; he could feel it every time they were together. But she was stubborn, and she was still punishing herself for her past. If Jordan didn't give in, if she didn't capitulate and open herself honestly to their love, they might both end up facing a future marred by an insurmountable void.

"Stewart!" The voice cracked through the morning mist and startled Aiden out of his reverie. He stayed composed, as though he hadn't heard, and continued to walk down the street. He hadn't recognized the voice, but he could hear jogging footsteps bearing down on him. The voice barked again. This time he could hear the runner's breathing. "Stewart! Aiden Stewart!"

Now Aiden turned, slowly, cautiously, but curious to know the owner of the voice. His shock must have shown in his face when he saw who it was.

"Stewart!" said Christopher Fenton again, slowing to a walk as he approached Aiden. "Surprised?"

"Yes, as a matter of fact, I am." Aiden was surprised to see Fenton when he had assumed the man had left the town after he had lost out on the deal with ChatDotCom. Aiden was also surprised at the man's physical condition. Fenton, dressed in sweat pants and a T-shirt and running shoes, was obviously a fitness enthusiast, his arms and chest characteristic of somebody who spent a fair amount of time in the gym. It was an odd contrast with his thin, pointy face and small features. There was an air of something about the man—Aiden couldn't quite put his finger on it—that was a little scary.

"Just out for a morning jog," Fenton said in explanation. "I've been wanting to talk to you, Stewart." He was grinning broadly.

"What about?" The last thing Aiden wanted to be doing was talking to Christopher Fenton. The man was odious.

"Let's go get a cup of coffee," said Fenton. "The Inn is open for breakfast."

"I just had my coffee," lied Aiden, wishing he hadn't abandoned his cup at Jordan's office.

"Well, then, we can just walk."

Aiden headed back in the direction of the Inn. "Look, Fenton, I've got to book myself a room. With your network, I'm sure you've heard that Gene Palmer has died."

"Yes, I heard. Too bad. Too bad. A real old time entrepreneur."

"What do you want?" Aiden was beginning to feel irritated.

"It's simple," Fenton said. "You and I got off on the wrong foot. We were stupid. We should have done this at the very beginning."

"Done what?"

"Pooled our resources. Gotten together. Why were we fighting over this company? We should have just joined forces, taken the company over, and spread out from there. Nothing could stop the two of us."

Aiden couldn't believe what he was hearing. "What are you talking about?" asked Aiden tersely. "Fenton Enterprises never approached Trade Winds. You were willing to do anything to keep us from getting Chat."

"And that was my mistake," Fenton replied jovially. "Yes, I do make a mistake here and there." He laughed at his owned presumed joke.

Aiden felt compelled to get away from him. "And now you want to buy an interest in Chat from Trade Winds, is that it?"

"Well, not exactly," said Fenton, slowing his pace. "I want you to put me in as CEO of ChatDotCom. I'll work with no salary until I put the first deal together. I'll get a percentage of that deal. Then, maybe we can talk salary, you know, after I prove what I can do for the company."

Aiden could not process what he was hearing. Fenton as CEO? Of Chat? Was the man delusional?

"I know, I know!" declared Fenton with the same odd smile on his face. "Sounds crazy, but listen, there's a method to my madness." Aiden really didn't want to hear any more, but Fenton kept talking, an urgent tone in his voice. "I've got two deals all set to go. They revolved around Fenton Enterprises acquiring Chat. Now that the decision has been made to sell to Trade Winds, I wanted you to know. I think we could work a deal that would be beneficial to everyone. I could pull off these deals as CEO of Chat."

"Jordan Fitzgerald is CEO of ChatDotCom. It's written into the contract. Besides, Trade Winds has no plans to replace her."

"You and I both know contracts are meant to be broken, Stewart," scoffed Fenton. "We could rearrange things so her feathers wouldn't be ruffled. And then you and I could join forces and get some real business done."

Aiden felt anger rising in him. "Not an option, Fenton, and need I remind you about how you drugged Jordan Fitzgerald with the pure motive of seeing her undone in the eyes of Trade Winds and Gene Palmer so you could advance your own position? Why would I be interested in any kind of proposal from you?"

"Hey, we've all done things we're not proud of to get what we want. I know you're, how shall we say, sensitive on the subject of Jordan Fitzgerald, but surely it's not an insurmountable problem."

"Fenton, stop right there." Aiden spoke softly but the warning in his voice was unmistakable. "Leave any talk of Jordan Fitzgerald out of this. She's not a commodity. She's the CEO of ChatDotCom, and she's staying in that position. As for any affiliation between yourself and Trade Winds or Chat, I'm not in favor of it. In fact, I'm going to repeat myself: It's not an option. And, you seem to forget, Trade Winds doesn't belong to me anyway. It's my father's—lock, stock, and barrel—but I can assure you, he would feel the same." Aiden would normally find a polite way to cut the conversation short, but any thoughts of politeness were far from his mind. "I don't know what you're up to, Fenton, but I'm done here. Trade Winds and Chat-DotCom finalized the merger yesterday. We have specific corporate goals and will pursue them. The position of CEO is filled, and there are no other positions open or any plans for negotiations beyond what we've already accomplished. Now, I'm going to book myself a room at the Inn and take a shower. Good-bye, Mr. Fenton."

Fenton's face flushed angrily, but Aiden turned away, the conversation over as far as he was concerned. "You'll regret this, Stewart! I'm giving you the chance to get in on the ground floor of a big thing. You'll regret this!"

Aiden let him have the last word. Without looking back, he walked down the street and up the steps to the lobby of the Inn.

Susan Noyes was behind the desk. She recognized him and smiled. "Mr. Stewart! You're back. Breakfast?"

"That would be nice, but I need a room first, thank you." Aiden forced a smile. It wasn't Susan's fault that he still carried an uneasy feeling from his conversation with Fenton.

The woman's face grew sober. "I suppose you're here because Gene Palmer has died," she said.

Less than twelve hours, the body hardly cold, thought Aiden cryptically. *The whole town probably knows. Well, less explaining to do, just like Jordan said,* he thought.

"Yes," said Aiden, "my company and Mr. Palmer's company have merged. It's too bad to have lost him so soon. I'm waiting to hear funeral plans."

"From Jordan?" asked Susan, smiling again.

"Ah, yes, from — from Jordan. She's the CEO." Aiden paused as he got out his credit card. "And my mother and father will be coming into town this afternoon. Could you reserve a room for them, also?"

"She's such a sweet thing," Susan remarked, not seeming to hear the request regarding his parents. She handed him the key. "Smart, too. She was Gene Palmer's right hand. His own kids never had any interest in it. Seems strange, doesn't it? You'd think…oh well. I'll send her up when she gets here."

Aiden blinked. *I give up,* he said to himself. "Thanks." He smiled at Susan as he took the key from her. "I'm not expecting her. Her secretary will call me."

"I'll have your parents' room ready by the time they arrive," said Susan as he started up the stairs.

It was the old, familiar Room 21. *Ah, the memories,* thought Aiden sardonically as he closed the door behind him. His eyes fell, as they had the first time he had entered, on the picture of the couple under the apple trees. *Banns.* He ran his fingers through his hair. A shower and a cup of coffee would revive him. The creepy conversation with Christopher Fenton still echoed in his ears. It didn't make sense. Aiden wondered if he had heard the last from Fenton. It wasn't like the man to drop things. According to all he had heard, Fenton was like a dog with a bone. Aiden made a mental note to speak to his father about it.

His stomach was beginning to growl; the sooner he got some food, the better. He stepped into the bathroom and turned on the shower. Thoughts fought for priority in his mind as he stepped out of his clothes and wrapped a white towel around his waist. He needed to address the employees of Chat and answer their concerns and ideas following the merger. He needed to properly represent Trade Winds at the funeral of Gene Palmer. He had no idea where he stood with Jordan at the moment, but he did know that they had to put their own emotional involvement aside long enough to make sure the daily workings of Chat were efficiently coordinated and assimilated into the machine that was Trade Winds. And now there was this morning's disturbing appearance by Fenton, which had left him feeling uneasy. He wandered to the window and looked out onto the garden. The lilacs were in full bloom, and their delicate scent permeated the air, reminding him of how his mother had always tended the gardens at home. He felt soothed, and he lay down on the bed and sighed.

Chapter Fourteen

Just as before, Jordan was nervous as she approached Aiden's room. This time, however, she came to him with a clear head and solid resolve. She rapped on the ancient wood. "Aiden, are you in there? It's me."

In a moment's time, Aiden opened the door. Jordan gave him a flirtatious smile, and he smiled back at her as she entered the room.

"Susan Noyes said you'd be coming," he said with a laugh.

"Susan knows all." Jordan laughed back, cocking her head coquettishly to the side. She turned and stepped closer to him, laying her open palm against his bare chest. She could feel his heart beating, feel the muscles moving under the skin. "I came to tell you something," she said, looking up at him.

"What is that?" he asked softly, his voice enticing.

"I came to tell you that I love you."

He caught his breath. "You love me…but?"

"No buts," said Jordan, slipping her hand down the hard muscles of his stomach until it rested just above his groin. She felt the muscles tense and savored her power to make them respond to her touch. "I love you. It's that simple. It has nothing to do with Mr. Palmer, or Chat, or my job, or even Grace, for that matter. It's a thing on its own. I can't deny it. It would be foolish to, and it would work against me in the end."

He was silent, letting her speak. Jordan bent her head to his chest and kissed him gently above his heart. She lifted her eyes to his again, searching his face as she spoke. "I want us to be together, Aiden. I see now that I'm not weak or selfish for wanting that. Love is never selfish. It can only make us stronger. We'll work everything out. Jobs, babies, business, families. It doesn't matter. Together we can do it. All this time I've been worried about compromising my reason, my power, by letting you in. That was so wrong. I've compromised myself by trying to keep you at a distance. I've compromised us, and I apologize."

"No apologies necessary," Aiden said hoarsely. He dipped his mouth to hers and kissed her deeply. Her lips grew warm under his. He pulled back and smiled down at her. "You look like you could use a shower," he said.

She giggled as he slipped the white T-shirt over her head in one deft move. He unclipped her hair, letting it fall in cascades over her shoulders. She stood, trembling almost imperceptibly with anticipation as he unsnapped her jeans and, kneeling in front of her, slid them down her legs. Her breath caught in a little gasp as he pressed his lips between her legs and kissed her through the white lace panties.

Aiden reached up and undid the clasp on her bra. She slipped her arms free, and it fell in a lacy heap on the floor. He kissed her taut nipples tenderly, one then the other, pulling gently at them with his teeth. The embers of desire that smoldered within her burst into flame. She gave a little moan as his lips traced a path from between her breasts to her navel.

Aiden stood up and, taking her by the hand, led her into the bathroom. He pulled the towel off, revealing his impressive erection. Instinctively, she reached out, longing to feel it in her hand, the sleek, smooth hardness of it, like silk over iron, but Aiden took both her wrists before she could touch him. He stepped into the shower, drawing her in with him. The steamy water felt almost cool as it fell on her hot, flushed skin, and her body prickled with the sensation of her mounting passion.

Aiden turned her around, and she leaned into the water, feeling it rush down her back, soaking her panties. She struggled with the heat between her legs, twisting her hips, pushing her buttocks against his groin. She ached to be filled with him. Now she felt Aiden's hands on her, playing with the wet lace, drawing the panties up between her rounded cheeks until the pressure on her pulsing center threatened to take her breath away. She groaned out loud, twisting in an agony of lust. She felt him move behind her, felt his lips on her back, moving down, down with the water as it cascaded over her body. Then, tiny nibbles and nips of beautiful pain heightened her frenzy. She couldn't see or hear; she could only feel.

She felt the panties being stripped off her and the incredible relief as Aiden's hand slipped between her legs and his fingers probed her secret recesses, slipping in and out, mixing her own hot wetness with the steamy water. Finally, just when she thought she might die of pure animal need, his fingers found the sensual center of her being. He began stroking, squeezing, working the spot until she gave a little shriek, begging for him. He withdrew his hand, and taking her by the hips, pulled her back onto his own hardness, filling her with himself and all his passion. His thrusts became faster and faster until she felt as though she were spinning down a warm, dark tunnel. She met him thrust for thrust until he began to slow, savoring the time, teasing her, urging her to topple with a crescendo of ecstasy.

Jordan read his mind and abruptly slipped from him. She turned around and knelt down, taking him into her mouth. The water beat down on her, tickling every nerve in her skin until she felt on fire. She slid her lips up and down the shaft, savoring the taste of him, the feel of him in her mouth. He groaned, moving his hips to match her caresses.

Finally, he lifted her to her feet. Backing her against the shower wall, he raised her leg, draping it over his arm. He braced himself, hands on the wall on each side of her shoulders, and drove into her, face to face, his mouth on hers. That was the peak. Jordan felt her body spin out of control with his first thrust, and the waves of her climax washed over her, again and again, with a force that transported her to a place where she had never been before, even with Aiden. She leaned back, her eyes closed, glorying in the sensation while he brought himself to the fulfillment of his own passion.

They stood under the water, leaning against the shower wall, until their breathing slowed. They finished the shower together, tenderly soaping each other's bodies, enjoying the feeling of being the only two people in the world.

Later, as they dressed, Aiden said, "I need coffee."

"I can get a cup of coffee with you downstairs," said Jordan, "but then I want to go home and be with Grace. Would you come with me? My parents have to go up to Burlington to see my brother at the University. It's a parents' weekend, so they'll stay and come home in the morning."

Aiden took her hands in his and kissed them. "I'd like nothing better than to come with you, but isn't that what we just did?"

Jordan laughed out loud. "Don't give up your day job to become a comic!"

Together, they went down into the dining room.

"Would you like to sit out on the garden terrace?" asked the young hostess.

"That would be lovely, thanks," said Jordan.

They sat at a small, glass-topped wrought iron table. The hostess put menus in front of them, and a server came by with a pot of hot coffee and filled both cups.

"I can smell the lilacs," Jordan said, closing her eyes and drawing a deep breath. "I think they're my favorite flower."

"They always remind me of home." Aiden picked up his menu.

"I hope I didn't offend your parents," said Jordan as she reached for her menu. "I left in such a state."

"Not at all. They were worried about you, though." The server returned, and Aiden gestured to Jordan.

"I'll have the eggs Benedict," she said.

"And you, sir?"

"I'll have a large orange juice and blueberry pancakes with a side of bacon."

"Thank you." The server nodded and put her note pad into her pocket as she left.

Aiden sighed deeply.

"Something wrong?" asked Jordan.

"I don't know."

Jordan's brow furrowed. "What do you mean by that?"

"Well, Christopher Fenton stopped me on the street this morning."

"What?" Jordan was aghast. "He's in town? I thought we were done with him."

"It gets stranger," explained Aiden. "He wanted to talk to me. He wanted, well, it sounded as though he wanted a job at Chat."

"What do you mean? What did he say?"

Aiden related the conversation. "It was totally weird. Kind of spooked me. He had a strange look on his face; made me wish we'd reported that incident to the police."

"This is just bizarre!" exclaimed Jordan. "He wanted to take my position as CEO?"

"That's what he said. What gave the guy that idea? What's the ulterior motive here?"

The server returned with their food and set the plates down in front of them, and they both began to eat.

"I don't think he's mentally very stable," said Jordan between bites. "Although, I'm guessing he's probably just trying to get a foot in the door and take over from the inside out. Mr. Palmer said he would stop at nothing and then he told us about Fenton's nefarious past dealings. I hope he's gone now. I can't forget what he tried to do to me and what might have happened." She gave a little shiver.

"Me, too. Is Chat looking for new hires of any kind?"

"No. At the moment, there's nothing available."

"Good. Let's keep it that way. It would be just like Fenton to try to plant a spy within the ranks at Chat. Let's not hire any new people for a while."

They ate in silence, each enjoying the close proximity of the other. To Jordan, it felt as though she belonged with Aiden. She had stopped fighting, stopped trying to love by rule of thumb. They would work things out. They would be guided by their love for each other.

It was one of the most idyllic days Aiden had ever had. They went back to Jordan's house. Grace had just woken up from her nap. Jordan dressed her, and they took her outside to play on the lawn. Aiden sat, mesmerized, watching Jordan as she watched her daughter, his body remembering all the exquisite details of her body and the euphoric heights his passions had reached until his desire began to stir again. He reached out and caressed her neck, running his hand down to the small of her back. She turned and smiled at him. It was all he could do to keep from rolling on top of her right there in the sweet, spring grass.

Later, after Grace had eaten her lunch, they put her in the stroller and walked the mile and a half into town. On this sunny Sunday afternoon, there was hardly a person or a car to be seen. It occurred to Aiden that the strangest thing about this little outing was that he didn't feel strange about it at all. He smiled to himself, reflecting that on most Sunday afternoons, he would be pursuing some seasonable activity on the mountain, in the woods, on the ocean, and would most likely be taking some girl to bed in the evening.

This immersion into sudden domesticity should have jolted him somehow, but instead, he felt calm and surprisingly at ease. When Grace squirmed and fussed in the stroller, Aiden bent down and picked her up. His strong hands, which had only held his nieces and nephews on occasion, handled baby Grace as though he had been carrying babies daily all his life. Her chubby little body fit easily into the crook of his arm, and she sat there, instinctively feeling safe, looking down on the world around her with the air of a queen looking down from her throne.

They walked back to the house this way, Jordan pushing the empty stroller and Aiden walking beside her with Grace cradled against his hip. The rest of the day was spent in a golden haze, any thought outside their own little sphere far from their minds. They were oblivious to anything except the tiny magical bubble in which they found themselves. They drank beer and talked. They laughed. They touched and kissed, happy to not have to contain their affection, happy in their own company.

When the sun began to slide behind the hills, Jordan fed Grace her supper, bathed her, and after reading a couple of stories, put her to bed in the little nursery across from her own room. The spring night was balmy. Aiden stood in the doorway as Jordan opened the window a few inches to let the fresh air in, and he joined her at the side of the crib until Grace fell asleep. They lingered for a bit, and Aiden marveled at the connection between mother and child. Finally, Jordan sighed contentedly, and she and Aiden left the room, leaving the door open a small crack.

"Are you hungry?" Jordan asked Aiden as they walked back into the living room. He was standing at the big window, gazing out over the hills. The sun had set and the warm spring evening was washed in the deepening blue of the encroaching night. Aiden could see the lights from the town and here and there, the warm yellow glow from neighboring homes as people enjoyed their supper hour.

"I could eat something." He came up behind her as she stood facing the open refrigerator door. She felt the little thrill in her soul as he put a hand on each of her hips and kissed the back of her neck. "I could eat you," he whispered. "That's all I need."

Jordan laughed. "That's for dessert. How about a steak? I can fire up the grill, and we can eat out on the deck. It's a beautiful evening."

"Sounds good to me," said Aiden. "I can do the man thing and grill the steaks."

"Good, then you get the grill going. I'll make a salad and some potato wedges."

They had a delicious and intimate meal. Jordan set the table with candles and opened a bottle of red wine. They ate slowly and laughed together softly as they enjoyed the peace and contentment that had settled over them.

Later, as they cleared dishes, Aiden noticed how easily they worked together. They had developed a natural familiarity that was testimony to their love. They went to bed early, slipping naked under the fragrant sheets of Jordan's bed. Aiden wrapped his arms around her, and they lay quietly, face to face, for some time, each listening to the other breathe. Finally, Jordan let her hand slip down his hip, over his muscled groin. He groaned contentedly as he felt the fire flare up between them.

This time their lovemaking was slower and more deliberate. The frantic, almost egocentric passion gave way to a need to discover each other, to understand who this person they so loved was. To Aiden, it felt as though he was seeing Jordan for the first time and that she was more beautiful than ever. Her large blue eyes were more luminous. Her ample alabaster breasts, flushed pink with desire, seemed softer. The heat from her body was more seductive, all because he was learning who this woman was. He could read her now. He trusted his soul to her.

Jordan gasped as Aiden's hand move down her belly, tickling her navel, skimming the surface of her skin as he sought the hot, wet place between her legs. She opened her thighs to allow him in. Aiden bent his head to that tender place between her thighs. The scent of her was intoxicating. He caressed her with his lips until she was writhing. He brought himself up and knelt between her legs, pushing into her all at once, seeking the hot vortex of her. In that moment, he wanted to possess all of her. He would have all of her that there was to have.

Jordan groaned and moved against his hips as he thrust into her again and again. They clasped each other as they would have clasped a life preserver in a flood, riding their own waves until their desire broke over them, drenching them both in a torrent of physical rapture, swirling their souls together as though they were froth on the tips of those waves of desire.

Aiden collapsed on her, trying to get as close as he could. He felt her relax under him, felt her hands resting so softly on his back. He rolled gently from her, careful to keep her cradled against him. He whispered in her ear, "I love you, Jordan. I love you."

Her head rested over his heart, and she kissed him there. "I love you, too, Aiden," she whispered back, just before they drifted off to sleep.

Chapter Fifteen

Aiden was wakened sometime later by an odd, sharp cry. It was like nothing he had ever heard. Panicked, he pulled himself up out of his sleep, fighting his way up through the layers of unconsciousness until he could open his eyes. The room was softly illuminated with moonlight. He saw Jordan pulling on a robe and rushing out the door. Then he heard a ghastly, strangled shriek.

Aiden vaulted out of bed and across the hallway, into Grace's room. Jordan was hysterical, throwing the bedding out of the crib.

"What is it!" he shouted.

Jordan wheeled, her eyes wide and frantic, the veins in her neck and forehead swelled and throbbing. She spoke in gasps of air. "Grace!" she gasped. "Grace! She's gone. Somebody's taken her!"

The room began to whirl. Aiden gripped the door jamb to steady himself. He turned, ran back into the bedroom, picked up his phone, and punched 9-1-1 with shaking fingers.

"Nine-one-one dispatch. What is your emergency?"

"There's been a kidnapping. Send the police immediately!"

"What is the location, sir?"

"1020 Stage Coach Road. The Fitzgerald residence. Hurry!"

"Your name?"

"Aiden Stewart. Look, can you just hurry up!"

"Who has been kidnapped, sir?"

"Please, send somebody now!"

"Sir, who is missing?"

"Jordan Fitzgerald's little daughter! She's been abducted! Please, hurry!"

"We're sending someone now. Please stay on the phone until they arrive, sir." Aiden glanced at the phone and purposely terminated the call. He ran back into Grace's room. Jordan was on the floor, her face in her hands.

"It's my fault!" she sobbed. "It's my fault! I opened the window when I put her to bed!"

Aiden reached down and brought Jordan to her feet. "I'm getting dressed," he said. "It just happened. I'm going to look for her. Wait here. Police are coming."

Jordan nodded automatically, and Aiden raced across the hallway. As he threw on his T-shirt and jeans, he heard the door slam and knew Jordan had taken off anyway. Quickly, he slipped on his sneakers and ran out into the night.

He could see Jordan at the far end of the yard, where the lawn was bordered by the woods. He was not familiar enough with his surroundings, but Jordan was. He ran and caught up with her.

"Did you hear a car?" Aiden's voice echoed in Jordan's head.

"What?...No, no, I didn't." Her teeth were chattering with fear and shock.

"Where are we? What's beyond those woods?"

"I don't know if anybody came this way. I don't know why I ran out here. Aiden, I don't know what to do!"

"What's on the other side of those woods?" he repeated, putting his arm around her.

"There's just a narrow strip of woods between here and River Street, the next street over."

"I'm going in there. I might still find something."

"You'll stay right here," said a quiet voice behind them. They both turned. John Giamo stood there, his young deputy, Tim Cully, in tow.

"John!" sobbed Jordan when she saw him. "John! Somebody's taken Grace!" She slumped into Aiden, and he held her with both arms.

"State police are already on River Street, Jordan. Can we go into the house? I need to ask you questions right away. We have to act fast. Cully, you scan the perimeter here and then go through those woods until you're on River Street. Check with State Police. See what they've found."

The deputy nodded and jogged off toward the wood line.

"Let's go inside," Giamo repeated gently. He led the way, and Aiden followed, holding Jordan.

The police chief sat down at the kitchen table. Aiden pulled out the chair across from him and guided Jordan, who clutched her robe around her, into it. Then he pulled out a chair for himself and sat beside her. Giamo took a recorder out of his pocket and set it on the table.

"Clark's Corner Police Chief John Giamo. Interview with Jordan Fitzgerald. May eighteenth, two thirty a.m.," he said. "We're taping this, Jordan."

Jordan nodded, glad to have the police chief there, ready to help. She'd always respected him; now she was relieved to have him by her side.

"When did you find her missing, Jordan?" asked Giamo.

"About half an hour ago. I—I heard her cry! I heard her cry! John, what if she's hurt? What will I do if she's hurt?"

Jordan's tears roll down her face. Aiden scooted his chair closer to her, his arm across her shoulders. She leaned into him, finding comfort in having him with her.

"Shhh, Jordan. We'll find her. We've got cops all over the place as we speak. You reported it right away." Giamo reached out and put a large hand over Jordan's small fist, resting clenched on the table top. Jordan nodded. She gave a shuddering sigh and wiped her eyes. Suddenly, she began to shake all over.

"Jordan, are you all right?" Aiden asked. Jordan nodded again, but her teeth were chattering. She couldn't seem to control the shaking.

Giamo looked concerned. "Look, why don't you just try to relax a minute. I'm going to get a call in to Cully and see if he's found anything." Giamo reached for his pager, and at that moment, a voice came crackling through.

"John, it's Becky. Call in, please." Jordan recognized the voice of Becky Dearborne, the local dispatcher and police department secretary. Becky knew everything of any importance that was happening in the town, day or night.

Giamo stood as he took out his cell phone and stopped the recorder. "Excuse me a moment," he said to Jordan as he called in to the department. "I'm here, Becky. What is it?" He walked into the living room, but they could still hear his conversation. The cold hands of panic clutched tightly around her throat as she visualized her daughter in the hands of a stranger. "You say Caleb's there? I'll get down there right away." He slipped the phone back in its carrier as he rejoined them in the kitchen.

"John, what is it?" Jordan held her hand to her chest, her breathing ragged.

"Becky got a call from Caleb Cochran. There's a fire at Chat. The building's on fire." He paused, and Jordan could see his frustration as he slowly drew his hand down his face. "Dayton reported seeing a man lurking near the building, and he said he thinks the guy may have been holding a child."

Jordan stood up. "I'm coming with you."

"You're not even dressed. Go ahead and get yourself ready." Giamo was already on his way out the door. "I'll meet you down there." He closed the door behind him.

Jordan dashed to the bedroom as the flashing blue lights disappeared down the drive. It took all her energy to shake off the fear that had paralyzed her. She forced herself into her clothes and captured her hair up in a ponytail.

"She's going to be okay, Jordan," Aiden said as they rushed out the door to the car. "Grace is going to be okay."

In spite of the leaden dread that threatened to sabotage any action she tried to take, Jordan's heart lifted. Somehow, she believed this man. She believed that together, they could do anything, including finding Grace. For the first time, she was feeling the power of real love.

They jumped into the car, and Aiden sped down the road toward Chat. As they approached the building, fear nearly strangled Jordan's new found hope once again.

The building was engulfed, with flames licking from the windows on the south end, along the far side of the parking lot. The scene was a melee of blue and red flashing lights, police cruisers, and fire trucks from neighboring towns. Jordan could hear men shouting. She felt Aiden's hand close around hers.

"Where's Giamo?" he said urgently. "Try to pick him out. We've got to know what they're doing to find Grace and if these two things are related!"

As Jordan strained to identify the figures silhouetted against the flames, a crowd had begun to gather around them. Vernon Gray, in charge of electronics at Chat, was there. So was Dayton Phillips. Jordan saw him wiping at his eyes. Joan Halloran was there, standing beside Mr. Palmer's oldest son, Dan.

"Jordan! Jordan!" Jordan and Aiden turned toward the voice, trying to peer through the darkness. Ashley was elbowing her way through the crowd. At last she reached them, taking Jordan's hands in both of hers. "I heard, Jordan! Oh, Jordan!" She embraced her friend, then stepped back and looked at Aiden. "I have some information that might help," she said.

"What is it?" he asked.

"I think Christopher Fenton is behind this. I did some research." Ashley held up some papers with a shaking hand. "It's all a house of cards! Fenton Industries is an empty shell!"

Aiden took the papers and began to go through them. Ashley went on, "The other day when Jordan saw Fenton, it set something off in me. You know how when you know in your gut something's really wrong. It even kind of scared me. I started looking up things about him, you know, Googling him and stuff. I made some calls to Verizon and Comcast and AT&T. I asked did they know ChatDotCom was up for sale. I pretended I was you, Jordan. I'm sorry. Then I found out that all these big companies thought Fenton had purchased Chat already. I found out that he was negotiating to sell off Chat in three different deals to these companies. And I dug further, into his personal history. Jordan, he's bad. He was accused of corporate espionage and fired from one corporation. Then he formed his own company, but it wasn't really a company. He made some small deals, got some cash, and did all the rest with smoke and mirrors. His last deal before he tried to get us was with a company in New York City. I found that they have a lawsuit against him for twenty-five million dollars! When I talked to them, they said the DA thought they had enough evidence to charge him with insider trading and corporate espionage, and they were going to try to bring criminal charges against him! Jordan, he's a phony, and he can't sustain the lies any longer. He's out of money and potential deals, and he's desperate! That's why he wanted your job at Chat! I think this has something to do with him."

Ashley stopped to take a breath. Aiden took the papers from Jordan. "This is all tied together somehow," Aiden said. "I'm taking this to Giamo. We've got to find out what they know about Grace."

"They won't let you across the bridge, Aiden," Ashley said.

"Oh yes, they will," said Aiden determinedly, but just as he started to cross, a man came toward them from the other side. The light from the fire illuminated him from behind: John Giamo.

"John!" cried Jordan running forward. "Have you found anything?"

Giamo took her hand. He was a father, too, after all. "We have a situation here, Jordan. I want you to listen to me carefully."

Jordan reeled. She gripped Aiden's arm and fought the nausea that overwhelmed her. "What is it?" Her mouth was so dry she could barely get the words out. Her heart pounded and fluttered at the same time. She felt faint and struggled to regain her composure.

"The fire is in the southwest corner of the building. I just talked to Caleb. He's directing efforts by the firemen to keep it contained there, but it's an old building. Caleb said there's the danger of it going up the inside walls. The sprinklers have gone off throughout the building, so that's a help. There's about thirty firemen there now. Now here's the problem: We did confirm that there's man in there. A couple of firemen saw him run up one of the staircases after they broke through the wall of the outer office. Jordan, one of the men thought he heard a child crying."

Jordan cried out and clapped her hands to her mouth. "No! No!" Ashley and Aiden supported her between them. "It's Grace!"

"And I'm sure the man is Christopher Fenton, Chief," said Aiden, handing him the papers that Ashley had brought. "Here's his motive."

"Fenton? You mean the guy who was trying to buy Chat?" Giamo took the papers.

"Yes," answered Aiden. "He's flat broke. It was all a sham. He was trying to negotiate a sale before anybody found out. I think he's unstable. He must have snapped."

Another fire truck arrived. Six or eight fully-outfitted men jumped out, dragging hoses behind them.

"Chief Giamo?" Ashley spoke up quietly. "Did you see Kyle? It's—it's his first fire."

Giamo managed a small smile. "He's sticking close to Caleb. Don't worry, Ashley. Caleb will take care of him." He turned again to Jordan. "Caleb is trying to divide his men. Some will contain the fire. The rest will fan out and try to find whoever's in there. Jordan, we're doing the best we can. I can't go in, and I can't let my men go in. Caleb's in charge now until that fire is under control."

Jordan nodded. Her knees were weak and she felt sick to her stomach. Giamo's radio went off.

"Giamo," he barked.

"John, it's Caleb," came the crackly voice. Jordan could hear it clearly. They all held their breaths. "We've got this guy up on the second floor. The baby's with him. I saw her. She seems unharmed, but I don't see them now. The fire's gone up the outside of the annex, and I'm afraid it's reached the third floor and it might cave. I'm going in to get them out."

"Careful," warned Giamo. "He may be armed."

Suddenly, a voice called out from the distance. "Stewart! Stewart!" Aiden looked around wildly, as did Giamo and Jordan. It was hard to see, hard to tell in the night air where the sound was coming from.

Then Jordan screamed, "Grace!" and, breaking away from the group, she ran onto the bridge.

"Jordan, stop!" commanded Giamo, but it did no good. Aiden started after her, with Giamo right on his heels.

Jordan had stopped at the far end of the bridge. The hot air, stirred up by the fire, was whipping her hair across her face. She was looking up as Aiden caught up with her and followed her gaze. The windows of the building had shattered under the heat of the fire. Flames flashed and jumped inside the structure, casting an eerie half-glow out onto the canal. Unidentifiable shadows loomed against the side of the building and danced crazily in frenetic patterns. Jordan strained her eyes, and her chest constricted with fear. There, on the old fire escape that hung out over the canal, stood Christopher Fenton. He clutched Grace like a ragdoll under one arm.

Jordan shrieked. "Please! Please, let my baby go! Please bring her back!" She turned to the police chief, now beside her. "John, do something! Do something!"

"Jordan, go back and wait. This is a criminal matter."

"I won't!" she yelled back at him. "It's my matter! It's my child!"

Giamo must have seen that it was futile to argue with her. He nodded his head, and then shot a look over Jordan's head toward Aiden. Aiden put a hand on each of Jordan's shoulders and stood there.

"What now?" Aiden asked.

Giamo lifted his radio. "This patches me directly into Caleb Cochran. I'll tell him what's going on and ask him if he can get to the old second floor fire escape on the East side." Then he stepped forward to the bridge railing. "Fenton," he called, his voice calm despite the situation. "Fenton, can you understand me? Do you hear me?"

Jordan was overcome by a sudden onset of trembling. She stepped up beside the police chief and gripped the railing. Her teeth were chattering.

"Fenton," called Giamo again, "can you hear me?"

"I can hear you," the man on the fire escape yelled back.

"We're sending firemen up to get you and the baby. Cooperate with them, Fenton."

Fenton laughed back. "And why should I do that? Nobody's cooperated with me. That's directed at you, Miss CEO. What a fool you are! I offered you the best deal you could get, and you screwed everybody over because you were screwing the competition! I could have made your company more money in one year than you could have in fifty! Now you've ruined me. You've ruined everything I spent my life building. And I'm going to ruin yours. You think about that!"

Jordan slumped against the railing of the bridge. Her heart was pounding so hard she could hear it and her mouth was dry with primal fear. *I can't let this happen,* she said over and over again to herself, *I just can't let this happen!*

Aiden signaled to Ashley, motioning for her to stay with Jordan. He then stepped up beside Giamo, listening to the conversation the chief was having with Caleb Cochran over the two-way radios.

"I'm working my way up there now," Caleb replied. "I should be there in about five minutes. Just keep him busy. I'm sending my men back down. It's too dangerous. I'll go myself." The radio went dead.

Aiden approached Giamo and relayed the conversation, adding, "I'm not sure he can make it up there."

Giamo gazed up at the burning building and the hysterical man perched on the rusted fire escape, holding the squirming baby under his arm. It was a desperate situation. "Don't worry about Caleb," he said. "He's not an ordinary man."

Police from the state barracks and the surrounding towns had responded to the call. Aiden looked around; everywhere he looked there were flashing lights and men yelling to each other. He had never felt so hollow, so stymied and useless.

The words of John Giamo echoed back at him through the melee. "He's not an ordinary man." Aiden shook his head and ran both hands through his thick hair. Something clicked in his soul as though he were suddenly reminded of who he was and where he came from. He came from people who met every day head on. He came from people who, despite adversity, figured their way out of difficult situations at every turn of the road. He came from people who didn't give up, didn't give in, and didn't allow other people to solve their problems. He came from people who succeeded.

Aiden walked back to the railing and stood beside Jordan. He ascertained the scene with a critical eye. He saw the fire escape. Long abandoned, it hung out just over the canal, and the stairs led down to a narrow ledge which had probably originally been a walkway before the building had been widened over it. He put his arm around Jordan and bent his head to her ear. "I have a plan. I'm going to get Grace."

"Not without me," she said.

"It's too dangerous. I've got to go out on that ledge. You stay back here."

"No way, Aiden. I love you and I trust you, but Grace is my life. I'm going with you."

Aiden could see the resolve in her face. It would be futile to try to dissuade her. He met her eyes for a moment, then gave the hint of smile. "Okay," he said, "but only so far as I can keep you safe."

Aiden saw Giamo, still absorbed in trying to keep Fenton distracted until Caleb was able to access the fire escape. It was their moment of opportunity. While Giamo played Fenton like a fiddle, Aiden and Jordan walked quickly across the bridge, the shadows hiding them. Giamo, as intent as he was on keeping Fenton occupied and Grace safe until Caleb got there, didn't see them as they slipped into the darkness under the bridge.

The inky darkness folded around them like a cloak. Jordan clutched Aiden's hand and felt his strength pouring into her. She felt, rather than saw him, creeping along the edge of the canal ahead of her.

"Are you all right?" he whispered over his shoulder to her.

"Yes, yes, I'm fine," she assured him.

There was a cement retaining wall on their right. Aiden stopped about fifty feet from the dangling end of the fire escape stairs. "We have to jump up on the lip here. There's room enough to walk as long as we're careful." He turned toward her. "Can you make it?"

"Yes."

"Be careful."

Jordan watched Aiden hoist himself noiselessly up onto the narrow ledge that ran along the foundation of the building. She waited as he braced himself against the brick wall. A moment later he reached down to her. "Take my hand. I'll help you up."

Jordan stretched out her hand and grasped his wrist. She clutched at the lip of the ledge as he drew her up, and then gathered all the strength she had and gave a jump. Twisting in mid-air, she landed on her rear end beside Aiden on the ledge. "Nice job," he whispered and smiled at her. For the first time since this nightmare had begun, she felt a surge of hope.

"Now what?"

"He's facing away from the stairs," said Aiden. "I think I can sneak up the old ladder stairs here and get behind him. I can grab Grace before he knows what's happening."

"Oh, Aiden, that sounds too dangerous! What if he sees you and throws her into the canal?"

A strobe light washed over the fire escape. Aiden and Jordan shrank back into the shadow of the building.

Fenton screamed, "Get that light out of my eyes! Get it off me!"

Jordan saw Giamo wave his hand and the strobe light dropped to the water's surface. Across the canal, she could see men lowering a rubber raft into the water.

"I know what you're trying to do down there!" Fenton's voice was full of panic. "Stay away from me!"

"We just want the baby," called Giamo. "Fenton, just hand over the baby. We'll help you. Things aren't as bad as you think they are. You can get through this."

"You're not listening to me! My life is ruined! I'm going to ruin hers! I want to see her ruined!" Fenton moved to edge of the dilapidated railing and Jordan heard an ominous, metallic groan. The fire escape was straining with the weight of the man. The escalating heat inside the building was weakening the outer walls to which it was fastened. Grace began to cry.

"Aiden! Aiden!" Jordan cried. "Aiden, I think the fire escape is going to collapse." She was nearly paralyzed with fear. She could feel the heat from the blaze now, at her back.

She and Aiden glanced up. Through the grate, they could see Fenton holding Grace. Then they noticed something at the broken window at the rear of the fire escape. A man stood in the shadows, the eerie undulating glow of the fire behind him: Caleb Cochran. Fenton had not seen him.

Fenton screamed at Giamo again, "Tell them to get that boat out of the water! If they don't get it out of the water, I'll throw this baby right into the canal! Then they'll have something to fish for!"

Before Jordan could react to Fenton's heinous threat, an unearthly screech filled the air. Aiden's arm flashed across her chest, flattening her against the brick wall. A loud bang followed. Bits of brick, splinters of wood, and rusted metal shards rained down on them. Jordan felt something graze her cheek, but she was oblivious to the sting. The fire escape had collapsed.

All around her, chaos reigned. She struggled to keep her grip on reality, to sort things out. *Grace! Grace!* Her baby's name thundered through her head over and over. Jordan had no idea she was screaming it out loud. She tried to move, then realized a piece of twisted metal held her leg tight to the wall.

There was a splash and Aiden disappeared from beside her. She struggled to see through the darkness. She heard the police chief shouting.

"I need spotlights! God damn it! I need lights here!"

Spotlights immediately flooded the area. Aiden was in the water. Jordan watched him take a breath and go under, then pop up a few seconds later, cradling Grace in the crook of his arm. He lifted the baby as high as he could, trying to keep her above the water line. With his other arm, he gripped a piece of the disintegrating fire escape that hung, twisted crazily, out over the water.

"Jordan!" he yelled. "Can you reach her?"

With more strength than she ever could have imagined she had, Jordan reached down and wrenched the metal detritus from around her leg. She was free! She inched along the ledge, getting as close as she could. The black current of icy water swirled around Aiden. She dropped to her knees and stretched her arm as far as she could, but she was still three or four feet from being able to reach them.

Then from above, she heard Caleb's calming voice, deep and slow. "Jordan, I'm going to lower this rope to you. It has a grappling hook on it. Toss it out to him. Then hang on. I'll lower myself and pull them in."

Jordan nodded. She could see Caleb through the broken window, silhouetted against the glow of the burning interior. Caleb stepped to the edge of the window and slowly lowered the hook and rope. Jordan snatched at it and caught it.

Her eyes stayed fixed on Aiden and Grace, and Caleb called to Aiden, "Stewart! Are you there? Jordan has a hook. She's going to throw it to you. Grab hold but don't move until I get down to the ledge. Okay?"

"Okay!" acknowledged Aiden. The spotlights and eerie glow from the flames illuminated the scene, and Jordan could see that the freezing water was beginning to take its toll as Aiden fought to keep Grace as high as possible. She wasn't even sure her daughter was conscious, but she buried that thought lest it interfere with her need to act. Around her, lights flashed. She could hear splashing and men running and yelling.

Jordan shouted, "Aiden! I can see you. I can see you and Grace. I'm throwing the hook. Here it comes." She knew Giamo was struggling to keep the spotlights on them, but the shadows distorted her view. She aimed for the metal stair frame that Aiden gripped and heaved as hard as she could. The effort nearly knocked her from her perch on the ledge. As she struggled to keep her footing, she heard the clatter of steel on steel. A few seconds later, Aiden yelled, "I got it!"

Jordan braced herself back against the wall, gripping the rope. She could now see Aiden more clearly. He must have been standing on a part of the wreckage under the water. His torso was above the rushing black torrent. He held Grace in his right arm, steadying himself with his left arm hooked through the remains of the fire escape.

"Hold on!" Caleb called from above. "Don't move, Aiden. I'm coming down. Jordan, hold on. Are you all right?"

"I got it," muttered Jordan through chattering teeth. She was hanging on for Grace's life, for Aiden's life, for her life.

Jordan glanced up and saw Caleb sink a hook around the crumbling window casing and begin his decent down. After what seemed like an eternity, she heard his boots hit the ledge pavement. Then, his gloved hand was over hers, gripping the rope. She drew a shuddering deep breath but she couldn't let go. Caleb said gently, "Step back, Jordan. Get ready to take Grace. It's okay. I've got it."

The mention of Grace's name snapped Jordan out of her trance. She relinquished the rope to Caleb and stood ready.

"Let go of the railing, Aiden," called Caleb. "Hold onto the rope. I'm pulling you in. When you get to the edge of the ledge, hand the baby to Jordan. I'll pull you up. Can you hear me? Can you do that?"

Aiden called back through the darkness. "Yes, yes. I'm ready. Go ahead."

Jordan couldn't breathe. She knew neither Aiden nor Grace could last much longer. Only Aiden's courage must be giving him the strength to hold onto the rope and onto Grace. She also knew the dangers of hypothermia, that it wouldn't be long before he lost consciousness in the frigid water. "Go ahead!" she heard him call again. Her heart pounded. *Please, God, let them both be all right.*

Caleb began to methodically haul in the rope. Jordan could see the current splashing up against Aiden as he held Grace tight to his chest with one arm and the lifeline with his free hand. Jordan dropped to her knees at the edge of the ledge and held out her arms. With one final pull, Caleb brought Aiden in to the abutment, and Jordan's hands were on her baby, lifting her up to safety. She crushed Grace against her and began to cry.

Then she heard John's voice cutting through the night. He stood at the end of the ledge where she and Aiden had walked out along the canal. "Jordan, come this way!" he urged. Two men stood behind him, holding blankets. "Jordan! Hurry! Come this way. Be careful!" He started out on the ledge to meet her. Then his arm was around her, guiding her to solid ground. The two paramedics quickly swathed her in blankets, wrapping both her and Grace tight. "Let's get you to the ambulance so they can make sure Grace is okay."

"Aiden! Aiden!" Jordan craned her neck as she was shuffled away. She needed to know that this man who'd risked his life to rescue her daughter, this man she loved desperately, was going to be all right.

"I've got him, Jordan," Caleb called out. "Go with the paramedics. I'm bringing him through. John, give me a hand, here." Jordan looked back just in time to see the two men pull Aiden's limp body from the water.

The paramedics continued to usher her away from the scene. "Aiden!" she screamed, but he didn't answer.

Chapter Sixteen

The town's four police vehicles, lights flashing, led the procession, followed by fire trucks from Clark's Corner and three surrounding towns. The hearse followed the fire engines. Small American flags fluttered on each front fender. Behind the hearse, the mourners followed. The traffic line stretched a quarter of a mile down the main street, and each car was packed. The first three cars behind the hearse held the family.

Jordan sat in the back seat of one of those cars, staring out the window. She was dressed in a black suit, her hair subdued in a low chignon at the back of her neck. High on her cheekbone, a small bandage covered the stitched-up gash inflicted by the falling rubble from the night of the fire. Grace, dressed in a daffodil-yellow ruffled pinafore, squirmed on her lap and sucked her pacifier.

Tears brimmed at Jordan's lashes. She tried to blink them back, but one breached the delicate dam of her soft eye lid and slid down her cheek. She felt a gentle touch to her cheek, brushing the tear away. She turned and smiled at Aiden. He smiled back and took her free hand in his.

"Thank you for riding with me today," she said softly.

"I was flattered that Mrs. Palmer asked me herself," he answered.

"It still doesn't seem real to me," reflected Jordan, holding Grace with both hands and bouncing her gently on her knees. "I mean, so much has happened over the last three days. Mr. Palmer dies, Fenton goes crazy, kidnaps my baby, and sets the company on fire." She heaved a deep sigh, then turned and looked Aiden directly in the face. "And I almost lost you," she whispered. "I almost lost both of you. I don't know what—"

"Shhh," Aiden interrupted her. "You didn't lose either one of us. We're both still here, where we should be. With you."

"I can't help thinking about it, though. Especially today, when we're burying Mr. Palmer."

Aiden peered out his window. "Looks like we're turning into the cemetery now. I think most of the people who were in the church are going to be here too."

"There's a big reception at the fire station hall after the burial."

"That's a funny place to have it," said Aiden. "Isn't there any place a little more…sophisticated?"

"Mr. Palmer donated the money to restore that building and buy a new fire truck. It's only fitting that the reception be there."

"Hm," Aiden mused. "He was a surprising man."

The procession halted along the stone wall of the old cemetery. Only the hearse entered the peaceful grounds, scented with lilacs and lily of the valley. It came to a stop beside the open grave. People filed in quietly and stood around in familial groups. Aiden and Jordan stood with their parents as the casket was lowered into the ground. Ashley and Kyle stood with them, holding hands.

As if on cue, the morning mist began to dissipate. The sun glowed through, glistening off the remaining droplets of fog that hung in the air and making little rainbows on the dewy grass.

The priest gave a short eulogy. Jordan couldn't hear what he said, but she didn't have to. She held her own thoughts in her heart. At last, the Palmer family collected together. Dan, the oldest son, spoke to the crowd. "Please come to the fire station hall for a remembrance reception," he said. "We hope to see you all there."

Mrs. Palmer took her son's arm and walked with the rest of her children and grandchildren back to the cars. She wasn't crying, but her eyes were dull, her face stricken with unfathomable sadness.

"I'd rather we rode back with you," said Jordan to her mother.

"We'll see you there, Jordan," Ashley said. She looked up at Kyle, telegraphing something to him with her eyes. They walked hand in hand back to their truck.

The reception was cheerier than the cemetery had been. People poured drinks, ate brunch food prepared by the firefighters, and gradually began the celebration of the town's father figure. Aiden and Jordan noticed that Mrs. Palmer sat with her youngest grandchild on her lap, smiling and talking with her daughter. Jordan put a fidgety Grace down and began a giggle-filled game of chase around the room.

Aiden nibbled at a bagel with lox, capers, and onions, watching Grace repeatedly evade her mother. He was deep in his own thoughts when he felt a hand on his shoulder. He turned around. A man with short dark hair and hazel-green eyes, wearing a fireman's dress uniform, put his hand out.

"I'm Caleb Cochran," he said. "I want to thank you for being there for that baby."

Aiden set his plate down on a nearby table. He gripped Caleb's hand. "I didn't recognize you without your gear. I'm the one who should be thanking you! You saved our lives. I couldn't have held on much longer."

"You came around fine. Just got a little cold." Caleb laughed. "I was just doing my job."

"Well, thank you, anyway," Aiden said, not wanting to embarrass him. "I'm getting to see what kind of people live in this town."

"It's a pretty special bunch," answered Caleb. "It's a tight community. We take care of each other."

Aiden looked around. "I can see that." Then he broached another subject. "What about Fenton? Was the body ever found? I haven't heard."

John Giamo, approaching the two men, answered the question. "Actually, I just got word as we left the cemetery. State police found the body this morning hung up in a blowdown at the side of the river about a mile downstream. That man really cracked. We were fortunate. Fortunate to have you and Grace and Jordan with us today." It was a characteristic of the chief to heave a deep sigh whenever his thoughts grew heavy. "Burying somebody is always hard, but it's easier to bury an old man than a young one, or a child."

The weight of his words kept them silent for a moment, until a pretty young woman, sporting an obvious baby bump, came up to

Caleb and slipped her arm through his. Caleb said, "Aiden Stewart, this is my wife, Lauren." He turned to his wife and explained, "Aiden's company recently merged with ChatDotCom. Aiden saved little Grace Fitzgerald the night of that debacle."

Aiden smiled, "Pleased to meet you."

Lauren smiled back. "I'm so glad to meet you as well," she said. "You're to be commended. That took courage."

"I guess it was more like instinct. Good thing your husband was there to back me up!"

Caleb laughed, and the small company dispersed, morphing into new groups as they all worked their way through the room. Finally, Aiden found himself sitting at a corner table with Jordan, Ashley, and Kyle.

"We were just talking about Chat," Jordan said as Aiden sat down.

"What's the damage assessment?" asked Aiden.

"Not as bad as it might have been," Ashley replied. "Most of the damage was to the lower end of the building, which wasn't fully restored anyway. It was used for storage, miscellaneous stuff, and equipment. It wasn't cleared for any kind of occupation, as you found out when that old fire escape gave way."

"So it's business as usual?" asked Aiden.

Kyle answered him. "The fire marshal will have to inspect it and clear it. Then it'll have to be cleaned to get the smoke smell out of it. There's some electrical and plumbing damage. I'd say in a week to ten days, everything will be up and running same as before."

"I hate to lose a lot of time," said Jordan.

"Don't worry," laughed Ashley. "It's digital. We can do most anything from our garages if we have to!"

Little by little, the clots of people broke up, reformed, and graciously took their leave. It was nearly one when Jordan pulled Aiden aside. "I need to get Grace home for a nap before she comes undone. Mom and Dad are ready to leave, and Dan just left to take his mother home. It's time."

Aiden was standing with his mother and father. "You go on ahead. I'm going to go back to the Inn with my parents. I'll call you in a little while." He leaned forward and kissed her upturned lips. It was their first public kiss, and in Aiden's heart, it signaled the end of one era and the beginning of the rest of their lives.

After she had gone, the Stewarts made their way out of the building. "What're you driving, Dad?" asked Aiden with a wink at his mother.

"We're driving your mother's car," the old man grumbled. "I don't like your mother's car. Too small. Cramps me up. Smart ass."

Aiden laughed and got in the back seat. When they reached the Inn, Gordon looked significantly at his wife. Aiden caught the glance but didn't understand its meaning. "What?" he asked.

"Your father and I want to talk to you a minute, Aiden," Nell said. "And, we've got something to give you. Something that might come in handy."

"Oh," said Aiden simply. "Okay. What is it?"

"Come over here and sit down a minute, son." Gordon led the way to a grouping of an overstuffed sofa and two chairs in the corner of the lobby.

It wasn't like his parents to be mysterious. They were usually upfront and direct about anything they had to talk about. Obediently, he sat down on the sofa beside his mother. Gordon settled himself in the chair.

Nell turned to her son. "Aiden, your father and I have been talking. We know how you feel about Jordan, and we want everything for your happiness. It's something you and Jordan will have to work out yourselves, find your own way together, if that's what the two of you decide you want to do. I guess what I'm saying, Aiden, is that your father and I are behind you whatever you decide." Her voice caught at that moment. She reached for his hand. "Aiden, your actions in rescuing that baby the other night made us so proud, but when your father and I realized the danger you had been in...Well, I can't begin to make you understand the anguish we went through thinking about what might have happened. We've always been proud of you, so we want you to have this...in case...in case you need it." She smiled at him as she reached into her purse and brought out a small, worn, brown velvet box.

Aiden's eyes widened in recognition. The box had always been kept in his mother's vanity in her bedroom. It housed her grandmother's engagement ring, which Nell wore sometimes on special occasions.

"Mom!" he said.

"Take it, Aiden," said Gordon. "I have a feeling you might have plans for it soon."

Aiden took the old box from his mother and opened it. There was the ring: a one carat rose-cut diamond, set in a delicate filigree and flanked by two baguettes. Feminine and elegant, it reflected the era in which it was crafted, and yet there was a contemporary-looking flare that resonated from it, a modern flash that mirrored the energy of the woman on whose finger Aiden pictured it.

"I don't know what to say," he murmured humbly.

"Well, you can say thank you to start," said Gordon as he rose to his feet, "and then just let us know what happens."

"Thank you," said Aiden, smiling at them both. "I can't say what will happen or when, but I'm hoping I'll be using it soon."

"Good, then," said Gordon. "Now help us with our bags. We've got to get going so we can get home before dark. I don't like driving in the dark anymore. In fact, I don't even like driving much at all. Especially your mother's car."

Aiden laughed. "I'll bring your car back as soon as I can, Dad. Jordan and I will have to assess the damage from the fire and…and work some stuff out."

Gordon nodded and clapped Aiden on the back. Aiden slipped the ring box into his pocket. A few minutes later, he stood watching his parents' car disappear down the main street, headed back home. Oddly, Aiden felt quite at home where he was. An aura of warmth and comfort settled around him. He smiled to himself and made his way to his car. It was as good a time as any.

When he reached Jordan's home, her mother met him at the door. "Jordan's down at the company, Aiden," she explained. "I expect she's trying to make some sense of all this. I know she'd appreciate your being there with her."

It took Aiden five minutes to get to the Chat parking lot. He pulled in beside Jordan's Jeep. The place looked deserted, but he knew she was there somewhere. Aiden walked around the back side of the building, where most of the damage had occurred. Jordan was standing in the narrow service alley, looking up at the charred and crumbling outer wall of the annex. She had changed from her funeral clothes. Aiden's stomach gave a little leap at the sight of her round rear end encased in snug-fitting jeans. A light cotton white T-shirt and silver flats completed her simple and very sexy outfit. He stood looking at her for a minute, remembering how she felt naked in his arms.

"Looks like we'd better get our hammers out," he called.

Jordan swung around to face him. Her face, perplexed when he had been standing there watching her, broke into a smile. She walked toward him with a graceful, fluid gait and held her arms out to him. He caught her up in an enthusiastic embrace, lifting her off the ground and kissing her mouth.

"It's a mess," she said, as he set her down. "I don't know where to start. My office stinks like burning tires."

"Don't worry," Aiden answered her confidently. "The fire marshal will be here tomorrow. After that, we'll get a cleaning company in, and then we'll rebuild. I think they'll let us build some type of temporary partition between the part of the building that was destroyed and the offices, so we can continue to work."

"I hope so," she murmured dubiously. "When Mr. Palmer was alive, it was easy to figure things out. I guess I knew I could always run things by him. Now I'm kind of on my own."

Aiden snorted. "You wound me! You're not alone. I'm here. We're in this together."

Jordan gave him a small smile. "You know, it's habit, I guess. I brainwashed myself into thinking I had to do everything myself. I apologize, because in the end, none of this matters. When I really think about what I might have lost, none of this matters at all. And the only reason I didn't lose everything, Aiden, was because of you. You pulled Grace out of the water. You saved her."

Aiden took her hand. "Come with me," he said. "We have to talk."

They wandered down next to the canal and stood, staring at the black water. The remnants of the fire escape still hung in the water.

"I've been thinking a lot these last couple of days," Jordan said. "That is, when I can bear to. Sometimes, it's just too much to imagine my baby so near death. I have to shut it out of my head, or I go catatonic."

"What have you been thinking about?"

"I've been thinking about you and me. Where are we going? I know I don't want to be with anybody except you, ever. I hope you feel the same, but I'm a realist. We've known each other for about two and a half weeks. I know we'll have to let it evolve, see how we hold up under a long-distance relationship. You have your job in Maine, and I have mine here. That's pressure, Aiden. Not too much for me, but maybe it might be for you." She sighed. "I love you, Aiden. I truly do."

Aiden took her hands in his. "I love you, Jordan Fitzgerald, and I'll do whatever has to be done to make sure you keep loving me. For starters, I'm going to stay here for now. I've been thinking, too. I'll rent a place, or stay at the Inn, or something. We'll oversee the renovations together. Things will make themselves clear and everything will work out. I know it will. We'll get the company back on track. It's like my mother said; we're stronger together than we are apart. Two is stronger than one. And, for your information alone, I would be totally useless if I couldn't hold you next to me, if I couldn't kiss you, feel your skin, smell your scent. I need you now. You're already a part of who I am, who I will be. And I have something to prove it. It's May, Jordan. Almost June. We've got a lot of work to do, and we've only got three months before the big event, but I think we can do it."

"Wait!" Jordan blurted. "What are you talking about? What big event? I must be losing it. What event is that? Was it in the merger contract?"

Aiden laughed. "No, but it should have been." He slipped his hand into his pocket and brought out the old velvet box. Taking her hand, he placed the box gently in her open palm, closing her fingers around it. "Will you marry me in September, Jordan? I can't wait longer than that."

Jordan stood as though turned to stone.

In slow motion, she opened the box. The diamonds flashed and glittered in the evening sunlight. She stared at it.

"Put it on," urged Aiden. "I want to see if it fits."

With trembling fingers, she took the ring out of the box and slipped it onto her finger. "Oh, Aiden," she breathed, "it's a perfect fit." Tears of happiness blurred her vision as she gazed up at him. "I will marry you, Aiden. I will!"

He bent and kissed her tenderly on the eyelids, cheek, and lips. It was mutual, Aiden knew, this indescribable feeling of love, confidence, and security.

"Where did you get this ring? It's so, so beautiful!"

"It was my great-grandmother's," he explained. "My mother gave it to me to give to you."

"Oh, Aiden! I—I don't know what to say. It's fantastic! I love it! Oh, Aiden, I love you!" Jordan wrapped both arms around him and kissed him soundly. "Yes, I will marry you in September, even if we have to elope!"

"Let's go tell your parents."

They walked, hand in hand, to his car. As they drove slowly back to the house, Jordan said quietly, "I was thinking about something else too. Something hard for me to think about."

"What is it?" asked Aiden. His heart was calm; he had what he wanted now. He felt very strong and confident. He would help her through anything. They were together now; that was what mattered.

"What you said about Grace needing to know her father's family. Aiden, she might have died, and they would never have known she had been born. I don't even know them, but I know that's just not fair. It was kind of an odd relationship, Mark's and mine. Sort of a friendship born out of loneliness and need, almost childish, now that I look back on it. But Grace came from that relationship, and I owe it to his memory to tell his mother and father that they have a granddaughter. Part of their son is a living, breathing, laughing little girl, and they need to know that. I don't know them. I know they live in Montgomery, up in the Northeast Kingdom. I have no idea what kind of people they are, or what they'll say. They might refuse to see or talk to me, but I have to try. Will you help me with this?"

Aiden cleared his throat, trying to conquer his sudden emotional response. He knew what to say, what to do. It was the honorable thing, the only thing, to do. His heart swelled with love for her, and he knew she saw it, too. The furtive, guarded, insecure Jordan was gone. In her place was a confident, self-assured woman who knew who she was. *Love will do that*, thought Aiden.

"Of course," he answered. "Of course I'll help you. We'll do it together. It will be a shock to them, so we'll have to plan it carefully for their sakes, but it needs to be done. They need to know. Grace needs to know."

They drove the rest of the way to the house in silence, each caught in their own thoughts. Aiden felt fulfilled, as though his life had started in earnest at last. And Jordan seemed happily surprised to find not a shred of doubt that this was where she was supposed to be, what she was supposed to be doing. Everything else was incidental, and they would figure it out as they went along.

It was two weeks later, a warm and sunny June afternoon, when Aiden pulled the Jeep up to the front of a neat, white frame house on a quiet, modest street in the tiny town of Montgomery. Vermont was awash with the vibrant green of full summer.

Two large maple trees shaded the home, and a carefully cared-for colorful border of annuals lined the walkway from the front door to the sidewalk. Jordan looked at Aiden. "Here goes nothing," Jordan said quietly as she got out of the car. Opening the back door, she lifted Grace out of her car seat. Cradling the baby on her hip, she started up the walk with Aiden following at a respectful distance.

The front door opened before Jordan could ring the bell. A gray-haired couple stood there, hand in hand. The woman was small and stocky with an open, pleasant face. The man was tall and thin with sad eyes.

As Jordan approached the couple, the man let go of his wife's hand and put his arm around her shoulders in a protective gesture, but the woman slipped out from under her husband's embrace and started down the walk to meet Jordan and Grace. She stopped just short of them, smiled and held out her arms toward the baby.

Grace giggled and buried her face in her mother's neck. Then, she extended her chubby little hands out to the woman and smiled broadly.

With tears in her eyes, the grandmother stepped forward and reached out for something she had thought she had lost forever.

Acknowledgments

Thank you to my publisher, Elizabeth Harper—again! Also many thanks to Cindy Campbell who patiently hammered it out with me when our editing programs didn't mesh! Also to Jennifer DeLucy for once again coming up with just the right music for my trailer. Thanks to the rest of the Omnific team, especially Coreen, Lisa, CJ and Kim and many, many hugs to Traci Olsen who has guided me through the confusion more than once, sometimes over tasty lunches!

About the Author

Linda Cunningham grew up a small town country girl and it is here where she's still most comfortable. She has written steadily throughout the years, although usually other peoples' speeches, articles, and grants, primarily for medical and agricultural trade journals. Now that her three children are grown, Linda is writing full time and writing the stuff she loves—Romance!

Linda lives in a romantic stone house in the Green Mountain State of Vermont, surrounded by her gardens and animals which include horses, dogs, cats, chickens, sheep, a parakeet, goldfish and the wild visitors who tiptoe through on a regular basis. When time permits, she also enjoys cooking, sketching, and painting.

←⠂⠂→Young Adult←⠂⠂→

Shades of Atlantis and *The Ember Series: Ember* and *Iridescent* by Carol Oates
Breaking Point by Jess Bowen
Life, Liberty, and Pursuit by Susan Kaye Quinn
Embrace by Cherie Colyer
Destiny's Fire by Trisha Wolfe
Streamline by Jennifer Lane
Reaping Me Softly by Kate Evangelista

←⠂⠂→Historical Romance←⠂⠂→

Cat O' Nine Tails by Patricia Leever
Burning Embers by Hannah Fielding

←⠂⠂→Erotic Romance←⠂⠂→

Becoming sage by Kasi Alexander
Saving sunni by Kasi & Reggie Alexander
The Winemaker's Dinner: Appetizers and *Entrée*
by Dr. Ivan Rusilko & Everly Drummond

←⠂⠂→Anthologies and Singles←⠂⠂→

A Valentine Anthology including short stories by Alice Clayton, Jennifer DeLucy, Nicki Elson, Jessica McQuinn, Victoria Michaels, and Alison Oburia

It's Only Kinky the First Time by Kasi Alexander
Learning the Ropes by Kasi & Reggie Alexander
The Winemaker's Dinner: RSVP by Dr. Ivan Rusilko
The Winemaker's Dinner: No Reservations by Everly Drummond
Big Guns by Jessica McQuinn
Concessions by Robin DeJarnett
Starstruck by Lisa Sanchez
New Flame by BJ Thornton
Shackled by Debra Anastasia
Swim Recruit by Jennifer Lane
Sway by Nicki Elson
Full Speed Ahead by Susan Kaye Quinn
The Second Sunrise by Hannah Downing
The Summer Prince by Carol Oates
Whatever it Takes by Sarah M. Glover
Clarity by Patricia Leever
A Christmas Wish by Autumn Markus

coming soon from
OMNIFIC PUBLISHING

Divine Temptation by Nicki Elson

The Winemaker's Dinner: Dessert by Dr. Ivan Rusilko

The Englishman by Nina Lewis

Tangled by Emma Chase

16 Marsden Place by Rachel Brimble